I0584470

Distant Mountains

Settlers Book 2

Tricia McGill

Print 9781773626024
Amazon Print 9781772993561
Ingram Spark 9780228627760

BWL Publishing Inc.

Books we love to write ...
Authors around the world.

http://bwlpublishing.ca

Dedication:

The Settlers series was written as a tribute to the magnificent pioneer women who battled alongside their men to open new frontiers in far flung corners of the globe. It was inspired by letters sent from Australia home to England by these women who were often torn away from the family and homeland they loved, forced to endure all kinds of deprivation, but faced every struggle with strength and fortitude. In this day of washing machines, supermarkets and homes filled with mod-cons it is difficult to imagine a life without these amenities, let alone to perceive what it must have been like traipsing after your menfolk to settle in unknown parts, often over miles of dangerous territory.

Table of Contents

Prologue

Moreton Bay
September 1828

A kookaburra warbled its silly head off. Laughing, no doubt, at the stupidity of man. And the cruelty.

The sun beat down mercilessly as the cat-o-nine tails whirled and cracked. Dear God! Rem thought. What had he done to deserve this agony? What had brought him to this—fixed to this triangle like a carcass nailed to a barn door.

He tasted blood as he bit down on his lip. Bile rose in his throat. He wouldn't scream. Through the battering pain, he registered the quartermaster sergeant calling out stroke number thirty-six. Blood flowed freely down his back now, soaking his trousers.

The magistrate used the cat for revenge. Rem's offence was so piffling it was laughable—if a man felt like laughing, as the bird up yonder did. Fifty lashes were the most the magistrate had been able to impose for a single offence. Thank God.

Through the lancing pain, Rem knew he must not scream, must not blubber and forever be known as a crawler. Hanging onto consciousness by a thread, he sagged against the bloody, filthy bars of the triangle; a frame tainted by the blood of so many men, and now would carry his.

"Cut 'im down!" the scourger shouted, and through his agony Rem recognized his punishment had ended.

Tripping over the hole made by the scourger's feet during the vile beating, Rem was kept upright by Scab and Salty, the only two men he could vaguely term as mates in this hell. In a flagrant act of disdain, he spat at the feet of the man who had inflicted the agony he now suffered as he stumbled and was half-dragged away. The man who gave him the "red shirt" swore viciously, and before he lost consciousness Rem warned himself to watch what he did in future. These bastards would soon have him back on the frame if he didn't toe their line.

Chapter One

June 1826

Freedom was sweet.

The air was pungent after a short spell of rain. It was cold, the chill air biting, but Rem reckoned he'd never really feel the cold again. Not in this country, where the sun shone more often than not; where the coldest day only called for an extra layer of clothing. He had almost forgotten the biting winds and bone-chilling cold of London. The thoughts had receded into some dark corner of his mind, along with the memories that still periodically invaded his sleep. Memories of hunger and desperation; days of despair when he had wondered if life was worth all the bother entailed to get through each day.

"Uncle Remy, where are you?"

Rem grinned as he pushed himself onto his elbows. His nephew had sought him out again. Not that he minded; the boy was good company, always ready for a new lark. Seven come September, Tim was mature for his age. Boys grew up fast out here in this new land. Here a lad like Tim learned early on, as they all did, that he had to work the land; put every ounce of his energy into it to reap the benefits.

"Over here, lad." Rem watched Tim, hair the color of ripened corn drooping over his forehead, trotting toward the riverbank. One of the sheepdogs, a black and white mongrel, loped at his heels. Tim always had a dog nearby and it would be strange to see him without one of his perpetual companions.

"What you doing sitting out here, Uncle Remy?" Tim squatted on his haunches by Rem's side. "Mama was getting all of a fluster because you were supposed to be working on the new barn, and the foreman said you'd disappeared."

"Not disappeared, boy, just taking a break. And, we both know your ma can get herself into a state over the simplest of things. Don't the air smell good?" Rem put his head back and sniffed appreciatively.

Tim nudged him, sighing. "Air doesn't smell, silly. The cattle stink, so do the horses after they do a business, but air hasn't got a smell."

Rem ruffled the golden hair. Pushing himself to his feet, he hauled Tim up with him. "Come on, let's go make my sister happy," he said, swinging Tim easily onto his back. He strode up the hill with his burden, the dog yelping at their heels. The boy gripped him about the middle with his knees and shouted encouragement at his mount.

His sister, Bella, four months along with her fourth child was at this irksome stage. Her husband Tiger was often off with his shepherds, laborers, or field hands, and at these times she liked to know Rem was near at hand.

Rem had been out here beyond Bathurst with them for a year now, and she still often stared at him as if she couldn't quite believe they were together. He wasn't surprised by that—he often had to pinch himself to prove it wasn't a dream. At times he dreaded he would find himself in the hellish hold of the transport ship. Or worse, at Newcastle where he could even now be with the gangs quarrying stone or working down the coal mine. Worst of all he could be with the lime-burners; the convicts who burned the seashells used to manufacture the lime used as mortar. By all accounts, it was the vilest job a man could have.

Tiger could be a hard taskmaster at times, never letting him get off light with any job. Not that Rem would expect to. He would be eternally grateful for Tiger's intervention on his behalf. Tiger had seen Rem released into his care when the authorities were just about to send Rem off to the hellhole Newcastle had become. If at times he got itchy feet and the tasks became tedious, Rem only had to recall the awful days spent on the treadmill in Sydney before coming out to Tiger and Bella's property here, west of the Blue Mountain range.

Tiger had built Bella a fine house of stone, with two floors and a veranda that went right around its sides. It sat proudly on the ridge facing the river, outbuildings now springing up in its surrounds. The barn Rem was supposed to be helping to erect was the latest of these buildings.

"Here you go." Rem helped Tim off his back as they reached the six steps that led up to the front porch.

"See you later," the boy yelled as he ran off, his dog at his side.

"Where you off to in such a hurry?" Rem called after him. But Tim was already out of earshot, likely in a hurry to escape his mother's schooling. Not that he would be able to do that for long, Bella was strict about his lessons and set aside at least three hours a day for that activity.

"Remy?" Bella's sharp call brought him up short as he turned toward the almost completed barn.

"That's me." Changing direction, he grinned and mounted the steps. His sister stood by the open door, wiping her hands on the apron covering the front of her plain blue woolen dress. Rem didn't think he'd ever get used to having such a beautiful woman for a sister. Those around her didn't notice the limp she'd had since a bolting horse trampled her in Stepney years ago.

Her rich auburn hair formed a loose bun at the nape of her neck, but tendrils had escaped and framed her expressive face. Her green eyes sparked with merriment "Where did you sneak off to again?"

"I was just taking in the air, love. Isn't it a fine day?" He half-closed his eyes, looking up to the sky, where not a smidgen of sun peeped through the gray clouds.

"Fine?" She made a disparaging sound in her throat. "You've got a vivid imagination." There was a soft chiding note in her voice. His sister knew more than anyone that any day was fine while they were able to walk free and breathe the air of free men and women.

Yes, he was still a convict, with five years to go before he could claim his ticket of leave, but compared to life

11

before Tiger rescued him, this was the next best thing to being able to hold his head up as a free man.

Bella's nursemaid, Agnes, smiled shyly at Rem as she joined her mistress on the porch. Rosie, the eight-month-old and youngest of Bella and Tiger's brood, rested on Agnes' hip. Agnes, seventeen and a plain little thing, had been with Bella and Tiger since they set out on their epic journey across the mountains in 1824.

"Isn't it a fine day?" Rem asked the girl, knowing she would agree with him if he declared it was as hot as hell, and the sun had blistered his skin. It was flattering to be idolized. Bothersome at times, but nonetheless a wonderful thing to have a female willing to do anything he asked. Some devil inside him often wanted to see to what lengths she would go to please him, although his kind heart wouldn't allow him to do it.

"It certainly is," Agnes agreed, as he'd known she would. "'Tis a bit cool, but that's not to be sniffed at. Beats summer when the sun makes you shrivel."

Agnes didn't like the hot weather. She complained it burned her fair skin, brought her out in freckles, made her skin go blotchy, and made her feel weak as a dish rag. Although complained wasn't the right word to use; Agnes never did anything quite so definite. She was too mousy and insignificant. A small apologetic grumble was about as close to a complaint she dared to venture.

Bella nodded to Rem and went back inside the house. Agnes's skin turned to the color of a beet as she stared at Rem. Her eyelashes were so light they could barely be seen—this only added to her mouse-like appearance. She jerked the baby higher into her arms, and bobbed Rosie about on her ample hip until the child squealed. As if surprised at what she'd done, Agnes crooned soft words of apology to the baby.

Rem knew he shouldn't do it, but the girl begged to be teased. Moving within a foot of her, he gave her the smile more than one maid told him was appealing. "How's the little mother today?"

"I'm fine, and how are you?" She nibbled on her lower lip as her eyes adored him.

Rem shrugged. "Tell the truth, Aggie, I'm bored to my high teeth. There are few chances out here to ease the monotony. I know I should be grateful for Tiger taking me on and bringing me here, but I'm not made for the country life. I miss the noise and bustle of the city. Not that I wish to return to Stepney." When she shook her head and gave him a look of condemnation that he could be so ungrateful, he hastened to add, "But a bit of excitement would add spice to this dull existence now and then. If you know what I mean?"

"Seems to me the city life only brought you into more strife than a body needs," she scolded softly.

Rem moved in closer and ran a finger over the blush on her cheeks, chuckling at her huffy response. "True."

Glancing about, he bent in closer, until he almost touched noses with her. He could feel the heat coming off her rounded body, could practically feel the shiver he guessed ran through her at his closeness. "But there's strife, an' then there's other things the town has to offer."

"Rem O'Shea, seems to me you don't know when you're well off." She hunched a shoulder when he continued to stroke her cheek, but she didn't step out of his range, as any city miss would have done. She was a sweet little chit, unworldly and naïve.

Rosie reached out to grab at his hair, and he laughed as he took the tiny fist into his hand and kissed the tips of her fingers, which pleased the child, and made Agnes tremble even more.

"Oh, I know well enough. But don't you yearn for a bit of excitement in your life now and then, Aggie girl?" He watched with a kind of fascination as the blush fluctuated on her face. What a shame she wasn't more prepossessing. What a pity he didn't share her infatuation. That at least would ease the boredom that gripped him at times until he could yell. Of course, he liked to think he wasn't so fickle all he thought of was a wench's looks, but her temperament

13

was so bland. Rem liked his women with fire and fervor and a temper to match his own.

"Excitement? I get more than my fair share of that chasing after young Tim, Annie, and this little 'un." She glanced at the babe in her arms, smiling down at Rosie affectionately. The child pinched Agnes' nose, making it turn an unbecoming shade of red. "Then there'll be another one come November, so I'll have my hands full."

"Mm, my sister and Tiger certainly are helping to populate this part of the world, ain't they?" He laughed, chucking Rosie beneath the chin. "But looking after toddlers and tots ain't my idea of fun, Aggie. I had something different in mind." He eyed her plain garb, scuffed boots, and mobcap. Her clothes did nothing to enhance her round shape. "Don't you ever want to dress up and traipse around like the gentry?"

"I'm not gentry, and can't see the point in yearning after the impossible," she stated pragmatically, shrugging. "I'm happy to have a good home here with the missus and master. And you should be too."

Rem sighed and turned to stare where the mountains loomed in the distance, like an impenetrable barrier between him and the excitement he craved. She was right, of course. He should be happy, but he yearned for so much more out of life than tending sheep and building barns and tilling the soil. Tiger was happy enough building his empire, and Bella was content to stand at his side and bear his children. If only Rem didn't have to wait another five years to gain his ticket of leave, and his freedom.

Without another word he sauntered off to the barn, hands dug deep into the pockets of his breeches.

* * *

Agnes watched his broad back, her eyes feasting on the strong length of his legs, the width of his shoulders, his head of rich dark red hair that reminded her of burnished chestnuts when the sun caught it, turning it to flame. The familiar yearning weighed heavily on her heart. If only she

14

were even slightly pretty. If only she were more intelligent and bright as a penny, as were most other girls of her age. She'd learned a lot sitting in on lessons the mistress gave Tim every day, but knew she was still as unworldly as when first plucked from the orphanage nearly two years ago by the master, to come here over the mountains with them as nursemaid.

There weren't many young females around these parts, but the few who had come west with their kin were certainly more fetching than she, with her ordinary brown hair and face that wouldn't stand out in any crowd, large or small. Her bosom was too big for her body, making her top-heavy, or so it seemed. Her behind stuck out so she looked like one of the ducks waddling about. That the babies fitted snugly on her over-large hips was about all that could be said in her body's favor. Even if she forced herself into a corset, she doubted she would look any more attractive. No, an ugly duckling she was, never to become a swan.

With a drawn-out sigh, she pressed a kiss on Rosie's cheek. This would likely be her lot in life. To look after other folk's children, to die an old spinster out here in the wilds; never to know the joy of nursing her own babe at her breast.

"No use pining for things that will never be, eh?" she asked the child as she stepped back inside and walked along the passage stretching from the front to the back of the lower floor of the house. Entering the kitchen, she put a bright smile on her face.

The family's second child, Annie, who would be two-years-old in a month, sat on a rug near the stove that threw out a welcoming heat; the rag doll Agnes had made for Annie's last birthday was cradled in her arms.

The mistress was helping Gracie prepare dinner. The smell of roasting lamb filled the air. Gracie, in her fifty-seventh year, was as cheerful as a rooster surrounded by hens, and never seemed to yearn for things beyond her reach. Gracie came over on the same transport ship as the mistress, and the two were as close as two women could get without being sisters.

"'Ullo dearly," she chirped. "'Ow's about a cup o' tea, eh?" That was Gracie's answer to all ills.

Agnes pulled a face. Gracie was unmarried and seemed happy enough with her lot in life. She received an offer of marriage in Sydney, but chose to turn her suitor down in preference of joining the mistress in this part of the world the master was slowly taming.

"Thank you," Agnes said as the older woman put the steaming cup on the table. Bending, Agnes put Rosie in the cradle. She sat down and sipped the drink, one foot rocking the cradle, her mind on the tall man with shining red hair who held her heart in his capable hands but didn't want it.

Chapter Two

July 2, 1826

Rem stared at Sara Greenwood, unable to take his eyes off this beauty. She was, without a doubt, the most entrancing creature he'd ever seen. With hair and eyes as black as sin and flawless skin like pure porcelain, her face was that of a goddess. A bloom on her cheeks gave her face a vital sheen of good health. How his fingers itched to unpin her silken tresses from their neat coils. He ached to touch that skin to see if it felt as soft and downy as it looked.

She carried her youth and beauty with a proud bearing missing in so many of the young women in the colony; these women brooded and sulked, despairing of their lot in life after being dragged to this awful continent by their fathers against their will. Most had pasty faces they kept well hidden beneath large-brimmed bonnets to shield them from the sun they saw as an enemy to their complexions.

Rem thanked God it was a Sunday, and they allowed him to join the small gathering. The thought he might have missed meeting this goddess made him shudder. Tiger made a habit of inviting all newcomers to the district to his and Bella's home soon after their arrival. The Greenwoods had recently settled here after living in Sydney for five years. Bella met them briefly on a trip into town, and Rem knew by her remarks she wasn't particularly enamored of Edmund Greenwood or his timid wife Eleanor. Rem couldn't give a damn about them, but was already half in love with their daughter.

"So charmed to meet you," Sara was saying to Bella and Tiger, who were decked out in the finery kept solely for such occasions.

Extending her long, slender fingers, Sara took their welcoming outstretched hands one after the other. Turning to Rem, she offered the same delicate hand, and he bowed over it reverently. Her scent filled his nostrils, battered at his senses. Like a garden in full bloom, or a bowl of roses. Not very poetic, he knew, but she would forever remind him of a spring day; an English one, where rosebuds sent out their fragrance to entice the bees, and butterflies were entranced by the colors.

Rem realized his breathing was as uneven as his heartbeat. As he straightened, their eyes met, and for one infinitesimal moment Rem felt sure a message passed between them. Could she be as smitten as he?

"We are delighted to meet you at last," Bella said, and for a moment, Rem wondered what she was talking about. So entranced was he, everything had gone out of his head, except this vision of loveliness.

"How do you find it here in Bathurst?" Bella asked graciously as they all took seats on the porch.

Sara spread the skirt of her blue dress about her knees, her dainty feet clad in black pumps peeped beneath the hem. Those bewitching eyes, filled with a sort of devilment met Rem's as Bella continued, "I'm so glad the weather has seen fit to hold." She looked to the sky, where a weak winter sun tried its damnedest to shine through the gray clouds.

"As I'm mighty glad it's decided not to rain before we've had a chance to settle in our house," Sara's burly father said, as he settled his large frame on a chair, and huffed. "I must say I'm also glad we brought plenty of help with us to this godforsaken neck of the woods." He had a perpetual air of grievance about him, as if the world should have tried harder to do better by him.

"'Tis a good life, once you grow used to it, and if you're prepared to work hard for what you wish to attain, it's very rewarding," Tiger said, looking out over his land. It was obvious to Rem his brother-in-law was no more enamored of this man than he was. Edmund Greenwood was brusque to the point of rudeness and loud-mouthed.

18

How did an ugly brutish man manage to sire an angel like Sara? And how did her meek and homely mother ever produce such a beauty? Perhaps she had been adopted. The thought made him smile, and he glanced over at his angel in time to see her watching him, her delicate brows raised.

Turning to Sara's mother, Bella offered, "You must call on me for any help you need. We lean on each other out here where months can go by without us seeing anyone from the other side of the mountains."

The pallid, insignificant woman looked to be about sixty in age, but was more than likely only in her forties. Rem suspected years of living with a boor had etched those deep lines on her face. Her pinched mouth looked forever on the verge of protest. Though, Rem doubted she would ever dare to come forth with a complaint.

"Thank you." The words came out on a thready whisper. Glancing up like a scared hare, Mrs. Greenwood added, "I didn't want to come," earning a wrathful glare from her husband.

"Balderdash!" Edmund waved an arm, his brows beetling, and she seemed to shrivel even more. "You'll soon get used to it. And with kindly ladies like Mrs. Carstairs here" —he gave Bella a sickly, condescending glance—"you'll soon acclimatize."

"I found it very strange when I first arrived in the colony." Bella smiled at Mrs. Greenwood, and Rem thought, for the umpteenth time, what a lovely woman his sister was. "And please call me Bella," she invited. "Everyone does. We don't stand on ceremony here. Being so isolated we have to become friends."

Rem wondered if these people knew his sister and her husband had both been convicts, sent to the colony by the British Government, same as he had. No doubt they did, for news traveled fast despite the great distances. Gossip was rife among the Exclusives and the Emancipists.

"'Course you did. We all have to learn to change." Edmund gave his wife a look that said she would have to change, or accept his wrath. Her hands trembled, and she twined them together on her lap.

19

"And how do you like living so far from the town?" Rem turned to ask the beauty seated beside him.

She shrugged. Her pouting lips were as soft, full, and pink as the rosebuds she smelt of. His insides ached with the desire to see if they tasted half as sweet as they looked. Jesus, he wanted to ravish her, to strip her and taste every part of the delectable body he knew the wool of her garment hid.

Her eyes slid from his dark red curls to the boots he was glad he'd polished for the occasion. Something deep inside him began to shake with his response.

Barely past her seventeenth birthday, so Bella had told him, and already she wore the look of a woman in control of her life and her responses. How he would like to help her lose her cool control. He made up his mind that would be his driving purpose in life from now on; sure in his conceit he would win her no matter what.

"I would have liked to stay in Sydney Town. I have my governess and companion still, who accompanied us over here, so I will have to bear it. For a while." She sounded utterly bored, and Rem wanted to stand up and shout that he would take her wherever she yearned to go.

Her father gave her another of his wrathful glares and boomed, "Bear it, will you? 'Tis my belief there's too many wrong 'uns in the town now. Wanted to stay over there, they did." He jerked his head toward his long-suffering wife and his beautiful daughter and snorted. "You talk some sense into them, madam." His smile reminded Rem of a conniving crook.

"I wasn't too happy about leaving the town myself," Bella said, giving Tiger the special smile she kept for her husband; one that left everyone else out of the loving and intimate world the two shared.

Rem now knew the full story of how Bella lost her first husband, Dougal, and her second-born son, Dougie, on the dreadful journey across the mountains to settle over here. She battled Tiger every step of the way in those days, fighting her love for him. Rem knew that now she wouldn't consider going back to town, even if Tiger was to give her

20

the option, which Rem knew he wouldn't. His life was here now, with his family, expanding his empire. Oh, they argued often still, but their fights were the quarrels of lovers; and any onlooker, including himself, always knew the rows were made up as only lovers' tiffs could be reconciled.

"As with all things, it becomes better once you grow used to the isolation," Bella continued. "We have quite a few families settled here now. Our small community manages to get along despite the differences in our backgrounds."

"'Course they do," Edmund bellowed, as if no one would dare to argue the case with him.

"I hear you left a manager in charge of your business in town," Tiger said, successfully managing to conceal the disdain Rem knew Tiger felt for this brash man. Rem guessed this was likely now multiplied after seeing the way Edmund treated his wife and daughter.

"That's right." Greenwood preened as he smiled condescendingly. Tiger had told Rem and Bella of how Greenwood arrived in Sydney five years ago as a free man and opened a store stocked with merchandise purchased cheaply at ports of call on the voyage over.

"My emporium is one of the largest and most successful now," he boasted. Grimacing, he shook his head. "If only we didn't have to put up with so much riff-raff in the people I'm forced to employ."

Tiger looked toward the mutton, roasting above a fire next to the garden, Bella's pride and joy. One of the hands signaled it was ready. "It looks as if the meat is about done."

They strolled to a table laid with cloth and cutlery, where Rem ensured he sat beside his beautiful enchantress. He saw Bella's raised eyebrows, but chose to take no notice of his sister's silent warning.

Gracie began to serve, aided by one of the new women brought from Sydney recently to help with the household chores. They served steaming dishes of turnips, carrots, and potatoes.

"You might be wishing you'd stayed in Sydney, but I can't tell you how happy I am you're here." Rem gave Sara his most beguiling smile, one nurtured in the past year. Agnes, usually the recipient of such smiles, tended the children at a smaller table set aside for them. Her antipathy toward the beauty at Rem's side was blatant. If looks were daggers, Sara would have been dead within five minutes of Agnes setting sight on her. Poor insignificant Agnes.

"I don't know which is worse, to be candid. I wished we'd never come out to this country of savages, but my father was convinced a fortune was waiting to be made." She flicked a glance at her father, now boring Tiger with a discourse on trading practices. Tiger's expression clearly showed his indifference to her father's monologue.

"And has he made his fortune yet?" Rem didn't take his eyes from her face. Every move she made entranced him more and more. He couldn't give a brass farthing for her father's possessions, but anything that got her talking was worth the effort.

"He's wealthy, if that's what you mean. My mother and I are allowed to purchase whatever we need to make us presentable in society."

"Society?" Rem laughed, glancing about. "Hardly that out here."

She picked sparingly at the food set before her. "You're right. We could all walk around in plain clothes and not give a fig for our appearance, and who would know or care? It really is a land of savages." The poignancy of her quiet statement struck him in the heart.

"I would care." Rem stared at her hard, and thought, such a hothouse plant should be pampered and spoiled, brought up amongst the society in London, not dragged to a godforsaken place like this. "Never change, sweet Sara. Always stay as beautiful and elegantly attired as you are now, no matter the cost or effort. Promise me."

"All right. I will promise you that." Her small laugh made his gut wrench. "Will you show me around the property?" she asked, glancing down the table.

The meal was almost at an end, and the others were still engrossed in a debate on the merits of sheep farming versus trading; Tiger enthusing about the price of fleece on the English market.

She had a way of fluttering her eyelashes that sent Rem's heart into a spin. Trying not to show his eagerness, and thus appearing like a smitten schoolboy, Rem rose slowly, bowing over her hand. "I would be honored." He pressed a kiss on her knuckle and was pleased to see her soft cheeks turn delightfully pink.

"Where are you off to?" Edmund bellowed, interrupting their discussion, as she settled her skirts about her with a pat of the hand.

Rem held his breath, expecting her father's annoyance to deter her, but then she said sweetly, "Rem is going to show me around, Papa," and gave Edmund a peck on his florid cheek. She smiled demurely at Bella. "And I need to walk after such a splendid meal. Thank you, Mrs. Carstairs. It was most enjoyable. But I shouldn't have eaten so much."

"Please call me Bella," Bella insisted, waving them on their way. "Go on with you, and enjoy your stroll." Rem grinned at Bella's meaningful look. A look that clearly stated he was to watch his step with this beauty, or bear the wrath of her father.

Rem knew Greenwood wouldn't make a scene in front of Bella and Tiger and smiled to himself. "Come, I'll show you the orchard Tiger planted soon after they arrived here." Offering his arm, he inhaled her fragrance as she hooked her hand in his elbow.

When they were out of earshot of the others, he said softly, "You smell as sweet as a garden full of blooms."

She tapped him on the chest with her fan and smiled, showing dear little dimples in her cheeks. "Hmm." With a chuckle, she wrinkled her nose pertly. "I'm surprised I don't stink like one of the horses, considering our mode of transport."

"There's no decent lanes or carriage ways yet. It's difficult for you to be jolted over the stubble in your wagon. Tiger's working hard at improving that. Soon there'll be a passable road connecting the properties on this side of the river. You should have seen it last year when I arrived."

"Is that how long you've been here?"

"Eighteen months to be precise. The house was half-built, and we lived in sod huts." He grimaced.

"Don't you get bored out here in the middle of nowhere?" she asked as he led her around the almond trees toward where the stone-fruit trees grew. They were well away from the house now, and he looked over his shoulder to see if they could be watched from the table.

"Truth is, bored out of my head, Sara." With a hand on her back he propelled her to a seat Tiger had positioned for Bella in the shade of what would eventually be a flourishing apple tree. She shivered, and he asked, "Are you warm enough?"

"It is cooler here." She hugged her arms across her chest.

"Would you like to go back?" he asked, praying she would say no.

"No, would you?" Slanting him a provocative look, she flashed him a wicked smile, her dimples more pronounced.

"I want nothing more than to be here with you." Rem took off his jacket and draped it across her shoulders. "Is that better?"

"Much." She shrugged into its warmth. "Now you'll be cold."

"Me? Not while I'm this close to you. You set my blood afire, did you know that?" Rem longed to plant a kiss on one of those indentations on her cheek, to explore it with his tongue. He held her gaze and reached for one of her dainty hands.

Her chuckle was charming as she tapped him again with the fan. "Gentlemen aren't supposed to say things like that to ladies," she admonished, but he got the distinct impression she wasn't the least affronted by his bluntness.

"I ain't a gentleman, Sara. I'm a convict, plain and simple. Does that bother you?" Sitting beside her, he pressed his thigh to her skirts. She didn't move away, although her look said she was slightly shocked.

"No, it doesn't bother me. Unless, of course, you intend to act like one and be brutish. What did you do to get transported?" she asked.

Rem shrugged. "Same as most. Not a lot. Pinched food to help my family. Most convicts are just like me, ordinary men and women charged with transportation for petty crimes." The memories, dulled in the past year, resurfaced. "Papa died in prison, our mum died the year I was sent out here, and one of our sisters died of starvation and the cold." Rem grimaced as he remembered the awful winters they had to endure; winters with no food, no heat, and the threat of disease a part of their everyday existence.

"How sad." She seemed genuinely appalled by his plight. "So is Bella all the family you have left?"

"No. We have another two sisters and two brothers still in Stepney, although Carlos, the eldest, will more than likely end up here soon. Likely the others will too eventually. It's the way of things. A fact of life."

"Carlos? What a foreign-sounding name. Why would your brother be named such?" Her limpid eyes turned on him inquisitively.

"Our papa was Spanish." Her eyes widened, and Rem quickly asked, "Does that bother you?"

"Bother me? Why, no." With a careless flick of the hand, she said, "But it does surprise me. Although it shouldn't really, for your sister's name, Isabella, is Spanish, is it not?"

"Right."

"And now that I look at you closely I can see you do have the appearance about you unlike most of the English men here in the colony." Her gaze roved over his face. He sincerely hoped she liked what she saw.

"And is my different look distasteful to you?" Rem knew he was seeking compliments from her, but couldn't help himself. How he yearned for her to be as entranced as he was by everything about her.

"Distasteful? Why, of course not." Leaning closer, she said in a husky tone that set his pulses to racing and his heart pounding at a fierce rate, "You're extremely handsome of face. But I expect you've been told so by countless women." With a sniff, she looked swiftly away.

Rem chuckled, feeling ten feet tall. "A few have assured me I'm not ugly. In truth, you're the first to tell me I'm handsome," he lied. "And I can't say how much it pleases me to know you admire my looks, for I must tell you that I find you the most entrancing woman on earth. You're beautiful, clever, witty…"

"Stop." With a laugh, she held up both hands then tapped him on his knee. "You'll turn my head with your compliments."

"I only speak the truth." Rem bent his head to whisper near her shell-shaped ear, "I love you with all my heart. And when I'm out of my term and a free man; then I'll ask your father for your sweet hand." He placed a kiss on her knuckle, and a tremor raced over her skin. He hoped it wasn't just the cool air causing it. He hoped she was as enamored of him as he was of her. "Will you wait for me?"

Her eyes widened at his impudence, but he knew without being told that his words captured her interest. "What nonsense. How can you speak of love, Remy? You've only just met me. How can you possibly have such strong feelings for me on such a short acquaintance?"

"Love knows no boundaries, of time or place. I'll feel the same fifty years from now as I feel at this moment," he swore with fervor, cupping her chin with his palm. Strangely, he knew his words were true. He had felt a strong attraction for a few women before, but nothing like this all-encompassing devotion that seemed to fill all his senses.

"I know not what to say." Her voice was low and husky. She made no move to remove herself from his touch, and that thrilled him to the core.

26

"Then say naught. Or say you return my feelings. But don't say you feel nothing for me, or I shall die."

"Stuff and nonsense. Of course you won't die," she said prettily.

With a hand over his heart, Rem sighed elaborately. "But I will. I thought females were more romantic than us men." Rem grinned.

"We are." She chuckled, a lovely sound that made his heart turn over. "We want men to fawn over us, to treat us as if we're hot-house plants."

"There you are." Rem touched a finger to her dainty nose. "I'll treat you as if you're the most precious person in the world. Just say you like me a tiny bit."

"Of course I like you." With smiling eyes, she examined his face until he felt foolish color rise up from his throat.

How ridiculous. Only females were supposed to blush.

"You're a personable young man. Far nicer than the other young bloods in town who fawned over me."

"Nicer? Ye gods! Is that all you think me?" Rem made a sound of disgust in his throat.

"Yes, nicer." She pouted, and Rem turned away. "In truth, I found some of the men who asked to court me absolute bores." As he faced her again, she wrinkled her nose. "All right, I think you the most handsome person I've ever set eyes on. But that's not to say I can return this love you foolishly claim to hold for me."

"Foolish? Jesus, you're enough to squelch a man's ego." Rem blew out a large breath. Still, she was so young. He would give her time. Soon her feelings would match his. At least while they were so isolated out here he could court her, woo her, and win her. In his heart, he had no doubt this would be the outcome.

"How am I to know these feelings you profess to feel for me aren't merely because there are very few women of our age out here," she said with a touch of hesitancy.

Rem held up a hand to silence her on that subject. 'No. Don't ever accuse me of being so fickle, I beg you. I'm twenty-three years old and way past pining over females

27

simply because their looks take my fancy. Believe me; this emotion within me will only grow with time I assure you. Allow me to know my own capacity for caring."

"You overwhelm me, Remy." It was true, he saw. Patience, he cautioned. They heard Greenwood's shout, and she looked behind her as Rem cursed silently. "There's my father calling me. We'd best go back now."

She rose and handed him his coat as he stood too. Her delicious scent of flowers still clung to it, and he pressed his nose to a lapel as he pulled it on.

"Sara." Catching one of her hands, he brought it to his lips. "Can I ask a favor of you before we rejoin the others?"

"A favor?" Her eyes were clear as she gazed up at him, leaving her fingers trapped within his.

"May I kiss you?" Rem knew that in polite society the question would have been received with absolute shock and disdain. But out here they were ruled by a totally different set of circumstances.

"You may kiss my cheek." She tilted her head. Rem placed his mouth over hers, smothering her small gasp of shock. Capturing her in his arms, he pulled her against his length, stifling her small protest.

This was heaven, paradise. Without thought, he deepened the kiss, tasting her with his tongue. With a smothered exclamation, she pushed at his shoulders. Rem released her slowly, stepping back a pace. Keeping his hands on her spine, he sighed deeply.

"A lady doesn't allow a gentleman to kiss her that way," she whispered, her cheeks flushed and her lips dewy.

He grinned. "I'm not a gent, we've already decided that. And don't tell me you didn't enjoy that as much as I did, or I'll call you a liar."

"I...I..." With a flustered movement, she pushed at a few strands of hair that had escaped her bonnet, which was slightly askew. "If my father knew you'd kissed me in such a wanton manner, he'd likely have you thrown into prison."

"Are you going to tell him?" Rem touched a finger to her bottom lip. She jumped and stepped out of reach.

"No, as long as you don't do it again."

Rem moved in on her, catching her fidgeting hands. "You don't mean that, do you? Swear to me you didn't like it one little bit, an' I'll promise never to touch you again." He swallowed hard. Jesus, if she did that he'd likely go barmy. Her lips were nectar, tasted better than the finest wine Tiger served at his table. They intoxicated him as no brew ever could.

She looked over his shoulder, nibbling on her lip again. "Perhaps I liked it a little. But you must never let my father know." Fear showed in her eyes. "He treats me as a child still."

"He wouldn't harm you, would he?" The thought of the brute setting a finger on her in anger had him ready to kill the man. Heat burned his cheeks.

"No, of course not." She fidgeted with her hair again. "My father loves me in his own way. But I fear what he would do to you if he learned you'd dared to kiss me."

"I'm glad you fear for me." That was surely something in his favor.

"My father wants me to marry a man of worth, Remy." There was a note of pleading as she said, "Promise me you'll watch yourself around him."

"I promise, but let me also promise this. One day I will be a man of worth. Then I'll ask for your hand, mark my words. And he won't refuse me."

Her sigh told him she wasn't too sure of that eventuality.

"Just a minute." Rem tugged gently on her arm as she began to walk back.

"What is it?" Halting, she gazed at him while he straightened her bonnet.

"There. If no one looks too closely at your pink cheeks they'll not guess you've been kissed by your future husband."

"Oh, Remy" She slapped at his wrist as he ran unsteady fingers along her cheek. "You're incorrigible."

"I've been accused of being that," he said on a laugh, as they walked slowly back to join the others. "Among other things."

Chapter Three

"Just what did you find to talk about that kept you with that young fella so long, Princess?" her father demanded, giving Sara a sidelong glance. It was apparent he had gotten into the rum or some other spirit with Tiger Carstairs, for his nose was more bulbous than usual, his cheeks florid with color she knew hadn't come from the stiff breeze.

Although spoiled by him since a child, he never showed her any real affection, and the realization had grown over a period of time that she didn't like her father very much.

Sara pushed uneasily at a stray tendril of hair escaping from her bonnet and blowing across her eyes. The wagon bounced and swayed over the ruts in the uneven road between properties. Her mother made a soft sound of distress. Sara could almost hear the poor woman's teeth rattling as she clutched at the iron side rail until her knuckles were white. How she ever survived the horrible trip over the mountains still puzzled Sara. Perhaps her mother possessed a streak of courage kept well hidden. Had she once possessed the bravado to stand up to this arrogant bully she married? Sara often wondered. Perhaps she had, but it was unlikely.

Rem was so different from her father; would he make a better husband? One could never be sure with men. Some of the wives she had met in town on excursions with her mother soon became disillusioned once the first glow of being a newlywed bride wore off.

"Rem was showing me their orchard, Papa. They have many stone-fruit flourishing." Thoughts of that wanton kiss and its effect on her senses made her blush. She turned away to look across the fields, a hand to her bonnet rim to hide her eyes. Her father was so insensitive to anyone's feelings it was unlikely he would spot the dreamy look in her eyes or her flushed cheeks. He saw only what he wanted to see.

"Humph." He cleared his throat noisily.

"He seems a likeable young man, dear," her mother ventured in that whining voice of hers that set Sara's teeth on edge at times. Why hadn't the woman learned to stand up to her husband?

"Likeable!" The poor horses received a slap with the whip for no apparent reason and increased their pace, which made her mother cling more tightly to the rail at the side of the bench seat, her bonnet now askew so she looked quite a pathetic sight. "He looks like the scoundrel he assuredly is. I don't want you getting friendly with the likes of him, Princess, hear me?" He glowered at Sara. "He's a convict, whether Mistress Carstairs likes to make out he is or not. He might be her brother, and Tiger's becoming a force to be reckoned with in the colony; but Rem O'Shea's still serving his term and don't you forget it!" He made a loud harrumphing noise. "Lord above knows what crime he committed to be sent here in the first place."

"He stole food to feed his starving brothers and sisters," Sara informed him tartly.

"Oh, yes." That earned her another glower. "That might be so, but he'd likely tell you anything to keep sweet with you. Anyway, you're only seventeen, not old enough to be going off alone without a chaperone, just remember that, my girl!"

"Meg Howe's only eighteen now, yet was married before we left Sydney last year, Papa." Why did she bother arguing with him? Her father had his own way of seeing life, and nothing she said or did would alter his one-viewed opinions. Sara knew well enough what she wanted and decided a long time ago that it was best to agree with him, and keep her secrets. Her mother never took her side for fear of earning her husband's wrath, and this added to

Sara's disdain of her. Sara would never saddle herself with a man who ruled her as her father dominated her mother.

Would Rem turn out the same? Sara doubted it, but had no way of knowing. Men told women all sorts of fancy tales to get their way. Something told her Rem would not be like that. Possessive he would likely be, but his sweet tongue would get him into any woman's favor. The thought of that sweet tongue, and how it had behaved while he kissed her, was enough to make her exceedingly hot around the collar of her cloak. A delicate shudder ran through her as she relived the sensation of his warm wet tongue touching her mouth, and his bold exploration within.

"He's too full of himself," her father snorted, pulling up in front of the porch. His complete lack of skill rattled every bone in Sara's body. Her mother straightened her bonnet with trembling hands. "He'll fall on his arse one day, mark my words."

Sara bit her lip as she turned away to stare back along the path. That was something she would never countenance from the man she married. No man but her father was ever going to tell her what to say and when to say it.

Edmund Greenwood grunted as he shouted for the stable lad impatiently. Dick came at a run, earning a cuff round the ear for his tardiness in not being on hand immediately.

* * *

Sara dropped her bonnet onto the chaise in her bedroom. She went to study her reflection in the long mirror and stared at herself critically. Without being conceited she knew she was pretty to look on, had been told so many times by those admirers she scoffed at. Her dark hair and eyes accentuated her pale skin—skin, she was pleased to know, held not one blemish to mar it. Running a finger over her mouth she paused as a tremor raced over her. Remy O'Shea was an experienced kisser. How many women had he charmed in the past? Was she right in thinking his lack of female company added to her attraction? How she hoped that wasn't so.

He certainly was good to look at, his dark complexion and rich burgundy hair giving him a gypsy appearance. That must be his Spanish blood. And what eyes—when he looked at her she got the feeling he was searching into her soul, could read all her secrets. After her father's sullen bigotry, Remy's readiness to laugh was so pleasing in a life lacking spontaneous laughter and fun.

"Help me off with my dress," she said. Josie, her governess and companion during her growing years, now begrudgingly acted as her maid.

The whey-faced, taciturn creature had come over with them from England five years ago. This was one person who definitely had never learned how to laugh; Sara doubted her thin lips ever curved. Sara viewed her as a jailer and wondered if her father ordered she follow Sara about like a shadow at all times. Since they left Sydney the woman was often so close at her heels Sara almost tripped over her when she turned suddenly. This closeness she would have welcomed if the woman showed one ounce of friendship or kindness.

When Sara was down to her petticoats, Josie asked, "Will there be anything else?" a sullen smirk twisting her mouth.

"No, that will be all." Knowing Josie hated being treated like a servant, Sara injected as much hauteur into her tone as she could muster.

The woman placed Sara's dress in the wardrobe, gave her one last reproachful glance, and silently left the room. With a sigh, Sara flopped onto her bed and idly turned the pages of a book of poems. Her father held strict ideas of what was acceptable reading material for her, and this book held stiff moralistic verses that bored her. Lord knows who advised him in his choice, likely the reverend.

The words blurred as her thoughts dwelled on Rem. She couldn't seem to think of anything else. At twenty-three, Rem was a man in his prime, obviously experienced in the ways of women. Had he learned how to kiss with convict women, or practiced on serving wenches he perhaps met in Sydney or even in London before his arrest?

His life had been so different to hers; he offered a touch of excitement, which she craved. In a house with her timid and often vague mother, surrounded by servants who feared her father too much to think of going against his wishes, she felt stifled. Often she fretted her life was slipping away without her tasting the things she knew were out there in the world beyond these oppressive confines. Turning onto her back, she stared up at the smoke-darkened beams, a hand to her fast-beating breast.

Would Rem come to call on her? He was brash and forward enough to do so, even knowing her father wouldn't sanction it. It hadn't been a lie when she said she feared for him. Sara sighed and chewed on her lip until she made it sore.

How could she meet him again? How could she get to experience his kisses, his special brand of humor and charm? With Josie constantly at her shoulder and the threat of her father's wrath if he paid an unwelcome call, the chances were minimal. That thought made her morose.

* * *

Rem shielded his eyes as he stood in the stirrups the better to see the approaching riders. There were two, and one looked to be a female, her skirts billowing behind the small gray horse she rode with skill. Yes, she rode side-saddle, and even at a distance, he could tell she knew how to handle a horse. Waving his cabbage tree hat, he plonked it back on his head and wiped his face with a corner of his neckerchief. It wasn't hot by any means, but the thought of meeting up with Sara was enough to bring him out in a sweat.

His heart began to thump in anticipation as they drew close enough for him to recognize her. Good God, what luck.

As they pulled their mounts back into a trot, then a walk, he saw her companion was a boy of about twelve, riding a giant bay cob.

"Good morning, Mistress Greenwood, what a pleasure on such a fine morning," he said, grinning.

Indeed, it was more than mere pleasure; it was an absolute delight. What a sight for his humble eyes she was, with her pink cheeks, shining eyes, and rosebud mouth. Dressed in a superb riding outfit of deep green, she looked as fresh and inviting as a mountain stream on a blistering hot day.

"Rem." With a regal nod of the head, she gave him a smile, curving those precious lips invitingly. "It is indeed a fine morning. Are you riding for pleasure, or at some task?"

Rem shrugged. "I rarely ride for pleasure. Tiger's a hard taskmaster, but I merely have to check on the shepherd guarding the flock over yonder." He nodded to where the creatures could be seen off in the distance, grazing. "I have to bring the fellow his food ration." He motioned to the bag hanging from his saddle horn. "Would you care to ride with me, or do you have to get back?"

Casting a glance at the boy, she grinned impishly. "I should be delighted to accompany you. Dick, you will stay at a distance." The lad's face turned a brilliant shade of claret at her suggestion. He looked disconcerted and uncertain, but gave a small nod.

When there was a reasonable few yards between them and Dick, Rem asked, "How is it your father allows you to ride out with a snip of a boy for company?"

"Dick is an expert horseman." Glancing over a shoulder at the boy, she said conspiratorially, "Father gave instructions that I'm always to be accompanied by a person who rides well. He cares not who that is."

"I'm surprised he doesn't forbid you to ride so far afield," Rem said.

With a delightful chuckle, she gave him a provocative smile. "He did, of course," she admitted carelessly. "But once we're away from the property, he can hardly follow my every move, now can he?" Breathing deeply, she looked to the sky. "Riding is the only occupation I can follow where I'm not constantly trailed by that idiotic companion of mine. Josie is terrified of horses." It was apparent this delighted her immensely.

"How fortunate." What an understatement. Rem couldn't believe his good fortune at meeting her. "I've been racking my brain to think of a reason to call on you without raising your father's ire." He leaned closer. "And here we have the perfect solution. Will you meet me again, Sara?"

"Hmm." She gave this some thought, stroking her gloved hand along her mare's silver mane. "I don't see any harm in that," she decided at length, and Rem blew out the breath he had been holding.

"Admirable." He cocked her a broad grin, whispering, "Now all we have to do is lose our friend Dick back there, and everything in my world will be perfect."

She eyed him thoughtfully, her fingers absently playing with the mane beneath them. "I have a feeling most things in your world work out to your satisfaction, am I right?"

"If I can make you care for me as I care for you; then I'll be able to say yes, but until then the answer must be no." Rem stared at the milling sheep before adding, "I've had a hard life, Sara. I've seen things no lady such as you could imagine. And things you most certainly should never know of. But I want to put that all behind me, be an upstanding citizen here in the colony."

"Then you will." He raised his brows in question and she added, "—become an upstanding citizen."

"I thought you meant I will have you love me one day as I love you." He let his gaze roam over her face.

With a small giggle, she moved her mare in, so close to his horse their elbows touched. His heart skipped a beat. "You'll have to teach me to love you, Remy O'Shea, for I have no notion of what being in love entails." Those endearing eyes of hers were wide with innocence. "Will you bring me presents and show your affection in small ways? Or will you try to kiss me as you did in the orchard?"

Rem realized she was truly innocent of what desire entailed and vowed, "Yes, I'll do that and much more." Lord knows when that would be.

They reached the stragglers from the flock, the shy creatures scurrying out of the way of the horses. Rem whistled and Mole looked up. The old shepherd sat propped against a towering gum tree, his two dogs at his side. They barked once, but then Mole offered a word or two to them and they lay down again. The old man rose slowly on arthritic legs. Rem knew not where Mole got his nickname, but nobody knew what else to call him. Wizened and toothless, he had come over a few months back with a party of newcomers, seeking to work for Tiger, whose reputation as a good sheep man and master had spread.

"Mornin'. Fine day for it," he said with a sly grin, his rheumy eyes taking in Sara at a glance as he touched a finger to his temple as a small salute of welcome.

"'Tis that, for sure," Rem agreed. "Your tucker." He passed the bag over and retrieved the empty one Mole held out for him. "Sheep all right?" Rem glanced at the milling flock, now settled back to grazing after the interruption.

"As right as they'll ever be. Stupid creatures." The old fellow looked over his flock with a touch of scorn Rem knew to be false. Mole was devoted to the animals.

"I'll see you the day after tomorrow then." Rem waved as he turned his mount.

"I'll be here." Mole winked. "Ma'am." He touched his forehead, and then resettled his tattered hat on his bald head.

"How can he bear to spend his days out here alone with just the animals for company?" Sara asked as they walked their horses back, Dick still at a respectable distance.

Rem shrugged. "There's all sorts of men out here in the colony. Men with sordid pasts they want to escape from. Men with secrets. And men, like Mole, who simply prefer the animals' company more than they like human folk."

"Perhaps he lost a love," she mused. "Or perhaps he killed a foe in a duel and had to flee from England. Perhaps he spends his life daydreaming of a sweetheart he left behind in England."

Rem laughed. "What a romantic little soul you are. No, 'tis more likely he got transported for stealing a nob's watch or for poaching on some gentry's land."

"Poof." She blew on her fingers and waved them at him. "You have no romance in your soul at all."

"Untrue. I'm the most romantic man you'll ever meet. Let me be alone with you for a few minutes, and I'll prove it." He winked mischievously.

"Remy O'Shea, you're a reprobate." She shot a quick glance to the boy riding just out of hearing. With a pensive turn of the head, she asked softly, "Just how would you prove it?"

She was adorable. "I'd shower you with kisses aplenty, and when you were breathless and begging me to put an end to my torment, I'd tell you in detail about your many bewitching assets—until you had time to catch your breath, mind." Rem heaved a sigh as he silently listed the many ways he would like to woo her—ways that would shock her senseless, let alone send her breathless.

"I may be wrong, but I have a feeling a gentleman shouldn't be saying such things to a lady," she scolded prettily, her dimpled cheeks a shade of pink that owed nothing to the wind.

"Ah, sweet Sara, something tells me you and I will never do or say what is considered the norm in respectable society." Rem reached across and took one of her hands, which he brought to his lips. "Am I right?"

With a sigh, she dragged her hand free. "You could be," she agreed.

* * *

July was drawing to a close. Three long weeks had dragged by since setting eyes on his beloved Sara. After discussing calling on her with Bella, Rem let his sister persuade him against it.

"No, Remy, I suggest you leave well alone," she said. "Her father's a hard man, a bully and a braggart. You'd gain nothing by calling at their home. He sees you as a convict, and let's be honest, you are. You'd only make life more difficult for Sara, believe me. It must be unbearable at times for a young vital girl like her to be in that house with him and her feckless mother."

Much as he hated to believe it, Bella was right.

Deep in thought, Rem let his horse meander while he morosely pondered his options. When his horse's head shot up and whinnied, Rem looked up and caught sight of two riders in the distance. His spirits lifted as he set his horse at a canter toward them. His spirits soared even higher when he knew it was Sara and her watchdog, Dick. When there were about fifty paces between them, he pulled up and waited for them to come to him.

"Good day, Mistress Sara, how are you?" Rem doffed his wide-brimmed hat, grinning. The wind blustered today and there was a nip in the air, and Sara's cheeks were delightfully pink from her ride.

"Good day to you. I'm well." Rem hoped the sparkle in her eyes was brought about by pleasure at seeing him, and not just the strong wind.

Rem dismounted and went to stand by her horse, his hand on its wither. Looking up at her, he urged, "Walk with me?"

She gave a small nod, and slid down her horse's side, into his waiting arms. Rem stifled a desire to crush her to him and smother her face with kisses. Congratulating himself on his restraint, he stepped back as she turned to order the lad, "Stay with the horses."

Dick's face was as red as a face could get when he dismounted and took all the reins in one hand.

They were on a flat stretch of meadowland with a few trees dotted sparsely around the landscape. Fervently Rem wished they could find a secluded spot so they could lose themselves. Still, perhaps it was for the best. At least now he would be forced to keep his hands to himself.

When they were a distance away from Dick, he said, "I was going to pay you a visit, but thought better of it."

"I'm glad you didn't." She put a hand on his arm and frowned. "Not that I wouldn't have welcomed your company, you understand, but my father would likely refuse you entry. He can be very belligerent."

Didn't Rem know it!

"Never mind, we're together now. I've done nothing but think about you." Rem steered her with a hand on her elbow toward the nearest gum tree. It wouldn't give them the privacy he craved, but at least he wouldn't feel as if Dick was spying on them.

She tapped him on the arm with her crop. "I don't believe that for one moment."

"It's the truth. I thought of riding over in the dead of night and throwing pebbles at your window."

With a hand to her chest, she turned to him, consternation clear on her face. "No, don't ever do that I beg you. My father would shoot you without asking questions, or his brute of a foreman would attack you. Promise me you'll never do anything so foolish."

There was true fear in her eyes. "All right, I promise. You're really convinced they would harm me, aren't you?"

"I know it for a fact. Luxton has no qualms about beating convicts senseless for minor offences, and my father lets him do as he pleases. My father sees all convicts as the scum of the earth, and there's nothing anyone can say to change his way of thinking."

"All right, I promise I won't come calling on you, but you have to promise me you'll find a way to meet me while out riding."

"I don't think I can do that." A sudden thought seemed to come into her mind, and she giggled. "How would you know which window to toss your pebbles at?"

Rem shrugged. "I didn't think that far ahead. I don't suppose you could visit Bella without your mother or that woman of yours accompanying you could you?"

"It's impossible. I think Josie delights in being horrible. The woman is sad and sour, and doesn't like to see me enjoying life."

"Come, let's sit here." Rem pointed to a grassy mound near the base of the gum tree. Glancing back, he saw Dick was sitting on the ground, while the horses in his charge grazed.

She settled her skirts about her as she sank gracefully down. Rem sat beside her and brought one of her hands to his lips, murmuring, "Such dainty fingers."

With a small laugh, she pushed gently at his shoulder. "You have a sweet tongue, Remy O'Shea. Tell me about your life in London, before you were sent here. How many girls did you kiss, and tell sweet lies to?"

"A lady doesn't ask such questions." He winked. "And any woman I might have kissed is forgotten. The only kisses I recall are kisses shared with you."

With a sigh, she looked at him from beneath slightly lowered lids. "Truthfully, tell me about your life. I want to know."

Rem went onto his side, resting on an elbow as he stretched his legs out. "There's things you wouldn't want to know. We lived from day to day, scrounging and thieving. How would you like to get up in the morning as hungry as when you went to bed the night before? I'll bet you've never been a whole day without food, have you?"

"Only when I've been poorly. I'll say that for my father, he might be stingy with his affections, but he's never skimped on the essentials of life. He's too much of a glutton for that."

"Where did he get his wealth from in the first place?"

Her nose wrinkled. "I'm not sure. I suppose his father left him an inheritance. We don't discuss such things in our home." Looking down at his hand curved around hers she asked, a slight quiver in her voice, "What is it like to live with people you know love you?"

"Ah, Sara." Rem brought her fingers to his lips. "When I make you mine you will know. I'll shower you with so much love you'll feel suffocated with it."

She studied him, her eyes grave. "You're so sure of yourself, aren't you?"

"It's called confidence. I have it in abundance." Rem sighed. "Some people would say I'm arrogant."

Those perfect shoulders of hers lifted in a shrug. "I don't think you're arrogant. I think your past shaped your character, and you've learned to look out for yourself and for those you love."

"And from this moment on, you belong with that band of people, for I love you more than life itself," he murmured, reaching up to curve his fingers around the nape of her neck to pull her down for a kiss.

When she pulled back, her cheeks glowing, she glanced around, looking flustered. "You shouldn't do that. Dick can see us."

"No he can't. I made sure we were out of his line of vision. I don't care anyway; he's not likely to go running to your father with tales, is he?"

"I…I'm not sure. I never know who to trust."

"Poor love." Rem stroked a finger down her blushing cheek. "When do you think you'll be able to meet me again?"

Nibbling on her lower lip, she frowned. "I'm not sure."

"Tell you what. We'll make this tree our meeting place. I'll come here every third day about the same time. I'll wait for an hour. All right?"

"Won't Mr. Carstairs be wondering where you're going if you leave your tasks so often?"

Rem laughed. "Aye, he'll wonder. But Bella will sort it out for me. My sister knows how to handle her husband." Rem cupped her chin in a palm and gazed into her eyes. "Now, kiss me again before I go out of my mind with longing."

She complied; yielding with an eagerness that convinced Rem he gained paradise.

Chapter Four

December 1826

Sara tried not to look across the table at Rem, knowing he was trying his hardest to gain her attention. In the five months since first setting eyes on each other, she had met him about a dozen times. Dick always hovered in the background. There was no way she could escape without her escort; it was trouble enough to ride as often as she did.

After their second meeting, she assured Remy it would be impossible to get out once a week, let alone every third day. Excuses had to be found for her mother, who couldn't see the point in riding in such heat as they experienced the past month. But then, her mother seldom saw any point in doing much in this life that was pleasurable. Lord, how she hoped her life would never become so colorless and meaningless.

"I must say it's unusual to have such a hot spell before Christmas," Tiger was telling her mother, who had been complaining about the weather.

"Please help yourself to more fowl," Mrs. Carstairs, who insisted they call her Bella, offered. Sara liked Rem's sister very much. The woman never put on airs or graces, never pretended to be any more than what she was, a sheep farmer's wife.

The dining table was set beneath a shelter erected in the garden. Bella said it was to protect them from the heat of the sun while they ate. She preferred to dine outside when the weather allowed so the children could eat alongside the adults. This was another of Bella's ideas Sara found admirable. Most wealthy families in Sydney seldom saw their children and perhaps spent half an hour with their offspring before dining formally each day.

"I swear I cannot find room for another mouthful." Sara shook her head.

"Oh, dear, I hope you have enough room left for the pudding Gracie's made." Bella said with a laugh.

"Perhaps you'd like a walk round the orchard, to give your first courses time to settle before you attack it," Rem said, standing and nodding in Sara's direction.

"What a splendid idea, that way I'll be able to do it justice. I'm sure Gracie's pudding is as tasty as the rest of this wonderful meal." Sara rose, smiling at Rem, who had rushed around the table.

"Good God, I never thought I'd get you alone," Rem muttered as he offered his arm, and they strolled away from those seated around the table.

"Can I come too?" It was Tim, Rem's nephew, and Sara smiled down at the boy. He was likeable, but definitely not wanted along today if the scowl Rem offered him was anything to go by.

"No, you cannot." When Tim tagged behind them, Rem swatted at the boy's fair head. "Go play with your sisters or brother."

"Sisters? Those two are busy playing with their dolls, and John is but a month old. Agnes is looking after him. I'll be glad when he's bigger, so I'm not surrounded by silly girls all the time." The sound he made clearly showed his disgust at the idea of spending time with his young sisters.

Rem laughed. "Then go play with your dogs."

"Dogs are for working, not playing," he declared with all the loftiness of a sheep-owner's son.

"Oh, aye, well go find some other activity. Here, I'll give you a farthing if you go find something else to do."

Tim whooped loudly as he snatched the coin and ran off, his dog at his heels.

"That was bribery," Sara said with a laugh.

"Don't I know it? But I'd give more than a farthing to get you alone. That was nothing. I'm fed up with having to put up with that dolt Dick hanging about when we meet. Can't you get rid of the pest when next you ride out?"

44

"Of course not." Sara twirled her parasol and made a small grimace with her lips. "I'm lucky my father doesn't send one of the older hands to watch over me when I ride. 'Tis only because he knows I can handle my mare well, and Dick is also an excellent rider that Papa allows me to ride at all. I daren't make suggestions, else he may curtail my rides altogether."

Rem sighed, lifting his broad shoulders in a shrug. He wore a white shirt today, the weather having necessitated the men removing their jackets earlier, and his muscles were clearly delineated beneath the soft linen. Sara knew quite well by now how those shoulders and chest felt beneath her fingers, and she ached to relearn their shape.

"How I wish you could slip away after dark so we could spend some time alone, Sara. Can't you possibly arrange it?"

By now, they were well away from the others, at the far side of the stand of apple trees. Rem suddenly dragged her about. With a swift look around to ensure they were alone he pulled her into his arms. "I'm on fire for you; I ache in every part of me when I'm away from you."

"Rem! I beg of you, they may be able to see us." Frantically she looked about. They could barely hear the murmur of voices from the dining table above the noise of the parrots overhead.

"They can't. I know how far you can see from the house and its surrounds. That's why I brought you here." Rem's gaze made her insides quiver. "I love you, Sara. I long for your kisses."

Sara still felt jittery. "What if Tim's hiding out behind a tree?" she asked. "What if he goes back and innocently tells them he's seen us kissing?"

"No." Rem shook his head. "Tim's a good lad. He'll not bother us now he has his coin." He tapped his brow. "The tyke's also very clever. He'll know that if he gives us away he'll not get paid again."

She laughed. "He's as outrageous as his uncle. That I can see."

"Not yet, he ain't. But he will be, one day, under my tutelage." His grin held that touch of mischievousness she adored. In fact, there was little about Rem she didn't adore, except perhaps his vast experience with females.

"You're very conceited, and I'm positive you're a rogue." With a sniff, she pushed at his chest when he tried to press her against him.

With a careless flick, he tossed her parasol aside, and then easily captured her by the wrists, successfully imprisoning her. Sara could feel his strength, his hardness through the layers of clothing separating them. Her heart did a quick turn, and she gasped.

"Kiss me, while we can." His murmured plea melted all resistance and she complied, meeting his mouth with her own. The world seemed to tilt. Or was she falling down a dark and pleasurable tunnel? How could the mere meeting of mouths bring forth such pleasure? Never in her childish dreams of romance and love had she dreamed it could be like this between a man and woman.

Breathing heavily he repeated her name again and again as his hot mouth moved over her face, worshipping every place he touched. There was a magic in the moment, as if time was suspended, and they were alone in the universe. Oh, how she wished at that moment they were somewhere private.

Taking her hands, he placed her arms about his neck, and then urged her closer with a gentle push on her back. An ache in her lower body made heat settle between her legs, and she squirmed. She shouldn't be allowing him such liberties, she knew, but how could she resist the sweet temptation he offered?

"I wish I could see you," he whispered against her throat. His wandering fingers had found the mound of a breast that had grown heavy, and he caressed it until she felt as if she would melt. Perhaps it was the sun that beat down from overhead, but she never felt so hot in her life; and that heat seemed to be collected where dampness pooled in the private place that seemed to be at the very center of her.

"I am here." Her own whispered response seemed to come from some place far away.

"But I want to see you naked, need to be able to touch your silken flesh." With that announcement, he shocked her to the core when his mouth traced a path over her upper breast where it peeped from her muslin dress, while his hand still caressed the other one through the fabric.

"No!" That was too much. "Remy, you mustn't do this," she implored, pushing away out of the silken web of desire he had trapped her in.

"Why not? Don't dare tell me you weren't enjoying it as much as I." Running his fingers through his thatch of hair, he sent it flying about his face until he looked tousled and wind-swept. A streak of color darkened his cheeks.

"Of course I enjoyed it. I would be foolish to try to tell you otherwise. But I'm sure young ladies of breeding aren't supposed to allow their suitors such liberties." Sara pressed her palms to her cheeks, finding them as hot as cinders.

"Piffle! We're out here miles and miles away from polite society. I want you. You desire me. I can see it in your eyes when you look at me, as much as you may argue otherwise. So, what's to stop us enjoying each other while we can?"

"I'll tell you what's to stop us," she said in a hot whisper. "My father, that's what, or who. If he were to find you've been kissing and touching me this way, I dread to think what he would do."

Sara knew deep down what he would do—he would likely kill Rem. A convict was less than the dirt beneath her father's boots. Regardless of what Rem was transported for, felons shipped out here were scum in his eyes. Her father wasn't a man to look at things from any angle but his own. And his bias was distorted beyond her understanding.

"We're young and alive, why not take what we can while we can, Sara," Rem pleaded, desire burning from his eyes until she felt the heat of them would sear her to the very soul.

"Because," she insisted, "despite what you say about us being out here in this primitive world we're still civilized people. We should at least try to adhere to the restraints put upon us by society."

"Not us, Sara." His nostrils flared. "Not you and I. We'll always make our own rules, people like us, and you know it." Again he reached for her. "Come now, another kiss before we have to go back to join the others."

"Rem," she whispered against his mouth in the moment before he covered hers. Then she forgot who she was, or where she was. Her hands wove into his soft hair, loving the feel of it between her fingers. He cast some sort of spell over her senses. Through a haze of desire, the realization hit her that no man would ever be able to arouse her this way.

"Rem!" The shout brought her to her senses, and she shoved at his shoulders. He refused to let her go and drew back to put a tiny space between them with a dreamy sigh, his eyes glazed with passion, his lips wet from their heated kisses.

"Damnation, it's Tim." He touched a fingertip to her lower lip, and Sara found it impossible to break free of the silken web surrounding her. "What is it?" he called, finally stepping back a pace or two, straightening his hair with quick strokes.

The boy strolled toward them, his dog panting at his side. "Sara's father's wondering what you're doing out here so long," he said. "Thought I'd best warn you he was set to send someone to search you out." Tim's eyes darted from Rem then back to her, with bright inquisitive interest.

"Thanks lad, you're a good 'un." Rem tousled the blond mane as Tim stood before him, a hand outstretched. "But you ain't getting any more coin off me today, so don't expect it."

"A boy can try, eh?" Tim said with a cheeky grin, pushing his hands into the pockets of his breeches.

"Aye, he can try. Right, off you go, we're coming along now." Rem gave him a soft nudge, saying, "And Tim, thanks."

Tim laughed again and jogged off.

Rem sighed heavily and brushed a strand of hair over one of her ears. That small caress sent shivers over her skin.

"We will become lovers, Sara. It's just a matter of when and where, not if." The passion in that statement stirred her. He was so confident.

"Don't be so sure about that." Sara felt the need to assert her authority. With Rem there was the need to let him know he didn't own her body and soul. Even if perhaps he did.

As they strolled back to the house, keeping a respectable distance between them, she knew she was fooling herself.

Remy O'Shea owned her soul already, and it was only a matter of time before he owned her body as well.

* * *

Sara picked at her food, letting her father's current tirade waft over her head. It was his habit to rant and rave at the dinner table while a captive audience was forced to listen to him rage about the convicts and tradesmen in his employ. It still puzzled her why he dragged them over the mountains when the business in Sydney was prospering. Presumably, someone convinced him a fortune was to be made in sheep. His land grant covered many acres, but compared to what they left behind in England, the house was a hovel. There were no polished boards beneath their feet, no sumptuous window drapes, no high-filigreed ceilings. To Sara it befitted the estate manager's residence rather than a man of property. She would have preferred by far to stay behind in town.

Until meeting Rem, she had preferred town life. Her mind wandered to their last meeting two weeks ago. How she missed him. Her father's suspicions were raised when that sour-faced woman of hers, Josie, divulged Sara was gone a whole afternoon riding.

"In this heat?" her father demanded. "What's wrong with you, woman?" He turned on his wife to shout the demand. "No decent young lady rides out alone in this kind of heat. It affects the men, makes them half-wild."

"I wasn't alone, Papa," Sara interrupted, earning a scowl from him. "I had Dick with me."

"That idiot? The lad hasn't half his wits about him." According to her father, everyone other than himself was half-witted. "How long has this been going on?"

Her mother began to tremble, her eyes widened as he continued to glare at her. "The girl likes to ride, Edmund. I can't accompany her, and neither can Josie, so I couldn't see any harm in letting…"

"Harm? You stupid woman!"

He turned on his wife with a fist raised, and Sara knew how her mother must have suffered his wrath all her married life. Sara felt a pang of sympathy for her. No man would ever treat her as her father treated her mother.

"The chit's gallivanting about this wild place with only a stable boy for company and you can't see the harm," he bawled.

Sara closed her ears to the long tirade that ensued, only catching the odd complaint about the staff and the convict labor he saw as flotsam of the community.

Sara was scared to go anywhere near the sheds housing the disreputable mob of laborers and farm hands. She also despised her father's overseer, Luxton, who made their life hell.

Chapter Five

May 1827

Rem made his way across the porch, stealthily avoiding the boards he knew creaked. He cracked his shin on one of Bella's wicker chairs and muffled an oath behind a hand.

A wraith-like shadow flitted across the end of the porch. Pressing against the wall, he concealed himself in the darker shadows. Tiger wasn't happy when one of his workers got himself drunk, and would be less than pleased with his brother-in-law for getting in that condition.

"Remy, is that you?" the wraith whispered.

Rem groaned low. Christ, it was Aggie. What was the chit doing wandering out here at this time of night?

"'Course 'tis," he mumbled. "What the bloody hell are you doing roaming out after dark, girl?"

"I couldn't sleep. 'Tis mighty stuffy in my room. Where have you been 'til this time of night? 'Tis after midnight."

Rem cursed again beneath his breath. "And what business is it of yours, may I ask? You ain't my wife to question my whereabouts, miss." He felt a momentary pang for snapping at her, but she tried his patience with her nagging.

When she stood in front of him, he saw she wore her nightgown, and a shawl draped over now drooping shoulders. With a jerk, she pushed her hair back, and he pulled his lips over his teeth, cursing his sharp tongue.

"I'm sorry," she mumbled. "Of course 'tis no business of mine what you do. But I worry for you. The master'll have your hide. You know how he feels about you men drinking spirits."

"Aye, I know." Rem grimaced as he plonked himself clumsily on the floor, patting the boards at his side. "Sit," he ordered, unsurprised when she obeyed without question, sinking down beside him, pressing her gown over her legs.

Tucking her legs beneath her, she asked timidly, "Where have you been?"

Her timidness riled him. He sighed. Why was she such a mouse? Compared to Sara she was plain, ordinary, and so compliant. Why, he knew that if he took her in his arms now she wouldn't dream of denying him all he asked.

Damn Edmund Greenwood to hell and back! If her father didn't hate convicts as a whole, Rem might stand a chance of courting Sara like a decent man instead of having to meet her on the quiet. These meetings were much too infrequent, and he damned the young fellow Dick for always hovering nearby like a sentinel.

"I've been playing cards with the laborers," he grunted, lifting his hands. "Lord knows there's little enough out here to occupy a man's time."

"Where did they get the spirits?" the mouse had the temerity to demand. "If the master found out..."

"Well, he ain't about to, is he?" he snapped. "Unless, of course, you take it into your head to inform him."

"You know I wouldn't do that, Remy. I wouldn't let you get into trouble. I just wish..."

The catch in her voice annoyed him. "Wish what? That I was a good upstanding citizen of this community?" He blew out a harsh breath. "Doubt I'll ever be that, girl."

"Don't be daft. Of course you will. You'll be something one day in these parts. Likely famous in all the country," she said fervently.

Rem let out a rough bark of laughter. "Silly chit." He tapped her chin, losing his balance as he bent forward. Straightening himself with a palm on the boards, he sighed. "Nice to know you have so much faith in me." Morosely, he stared at his booted feet. Shame Sara's father didn't share this chit's views.

"You know I care for you more than anyone else in this world," she said soulfully, tucking the shawl firmly beneath her armpits. "I know you don't give a fig what happens to me or how I feel, but that will never stop me from loving you."

"Christ, Aggie, don't go saying things like that." Rem pulled her clumsily to his side and squeezed her plump shoulders. "I'm no good, never have been. Probably never will be. You need an upstanding fellow who's steady and good like you. You're wasting your time caring for me."

"No, I'm not!" She pressed her cheek to his chest and put her arms about his waist. Rem could feel her heart pounding beneath the arm he held across her middle. Could feel her breasts. They were nice and full. He wondered how they would feel in his hands. Sara's were small and up tilted with rosy nipples that invited a man to sample their delights, and he loved them dearly, but Sara would never let him have more than the briefest glance. Aggie would allow him to fondle hers, he knew.

As slowly as he was able, considering he was well into his cups, he reached out a finger and ran it over the mound nearest to him. A shudder rippled through her, and she pressed her face closer to his chest, her hands tightening about him.

"I suggest my girl that you take yourself off to your bed. While you can." He hiccupped. "I have evil thoughts running through my head, and the best place for you is far away from me at this moment." He tried to push her away, but she clung like a limpet to a rock.

"I'd rather stay here with you," she mumbled, her breath warm through his shirt.

Rem swallowed hard. Christ! "Ah, girl, you haven't any more sense than what you were born with." He felt his burgeoning desire and knew that in his intoxicated state he had little resistance against her soft warm body. It was flattering to have someone care for you so selflessly. "Get going, now." With a hard jerk, he tried to untangle her arms.

She held fast, with strength honed by lifting babies and caring for mischievous toddlers, and it developed into a struggle of wills he knew he was too weak to win.

"I don't care if this is all I ever get of you, Remy, but please let me stay. Let me prove how much I love you," she begged, her voice throbbing through his chest. Raising her chin, she gazed up at him, the moonlight turning her hazel eyes to silver. She looked almost pretty in its glow, and Rem wished he could return her love.

"Aggie, you don't know what you're saying." A fire burned in his loins, and the blood rushed to where his cock strained against his breeches. Summoning a shred of sanity, he tried once again to push her away.

"Oh, but I do. I know you'll never love me. You'll only ever think of me as a silly chit, but I love you with all my heart; and I want to give myself to you."

"Don't be daft." Rem pushed her away roughly, this time succeeding. She tumbled sideways, and he tried to stand. His legs felt like saplings and gave beneath him. "Christ, let go," he bit out when she wrapped her arms about his calves, forcing him onto his knees. He landed with a soft thud that jarred up his spine.

"Please don't send me away." With a strength that belied her size she clung to him, those soft mounds now pressed into his side.

Rem cursed, closing his eyes as a shudder ripped through him. It had been a long time since he had a woman. Lily, the doxie, that Tiger and Bella brought across the mountains, serviced the men, but he wouldn't touch her with a twenty-foot stick. Not that she hadn't offered herself. Many times. Up to now, he managed adequately to steer clear of her. Lord knew what diseases she carried. But he was only human, and this girl was offering herself to him with a fervor that made his mind go blank. Blank except for the sinful thoughts brought on by the soft pliant, trembling body pressing against his.

With a shuddering sob, she pushed him backward until he lay flat out on the boards. A small part of his befuddled brain told him that to take what she offered would be a sin. But, ye gods, she was so soft, so curved in all the right places. And she was offering all he was willing to take, muttering small phrases of submission he couldn't decipher but nonetheless had little doubt of their meaning.

Before the last shred of sanity fled, Rem tried to get up, tried to force himself from her clinging embrace. "Aggie!" The reprimand came out on a small thread of sound.

When her lips covered his, all common sense took a running jump. In a dark corner of his mind, he tried to pretend this was Sara, his love, offering herself to him as he had begged her to so many times.

Then the baser side of him took over, and his hands wandered at will, tracing a path over the tantalizing woman, her untutored kisses exciting him. Her small whimpers of pleasure set a fire off inside him that knew but one way to quench its hunger.

God, he must go gentle. Some deep part of his brain told him this was a virgin. But she was so giving, so eager. He rolled them over, covering her body. Little moans now left her throat, urging him on, driving him to a kind of insanity that knew nothing of gentleness or reason.

With a rough tug, he discarded the garment she wore, sending it flying, so his palms could cover the full mounds of her breasts. "I knew they would fit my hands," he mumbled as he caressed her nipples to hard peaks.

Her whimpers became groans as his mouth roved over her until it found one of these peaks; while sucking on it, his body about to explode at the delirious sensations building within him. His cock was fit to burst, and after a fevered fumbling, he released the buttons of his breeches.

Her legs wrapped themselves around his middle as he thrust into her. She cried out, and her whole body stiffened as she whimpered his name. For a fraction of a second, before his lust over-rode all rational thought, Rem recalled how he meant to be gentle with her. Then all else was forgotten, all but the need that drove him on to fulfilment. With a shout, he sent his seed inside her warm body.

Aware she was crying, he bent and placed a soft kiss on her mouth, before rolling away, one arm thrown across his eyes. Darkness enveloped him.

* * *

Something jabbed him in the ribs. Rem realized hazily it was a boot, and he slapped at the offending foot, swearing loudly. "Get off," he grunted, peering up through slitted eyelids. Against the sky, he made out Tim's shape. It wavered, and he swallowed. His mouth tasted like cow dung.

"You'd best get off yourself," his nephew advised with a chuckle. "Mama will be out here soon enough, and your hide will be hung on yonder fence for getting into the spirits again."

"Smart little arse!" Rem groaned as he sat up, a hand to his head. A hundred hammers pounded away on his skull. "What time is it?" he mumbled.

"'Tis breakfast time." Tim leaned over him, hands on his small knees. His dog panted near Rem's ear, and Rem pushed it away irritably. "Mama's been asking where you are."

Rem opened and closed his eyes a few times as he shook his head, and then squeezed them shut as the world spun. What in hell was he doing out here on the porch? "Go off and tell her I'll be in shortly. But don't let on where you found me, will you?" Rem struggled to his feet, hanging onto the wall for support when his legs threatened to give way beneath him. Lord, never would he touch spirits again!

"Course I won't. But remember you'll owe me a favor." Tim laughed outright. For an eight-year-old he sure knew how to bargain like a seasoned trader.

"Fair enough." Rem stretched his spine and wiggled his shoulders. It was mighty hard on those boards. How on earth had he ended up sleeping out here? On all his binges, he had never failed to get into his bed at some stage of the night. "I'll go and throw some water over my head and find a clean shirt." He walked away as Tim ran off.

Water dripped from Rem's hair, soaking the collar of his fresh linen shirt. He felt slightly better if not completely human. Again, likely for the fiftieth time, he promised to leave the spirits alone in future.

When he entered the dining room, Bella was feeding a sloppy mess to John the baby. She glanced up, censure in her eyes, but he ignored it. Agnes sat spooning porridge into Annie's mouth while Rosie banged her fists on the table for attention. Agnes looked at him then her eyes slid swiftly away. Her cheeks glowed as red as the kerchief around his neck.

Christ! Aggie. Like a nightmare re-running through his head the happenings of last night came back in force. That explained why his breeches had been undone. It took all his willpower not to turn and run. Thank God Tiger was off about his business. It was bad enough having Bella here as witness.

"Good morning, Remy. You look as if you've had a bad night," his sister said smoothly, watching his every movement like a hawk watches a mouse. With an inward groan, Rem sat opposite her at the table, as far away from Agnes as he could get. He hated himself for his cowardice, but didn't want to get within touching distance of her. Wished devoutly he could run a mile.

"Bad dreams," he mumbled, helping himself to eggs and bacon from the dish Gracie put in the middle of the table. Only when he took a mouthful of the bacon did he realize his stomach was churning. Jesus, he felt sick. What a dolt! How was he going to extricate himself from this mess?

In all fairness, she had thrown herself at him. If he recalled correctly—and in his sodden state some parts were still hazy—hadn't she insisted she wanted him. He had tried to get away; told her adamantly to get to bed. Yes, she was more to blame than him; he tried to send her off. What was a man to do when a female seduces him? A female set on her course as Aggie had been was hard to shake off.

"Where were you last night?" Bella's eyes searched his face as if she might find an answer there. Did she guess? Lord, if she found out she would likely flay his hide. And he wouldn't blame her.

"I had a game of cards or two with the laborers. I won as it happens." He played with the eggs on his plate, and then took a swig of the tea Gracie poured for him. "That's why I was late in; I didn't want to leave while I was on a winning streak."

"I do wish you wouldn't spend so much time with the men over at their camp." Bella frowned at him before turning her attention to the baby rapping a spoon on the table.

"Don't nag, Bella. What am I supposed to do, for God's sake? I'd die of boredom here if it weren't for a game or two now and then." The tea had a slight settling effect on his stomach, but bile still threatened to rise.

"I can understand that. I know how it must get tedious for you out here miles away from the town." Bella smiled, and his guilt threatened to choke him. "Don't think I don't understand. But think on how things would be if you were still over there. You'd likely be down the mines at Newcastle if it weren't for Tiger rescuing you when he did."

Rem sighed. "I know that, Bella." Of course he knew that, thanked the Lord and Tiger every day for their intervention.

Agnes had finished feeding the girls. She wiped their faces then helped them down from their high chairs. During all this conversation, she barely glanced his way. Rem knew he couldn't ignore her and go about his business as if nothing happened the night before. Lecher he might be for taking her innocence, but he had to speak with her, make it clear what happened was not entirely his fault. Was more her fault than anything else. Hadn't she pestered him? In fact, wasn't she the one making cow's eyes at him since his arrival two years ago?

Stifling a groan, Rem tossed down the last of his tea and pushed his chair back, making a loud scraping noise on the boards that brought all eyes to him. "I'm off to help with the barn." He knew he was taking the coward's way, for Agnes couldn't leave the children right now. There would be time later to talk to her.

"But you haven't eaten more than a mouthful," Gracie grumbled as she picked up his discarded meal.

"I ain't hungry,' he said over a shoulder as he strode out, aware the three women watched him with varying degrees of interest.

* * *

"Are you ignoring me?" Agnes swallowed her nervousness and faced the man who had made love to her three nights ago and hadn't spoken more than two words to her since. If she hadn't managed to catch up with him as he left the house after dinner, she knew he still wouldn't have faced her.

"Of course not. Why would you think that?" He sounded belligerent, and she nearly fled.

"You run every time I draw near, and you seem to be dodging me." Agnes hated the note of pleading in her voice.

"Rot. I've been busy. The barn is nearing completion, and all hands are needed. I've been wanting to speak to you as it happens." He didn't look as if he wanted that at all; he looked more like a caged animal about to find freedom when its cage is left open. His beautiful eyes looked at a place somewhere over her shoulder.

"You have?" Agnes' spirits rose. Perhaps she was mistaken.

"Yes. Look, Aggie, about what happened." He ran a finger around his shirt collar, stretching his neck as if his neckerchief was strangling him.

"I'm not sorry, if that's what you think," she blurted, as he pushed his hair back from his wide brow and sighed.

"Well, I am. It should never have happened. I was drunk, and you practically forced yourself on me. I told you to get off to bed, and you refused to go." His lower lip jutted, and momentarily she hated him. Was it possible to adore yet hate someone at the same time?

"I forced you?" Agnes stared at him, hiding her trembling hands in the folds of her skirt. "How could a woman force herself on a man? That's nonsense. You're stronger than me, much larger, and weigh twice as much. What a thing to say."

"All right, it was the wrong way to put it." Finally, he looked her straight in the eye. She wished he hadn't when she saw the disdain there. "But, you can't argue that I gave you plenty of chance to go, and you insisted it was what you wanted."

"I agree. As I told you, I'm not sorry. I...I..." He was making this very difficult. With an agonized sigh she rushed on, "I love you, Rem, I wanted you to make love to me."

"I told you not to be so soft. I don't love you, Aggie, and that's an end to it. You caught me when I was full of spirits and not myself. There's no way I would have taken you if I'd been sober."

For a moment, all she could do was gape at him like some fool. His cruelty cut like a knife to the innards. It actually felt as if someone had plunged a blade into her.

"Thanks," she managed to splutter. She had always known he cared little for her, but after making love with him she hoped and prayed a small part of the love she felt would rub off on him. What a foolish, hopeless idiot she was to think the act of giving her body to him would change his way of thinking and open his eyes to what they could share if he cared half as much as she did.

"Look, Aggie, I made no secret of my feelings for you." He twisted the knife until she couldn't breathe with the pain around her heart. "We can't force ourselves to care for another when the feeling ain't there, now can we? And what we shared was an act of lust, no more. So don't go making more of it than there is. You were willing, and I'm a man, as weak as the next one. Especially weakened by spirits. Let this be a lesson to you, don't offer yourself to anyone unless you're prepared to let them take what's on offer." He wagged a finger beneath her nose, and she gasped.

Agnes knew her face had gone pale; she felt the color drain out of her skin just as her hopes drained out of her heart. The way he put it, so bluntly, so callously, made her sound like a whore. Perhaps she was, for giving to him what she should have rightfully saved for a husband. But hadn't she known what she was risking when she threw herself on him?

Of course, she had known. It seemed worth the risk. But what to do now? How could she go on, knowing he rejected her gift of love?

With a sob, she turned and ran, putting as much distance between them as she could. She heard his shout behind her, but she ignored it, heading for the orchard, tears blinding her.

Chapter Six

August 1827

Agnes put a shaking hand to her head. Sweet heaven! What was she to do? She had seen her mistress with child enough times to know all the signs.

How was she to tell Remy? The master would likely kill him. One thing was certain; Remy wouldn't be pleased with the idea of being a father. He had barely spoken to her since that night on the porch, and even less since she confronted him. There were times when she reckoned he wished she would disappear from his sight like some unwanted mongrel. It was obvious he managed well enough to put the incident out of his mind.

"Aggie, are you all right?" Her mistress's question and soft tap on the door made her jump. Lord, she would have to tell her, no sense in trying to hide it. It would be plain as anything soon enough. She was three months gone.

"Yes, ma'am, I'm coming now." Forced to run while feeding the babies' breakfast she had brought up all the contents of her stomach.

"Are you sure?" Her mistress opened the door and glanced around its edge, her eyes showing her worry. Agnes wiped her face on the hem of her apron and stood up, wobbling.

With a hand on the bedrail she said, "No, ma'am, I'm not." Pushing some stray strands of hair beneath her mobcap, she shivered, even though she felt feverish. Her hands wouldn't stop shaking.

"What is it?" The mistress frowned as she sat on the bed, pulling Agnes down beside her. "You're awfully pale,

Aggie, and I heard you vomiting. Shall I send to the barracks for the military doctor?"

"Aw, no, Ma'am." Agnes fidgeted with her apron strings and stared at her feet. "I done something dreadful. I have to tell you…I'm…" Swallowing the lump that felt like a great rock in her throat, she whispered, "I'm with child."

Color rushed into her mistress's face, and the shock written on her features made Agnes cringe. She loved this woman dearly and knew how disappointed she would be in her. And in her brother.

"No! Tell me this isn't true." Getting up jerkily, the mistress walked over to the tiny window overlooking the recently completed barn. "Who is the father? The master will have him flogged. Who did this terrible thing to you? What man violated you? Why didn't you come to me before and tell me when it happened?"

Agnes began to cry quietly, the teardrops splattering onto her fingers as they twined and twisted in her lap.

"Wasn't nobody violated me, ma'am," she whispered, and the mistress came back to kneel in front of her.

"Are you telling me you allowed a man on this property to get you in this condition, Aggie? I don't believe you. Who are you trying to protect? I know you care for Rem, but I can't think of…" With a groan, she put a hand on her head, and slapped it twice. "No! Not my brother?"

Agnes wanted to run, wanted to go and hide. How could she bear having her mistress think badly of her?

"Agnes." With a sharp movement, her mistress dragged them both to their feet. "Tell me it wasn't Rem, for God's sake!"

Agnes felt what little color that had been in her cheeks seep away. Unable to bear her mistress's scorn and distress, she pulled from her clasp, turning away. "I'm sorry, ma'am. Weren't his fault," she managed to get out.

"Not his fault? Don't be daft, girl. Whose fault would it be if he got you into this condition?" She looked ready to kill someone, probably her brother. "How long since you had your monthly flow? When did you lie with him? Or have you lain with him more than once? Don't tell me this has been going on beneath my nose, and I never guessed."

Her scorn was hard to take. Agnes wiped a fist across her nose and sobbed. "'Twas only once, mistress. And that was three months back. Remy was drunk, and I forced myself on him."

"Forced yourself on him? You little fool. Don't talk such rot. He's a man with a man's strength and desires. How do you expect me to believe he coupled with you because you forced him?"

"I did, ma'am. I knew he was too drunk to know what he was doing. I enticed him. I thought…"

"Merciful heaven." The mistress flopped down onto the bed, her face in her hands as she rocked back and forth. "I know you have deep feelings for him, Aggie, but I never reckoned you'd be that foolhardy. You know what men are like when they're in their cups."

"I know. But I love him." Agnes sat down again, her misery making her ache in every muscle. "What am I to do? Will the master send me away?"

"Send you away? Of course not. He won't blame you, he'll blame Rem, and that's for certain. Oh, Lord! He'll likely kill Rem." She dragged in a shaky breath.

"Oh, ma'am, please don't let him harm Rem, I love him. I'll take the blame. Or what if I say it was one of them shepherds who passed through a while back. If we don't tell him the truth, he won't be none the wiser."

"If only it was that simple. Let me think this through." With fingers pressed to her head, she bit on her lips until they turned white. "All right? Don't say anything until I've had a chance to think of something. I'll talk to Rem. Make him face his responsibilities. He's not all bad, he'll see sense, and marry you afore Tiger even knows the truth."

Agnes made a sound of distress in her throat. "He won't want to marry me," she sobbed. "I think he hates me."

"Rubbish! What he wants and what's his duty are two different things, girl. Right, wash your face and tidy yourself. We can't do anything 'til the men come in from the fields anyway. I'll get a chance to talk to Rem before the master gets in. It's not the end of the world; take my word for it. Wasn't I in the same position myself once, carrying a child and no husband? I won't see you end up in the same strife as me, Aggie, I promise you." Her mistress pulled her swiftly into her arms.

In that moment, Agnes knew she would give her life for her.

Once her mistress left, Agnes poured water into the bowl and sloshed some over her face. Perhaps she could find a way to get rid of the baby. Still, it was probably a bit late. That whore Lily would likely know a method that would do the trick, but Agnes had a feeling if anything was to be done it should have been done afore now. The thought of killing Rem's child made her feel sick again, and she vomited into her chamber pot until her belly hurt and her throat was sore. With a silent wail, she again wiped her face and then straightened her shoulders. The mistress was on her side; she would find a solution.

* * *

"Marry her? Are you mad?" Rem paced the sitting room, his fingers raking his hair until it stood up like stalks of corn.

After coming in from the fields, he had barely washed the grime from his hands and face before Bella demanded his presence in the sitting room.

"What's so mad about that? The girl's with child, and it's yours." His sister wore a look on her face he'd never seen before. It made him feel as low as a snake.

"How can you be sure of that?" he demanded, knowing that was close to the worst remark he could have uttered. Who else's would it be?

"Don't you dare stand there and ask me such a thing," she said. "Agnes is three months along. I've traced it back in my mind for she wouldn't tell me exactly what happened, except to say, silly little chit, that she forced you. It was that night you were so in your cups you passed out on the porch. The night you told me you'd won a fair amount."

Rem buried his face in his hands and groaned loudly. God, what a mess! "Is she sure?"

"Of course she's sure. She's been bringing up her food for days and is sick of heart as well as body. Claims you aren't to blame. Claims 'twas all her fault. Forced herself on you, she did." Her contempt stabbed him to the core. His dear Bella was so disgusted she could barely look at him.

"Oh, Lord, I'm sorry." Rem rubbed at eyes gone gritty. "But I can't marry her, Bella, you must see that. I don't care for her in that way, and we'd only end up hating each other."

She exhaled a sharp breath. "Seems to me I've heard that same sentence before somewhere." With a sigh, she got up and came to place a hand on his arm. "Sit down, Rem. I'll tell you a story."

A while later she left him alone. He had known she hadn't married Tiger until after their second child's birth, but until now hadn't known the full story of why they hadn't wed sooner. Now he knew Tiger didn't want to marry his sister when she found out she was carrying Tim. In his arrogance, he forced her to marry her shipboard friend, Dougal. It was a disastrous match from the first, and they grew to hate each other. A hatred that intensified when Dougie, her second baby, died from snakebite on the way over the Blue Mountains. Dougal cast all the blame on Bella, accusing her of caring for Tiger's child more than his. Bella conceived Annie after Dougal fell off the side of The Big Hill to his death. Bella refused Tiger's offer of marriage several times, unable to forget how he rejected her at first.

Rem could see what she meant about history repeating itself, but there had been a genuine and lasting love between Tiger and Bella, a love anyone could see surmounted all obstacles and seemed to grow with each passing day. He didn't even have more than a liking for Agnes. God! If he married the chit, they would both live to

66

regret it more than Bella had with Dougal. At least Bella and Dougal had once been good friends.

Besides, he loved Sara; more than loved her, worshipped the ground she trod upon and wanted to marry no one else. What an absolute disaster! Why had he taken what Agnes so willingly offered that night? Simple; he had been too far gone to have any control over his lecherous body, and the silly girl hadn't the sense in her head to know that.

* * *

Agnes stood still as a statue. She dare not move in case the mistress or Remy heard her. Agnes knew almost the entire story of what happened between her mistress and master, but hadn't known the master refused to marry the mistress when Bella found herself with Tiger's child.

There was no way in the world she would force Rem to marry her simply because of the baby she carried. She had seen her chance to have one night of his lovemaking, and had taken it, knowing full well it would likely be the only chance she ever got; knowing full well his feelings for her never matched her own. Never had she dreamed it would end this way, with her pregnant.

What could she do? If the mistress forced him into marriage, he would surely end up despising her, if he didn't already. And she would hate herself for forcing his hand. If she ran away, where would she go? No one would take on a maid heavy with child. There weren't enough settlers this side of the mountains for her to seek employment with them anyway—not that the mistress would see her working for someone else.

She could likely get a ride back to Sydney with the next party traveling across the mountains. But what sort of life would she have with a child and no income? Perhaps the mistress could secure her a position as a nursemaid where they would accept her baby.

Stifling a sob of despair, she made her way quietly along the porch and entered the house by the side door. The master was coming from the room he used as his office, behind the kitchen. "Agnes, what are you doing creeping about?" he asked, running fingers through his thick hair of gold. "Where are the children?" Usually at this time of the day, she was preparing them for bed.

"I...I was..." Unable to think of a sensible retort she hastened away and ran to the nursery.

Later, after seeing Tim, Annie, Rosie, and the baby, John, safely tucked up in their beds, she crept out of the house and walked in the garden. Pulling her shawl tightly about her to ward off the chill, she wandered aimlessly for a while, not wanting to go too far from the lights spilling from the house so she could keep an eye out for snakes.

A dark shape loomed before her, and she couldn't hold back a small shriek.

"It's all right, miss, I won't hurt you." She breathed easier when she saw it was one of the shepherds, Mole they called him, sitting on a log, puffing on his clay pipe.

"You frightened me. I thought I was alone," she said shyly.

"Not right for a lady to be wandering about after dark by herself," he said, eyeing her with interest.

"I'm not a lady." She looked up to the sullen sky. Not one star peeped through the dark clouds.

"'Course you are. Because you ain't gentry don't mean a thing. 'Tis the way you behave that decides whether you're fit to be called such or not. Now that doxie, Lily, she ain't fit to be called more'n what she is, a harlot. But I've seen you with the little uns, and you're a lady for sure. And no arguing." He smiled around his pipe.

Agnes had seen him about the property. Old as anything, he knew sheep, or so everyone said. In this country, where sheep were looked on with respect, a good shepherd was worth his weight in gold.

Agnes thought sheep the stupidest creatures God had seen fit to put on this earth. But the master made most of his wealth from them it seemed, or from their fleece, which he sent to the mills in England.

"So, what's the problem besetting your young head then?" Mole asked mildly.

"Problem? What makes you think I have one?" Agnes looked at him sharply.

"I can tell something's up with you, lass. You're shoulders are all slumped, and I haven't glimpsed a smile on your pretty face in weeks. I been away awhile tending my charges, but you was miserable afore I went a fortnight ago. And you're ten times worse this night."

"I'm not the least bit pretty, and that's at the root of all my problems." She gave a shuddering sigh and joined him on the log.

"Nonsense, it's all in the eye of the beholder." He wagged his pipe at her. "Some young blood turned you down, eh?"

If only it were that simple. "The man I love doesn't care for me," she blurted, and then wondered why she had told this to a shepherd—and probably a convict at that.

"What is he, mad?" He looked truly aghast.

"No, he's not mad, nor even simple. He's in love with somebody else, and I mean nothing to him." Shoulders sagging, she scuffed one boot toe in the dust.

"Oh, Lord, now don't let that upset you, m'dear. Look at my ugly mug." He pointed to his wrinkled face and grinned, showing many gaps in his discolored teeth. "I've probably been turned down by more women than I've had 'ot dinners, so I have. And that in the days when I was a lot more presentable than I am now." He chuckled. "But has old Mole let it get him down? Of course he ain't. You pick yourself up and go and make a conquest. There must be lots of young men hereabouts only too glad to set up house with a young lass like you."

"But, don't you see, I don't want them. I want..." Agnes bit her lip. She had said far too much to this old man already.

"'Tis the young mistress's brother you want, ain't it?" he asked solemnly, shaking his felt-capped head.

"How...how did you know?"

69

"Ah, well, ain't no secret really. You been mooning around after him since I came here last year, probably longer than that."

"I don't moon over him. I love him," she protested in a small voice.

"Love, hah!" He sent out a stream of spittle. His dog, which had been lying near his feet, shifted, circled, and then lay down again with a huff. "Strictly for fools, is love."

"Then I'm the biggest fool," she moaned.

"Forget the boy. He ain't fit for you, lass."

"If only it was so easy." With a drawn-out sigh, she stood up and prepared to walk away.

"Anyways, he has big eyes for the Greenwood lass. Ah," he muttered as it apparently dawned on him this was the whole crux of the problem. "That's why you're so down in the dumps. Because he's mooning over that lass, and you're mooning over him. He ain't worth it, girl," he repeated vehemently.

"Maybe so. But that's not all of it." Agnes sat by his side again, feeling the desperate need to confide in someone. "I'm a fool. I'm carrying his baby, and he didn't even want to lie with me. I forced myself on him, and now I'm having to pay for my sins."

"Hush, girl, what sins? By God, he's the one who's sinned. And as for your forcing yourself on him, that's a load of rubbish, if you'll pardon my language. No girl of your size could force a man to do anything against his will. I never knew he was that sort. Well, well, we live and learn." He puffed silently on his pipe for a while. The night creatures shuffled about and a few birds shifted their perches in the trees around them. His dog grunted as it settled itself more comfortably.

"What did the mistress have to say about it?" he asked at length, when she felt sure the subject was finished with.

Agnes bit her lip. "She's after him marrying me. But he'll not have that. And neither will I."

"Hmm, 'tis a tricky situation 'an that's a fact. Hard to know what to do. No sense in getting wed to someone you'll hold responsible for trapping you."

"I know that." Agnes rubbed at her temple, which ached with all the worry. "That's why I wouldn't wed Remy now if he pleaded with me."

"There's another answer. Marry someone else who'll look after you and the babe."

"That would be even worse. I couldn't bear to have another man touch me as a man expects to touch his wife,' she confided. "I'd sooner stay as I am."

"Hmm, you could marry someone old enough to be your grandfather." With a soft chuckle, he paused before adding, "That way the child will have a father, you'll have a husband with all the respectability that goes with it. And the man'd have a good young wife to cook his meals and keep his cabin clean."

Agnes shrugged and turned to stare at him. "I could never get wed for the sake of it, to someone I didn't care for."

"What's the alternative, I ask you?"

Agnes toyed with her shawl fringe. She had no answer.

"I've got it." His elbow nudged her gently in the side. "I'll marry you. Now what about that idea, eh?"

How could she marry a wizened old man with not many teeth, wrinkled skin, and the smell of sheep constantly about him? To tell him so would be unkind and rude, so she smiled and said, "Thank you for the offer, but I'll find another solution."

"Think on it, lass," he said softly as she got up and began to walk slowly back to the house.

Darkness enveloped it except for one shaft of light flowing from the sitting room window. How she loved this place and the mistress who had taken her from the orphanage where she had lived since she was a four-year-old. Her mother, caught stealing a yard of ribbon from a stallholder at the market, died on the transport ship. The mistress was the closest to a mother she ever had since. And now Agnes had disgraced herself and likely turned her mistress against her brother for what she would see as his lechery.

Lord above knows what the master would say about it when he heard of her condition.

Chapter Seven

"With child?" the master bellowed.

Agnes shrank back against the wall near the window to the sitting room.

"Aye, Tiger, she's three months gone. Poor child." The sadness in the mistress's voice brought tears to Agnes's eyes. With a fist over her mouth, she held back a sob.

"Poor child, is it? She's eighteen, Bella, love. Hardly a child, I'd say. So, who's the father?" He paused, and Agnes pressed herself harder on the wall. "If it's one of my men, I'll have him whipped and slung in chains!"

"Tiger, don't be so harsh," the mistress chided softly, her skirts rustling as she crossed the room. "It's not one of the laborers or shepherds…it's..." She stopped talking, and Agnes could sense she fought with her conscience.

"Then who the bloody hell is it? The girl spends all her time with the children and you, and barely spares a glance for any of the men. Except…Jesus! Don't tell me it's your brother." Agnes cringed at the string of muttered oaths he emitted.

"Tiger, don't be angry." The mistress's soft rebuke was filled with gentleness.

"I'm not angry," he shouted, proving he was angrier than Agnes had heard in a long time. "I'm disgusted. I'll kill him."

"You have a short memory, love." Agnes heard the sigh in her tone, and then the master's soft snort.

"It was different with you and me."

Agnes knew it hadn't been much different at all. The master refused to wed the mistress at first, forcing her into a loveless marriage with her first husband.

"Was it? Agnes loves Rem, fool that she is, even though I hate to admit it. My brother pines for Sara Greenwood, and Agnes moons over him. It happened while he was well into his cups. Agnes could no more stop herself from succumbing to him than I could to you all those years ago. What will we do, Tiger?" she wailed in a distraught voice. Agnes shuddered. "Rem doesn't want to get wed any more than you wanted to way back then. We can't force him to marry her. I wouldn't want to see them endure the unhappiness Dougal and I shared."

The master must have put his arms about the mistress for his voice was muffled, probably because his mouth was pressed to her shoulder. "I wish I knew, love."

Agnes turned and ran. She didn't stop until she reached her room. Sitting on the edge of her bed, she let the tears fall unheeded. What a mess. Did she really expect Remy to fall in love with her because she offered herself to him?

One of the children began to whimper, and she quietly went to the room next to hers. It was the baby. Picking him up she rocked him as she paced the room, crooning. "Hush John, my babe," she whispered. When he quietened, she placed him back in his crib, staring at his cherubic face for ages, while her mind went over and over what the master and mistress had said.

Even if they forced Rem to marry her, she wouldn't. Not now. Not if he went into it unwillingly. She loved him too much to make his life a misery. How she hated to be a disappointment to her mistress, the most beautiful person she had ever known. She knew what it was like to love and not have that love returned. But then, everything worked out right for her in the end.

Try as she might, Agnes could never see things working out right between her and Rem. He wouldn't have taken her unless drunk and she had thrown herself on him. She hadn't a lot of pride where he was concerned, but Lord, it would be purgatory to be wed to a man who hated her.

* * *

74

"Where's Aggie?" Bella turned to Rem. He concentrated on the food on his plate and shrugged. His sister then turned her attention on Gracie, who was placing a platter of roast lamb on the table in front of Tiger for him to carve.

"Said she's not feeling well, wants to lie down, she does," Gracie said, her eyes as solemn as Bella's as the two women appraised each other silently.

Why did women always seem to know what the other was thinking, Rem wondered. If only he knew what went on in their heads. Always a look passed between them and although no questions were asked, they seemed somehow to know what the other referred to.

"I guess we might as well bring this out into the open, seeing as the chit isn't here," Tiger said as he began to slice the meat. "What are your intentions where she's concerned?" His eyes turned to study Rem as the carving knife stopped in mid-air.

Rem ducked his head, groaning inwardly. Jesus, what to say? "Intentions?" he asked, knowing he was being cowardly.

Tiger sighed, returning to the carving. "Don't beat about the bush, man. She's with child. Your child. And I asked a straightforward question. Are you going to meet your obligations? Please tell us while she isn't here to feel insulted further by your refusal to make an honest woman of her."

"I can't wed her, Tiger. Don't you see?" Panic made him dizzy, and he swallowed. "She deserves better."

"Pity you didn't think more on this before you violated her innocence." Tiger waved the knife, and Rem eyed it. Both Gracie and Bella were still as statues while they listened.

"Violated? That's rubbish, Tiger." Rem glanced at his sister, now shaking her head, whether in sorrow or disgust he wasn't sure.

Tiger's laugh was scornful. "Spare me the stories. All right, I can understand fully why you wouldn't want to wed her when there's no feelings whatsoever for her. I wouldn't

75

force you down that path." He glanced to Bella and a meaningful look passed between them. "So, what's to be done, love?"

Rem stifled a retort. They were discussing this as if he had no say whatsoever in the outcome. No say in how the rest of his life shaped.

Bella sighed sadly. "I'm sure I don't know. I guess things go on as before. Another baby in the house won't make a lot of difference. We already have four, and that'll grow to five before the year is out. I'll tell her later when I go in to see how she is."

The food was passed around the table. They ate in silence.

Rem had lost his appetite. "I'm sorry, Bella," he said, rising suddenly. "I know as well as you that I'm being a selfish brute."

He left them, knowing he sank in his sister's estimation. He detested having her feel that way. Ye Gods, if only he had insisted the silly chit go when he told her to. Had she actually thought she could force his hand, force him to care for her? What a mess.

He wandered outside, walking in the softness of the late winter evening. A small sliver of light showed beneath the blind in Aggie's room and for a moment, he considered going to her, pleading for sense in this matter. She could still bear the child and be welcomed under Bella and Tiger's roof. There was no need to complicate matters by going through a wedding that would be a farce.

"Life can be full of difficult choices," someone said, and Rem jumped as he peered into the shadows.

"Oh, it's you, Mole. What you doing here still? I thought you'd gone with your flock." Rem walked toward the shepherd, who leaned against one of the trees, light from his pipe gleaming in the dusk.

"I'm off in the morning. I offered the lass marriage, but she turned me down. Can't say I blame her. Why would such a pretty wench want to saddle herself with an old man, eh?"

"You did what?"

"Asked her to marry me, I did. But she swore she could never marry anyone but the father of her child. That's the way a woman's mind works." He spat and grunted. "There's no logic in a woman's thinking. It's all a matter of the heart with them."

"Tell me something I don't know," Rem said. "I suppose you know who the father is. 'Tis likely everyone for miles knows and is castigating me for my selfishness, eh?"

"Aye, 'tis common knowledge, at least on this spread." Mole sighed and took a long drag on his pipe. "Can't say most of the men blame you for turning the wench down. Most would do the same. No man likes to be saddled with what's forced on him by circumstances beyond their control."

"I wish I could at least like her enough to say that we could try to make a reasonable match."

"Ah, well, 'tis no use crying over spilled milk. Wish the wench had considered my offer though."

Rem wished she had too, but wasn't about to tell Mole that.

They chatted for a while about the sheep, then Rem returned to the house. The others were gathered in the sitting room. Gracie sat over her sewing, scowling at him, and Bella seemed engrossed in her morose thoughts. At least Tiger seemed to be on his side in the matter, but Rem knew he would always take Bella's view in this. He was in no position to dictate to Rem, and knew it. After a half hour of the strained atmosphere, Rem decided to retire for the night.

If only he could find a love such as his sister and her husband shared. Sara admitted she cared for him, but knew her father would have an apoplectic fit if she considered marrying a convict, even presuming the law would allow it.

As he bade them goodnight, Bella rose, saying, "I'll check on Aggie, she can't shut herself up like this without supper."

"She wouldn't answer when I knocked earlier," Gracie said, putting her sewing aside.

Out in the passage that ran the width of the house from front to back, Bella put a hand on Rem's arm. "Oh, Rem, I hate to see you in this situation," she said on a sigh. "Heaven knows I would no more wish to push you into marriage than I would wish to send Aggie away, but the poor girl's so unhappy..."

"She'd be a bloody sight unhappier if we were to wed, and you know it," he said as they reached his door.

He went into his room, and Bella continued to the back of the house where Agnes had a small room beyond the girls' bedroom.

Barely had he undone his shirt buttons than he heard his sister's distressed cry, "She's not in her room. Agnes is not in her bed."

Chapter Eight

Agnes sobbed quietly as she walked. Her stride wasn't hasty nor did she dawdle. Strange how it all seemed so inevitable now. After overhearing the conversation at the table her way became clear as glass. So, the mistress would let her stay on, living in this house with Rem's child. Living here and seeing him each day, likely married to his dark-haired goddess one day while the mother of his child sat by and watched. Watched him with another woman and died a little every minute, every hour. No, better to end it all now—better this way than living a life in purgatory. So near the man she worshipped, but would never be able to touch again.

The river loomed before her, a dark abyss on this August night. Aggie remembered happier days when the family picnicked here on the banks, her ever watchful the little ones didn't venture near the water. A sob racked her; how she would miss her babies. Stupid cow! She would know nothing. But perhaps they would miss her and cry for her in the mid of night. Even that thought didn't deter her. With a purpose born of desperation, she plunged into the murky blackness.

So cold. The water was so cold, and it amazed her for a moment she could feel it as her feet slipped on the mud. She tumbled forward. Like a great dark cloak it closed over her, and her clothes dragged her down. Too late, she began to fight, thrashing at the water with hands grown numb. The strong current swiftly drew her down river. Away from all she had known and loved in this life. Too late for fighting; best let the water take her, away from pain, away from a sadness that had swallowed her soul just as the river was swallowing her.

"Remy." His name was on her lips as she went below the murky, swirling surface of the water, her arms above her head in a last futile effort to gain the surface. A silent scream ripped from her throat as her chest seemed to explode with its fight for air. Then blackness.

* * *

Rem wiped a fist across his gritty eyes as he drew his horse to a halt and stared ahead. Rain began to batter him, but he felt numb with weariness and guilt. Where the hell could the chit be? Some sixth sense warned him for the last forty-eight hours, while all hands had been set to search for her, that she hadn't run off and was hiding out while she nursed her sadness and feeling of rejection. They had combed the surrounding countryside for two days. Looked in every conceivable hiding place, questioned every home within miles. Not that there were that many neighboring houses to make inquiries at. The Greenwood's outbuildings had all been searched. He didn't have the heart to face Sara; his guilt weighed heavily on him.

Rem wiped a sleeve across his eyes as he turned his horse for home. There was no way she could have made it this far downriver on foot. The men would have to rest before continuing the search further afield.

A shout brought his head up, and he squinted through the downpour. Two men had dismounted where huge river gums draped their branches over the water. That patch was searched yesterday so Rem hadn't bothered going over the same stretch again.

He headed for them as one of the men began to wave his kerchief and yell at the top of his lungs. Rem knew even before he spotted the lifeless, water-bedraggled body that it was Aggie, and he rubbed a hand over his forehead, cursing vilely.

She floated half in and half out of the water, caught up in the twisted branches that dipped into the water. Her poor body was bloated, her face almost unrecognizable with streaks of mud discoloring it. The strips of weed and flotsam tangled in her hair, made her look like some repulsive gargoyle.

Sweet heaven! What had he done?

Never, if he lived to be a hundred, would he forget the sight of her pathetic body as the men hauled her clear of the tree and laid her gently on the bank. Her feet were bare, her skirt torn to ribbons.

The three of them stood over her, for a moment speechless, and then one of them said, "Gawd, what a state!" Rem jerked his eyes away. Indeed she was.

"Help me lift her onto my horse." His voice sounded as if it came from far away, not from him.

The forlorn party began the trek back to the house, Rem leading his horse and the two men trailing behind, talking in whispers. But Rem knew what they said; it was common knowledge he had gotten the chit with child and refused to marry her.

Bella must have seen the small procession from afar because long before they reached the edge of the garden she was waiting there, wringing her hands.

"Aggie!" she wailed. Her eyes held condemnation and anger as they turned on Rem.

He didn't blame her one bit; aside from his guilt he felt utter wretchedness. He brought this on and didn't know how he would ever live with himself.

* * *

Sara tightened the ribbons of her bonnet beneath her chin. Anger and another insidious emotion swirled inside her. By the saints, what had Rem done? Servants and laborers talked and gossip traveled in this part of the world much the same as in Sydney and London. When Josie had taken a perverse delight in passing on the latest news, disbelief filled Sara. Aggie, that mousy nursemaid who worked for Mrs. Carstairs had become pregnant. Like a cat savoring the last lick of cream, Josie stood, waiting for Sara to ask the inevitable.

Of course, Sara asked, "And who is the father of this baby?" Shock and disbelief made her nauseous when Josie imparted the terrible news of how Rem supposedly raped the nursemaid and then refused point blank to marry the chit, so bringing about the poor girl's demise by her own hand.

A shiver ran through Sara at the thought of taking one's own life. She doubted she could bring herself to do such a deed, no matter the circumstances. Then she put herself in Aggie's shoes and tried to envisage the humiliation of coupling with a man, conceiving his child, only to then have him reject you like a cheap doxie.

Unable to bring herself to believe it of him, Sara inveigled her mother into taking a ride over to the Carstairs' property. She still couldn't believe her mother agreed. Perhaps she was as interested in the goings on as most of the other settlers in these parts. Death was well-known in the colony, but it seldom occurred by one's own hand. The drama seemed to intrigue the whole population.

One of the laborers drove the wagon while Sara, her mother and Josie, looking smugly satisfied, sat in the back for the bumpy trip. The rain, sorely needed after a lengthy drought, had eased, so they didn't have that to add to the discomfort of the journey.

"What a pleasure," Bella Carstairs said as the driver helped them down on their arrival. Her usual smile was absent. In fact, she looked haggard.

When her mother seemed reticent to offer a reason for their visit Sara said, "We heard about the unfortunate death of your nursemaid and came to offer our condolences."

"Thank you. That's kind of you. Please come into the sitting room."

They followed her into the house, along the hallway, and into the comfortable sitting room overlooking the garden. When they were seated, their kitchen woman Gracie served each with tea, and then left quietly.

"It must have been a terrible shock for you all," Sara said.

"It surely was, and I don't know how I'll manage without her. Agnes…" Bella halted and took a deep breath. "Agnes became indispensable to me. We brought her over when we crossed the mountains, you know, and she's taken care of all my infants from the minute they were born. All except Tim, who was a toddler when she came into our lives."

They chatted on for a while, the subject ranging from where Bella would find a replacement nursemaid to more mundane things. Sara longed to ask where Rem was and whether he was about the house or nearby so she could speak to him. But how could she simply blurt out the query. It was only as they all prepared to leave that Sara got her chance to speak to Bella alone while the driver helped her mother and Josie into the wagon. "Do you think you could give this to your brother?" Sara passed the note she had written earlier across to Bella. There was no mistaking the look of surprise on Bella's face as she took the folded sheet of notepaper.

"I suppose you've heard the gossip?" Bella turned the note over in her fingers and then put it into a side pocket of her skirt.

"No sense in denying it. Talk travels fast wherever one lives, and faster I daresay in these parts where women are cursed with boredom. Is it true? Was Rem the father of the child Agnes carried?" No point in mincing matters.

For a moment Sara thought Bella wouldn't answer; her shock at the bluntness of the statement obvious.

After a lengthy pause while she seemed to toss up what to answer, she said, "Best let Rem tell his side of the story. I take it your message," she tapped the pocket holding the note, "is for a rendezvous with him?"

Sara nodded. "Does that shock you?"

"Of course not. I have eyes, I saw where his feelings veered, and I know the two of you have become good friends."

More than friends, Sara wanted to say but silently stared at the older woman.

"I'll make sure he gets your note, don't worry," Bella said in a whisper as they went to the wagon where her mother waited impatiently.

* * *

"How could you do such a thing?"

Rem knew the question was bound to come, and try as he might hadn't been able to come up with a feasible answer.

Sara's note begged him to wait for her at their usual meeting place. So here he was, alone with her beneath a stand of wattle trees, a fair distance from the boy, Dick, who, as always, accompanied her on her rides.

"I have to explain how things were, Sara."

"So explain. You pledged your love to me; told me you would love no other all your life—and at the first opportunity you lay with a serving wench, a nursemaid!"

"Don't talk about Aggie that way. All right, so she was just a nursemaid, but she was also a gentle, kind soul, and I'd give anything to have had this all turn out differently. The first thing you must understand is the night I took her I was full of spirits. You're an innocent maiden and don't know about the ways of men and their lust. The silly chit thought I'd fall in love with her because she gave herself freely to me like that."

"And what of the baby?" Sara demanded. "Is it true she carried your child when she drowned herself?"

His large hands covered his face, and she watched as a shudder ran through him. "Yes," he mumbled. Then louder, "Yes. And the awful thing is even knowing that, I couldn't bring myself to wed her. I love you, Sara, and I would have made her life hell."

"Oh, Remy, what are we to do?" Sara wailed, stepping closer and wrapping her arms about him. "Everyone in these parts knows the truth. My father's been gloating since he heard."

"No doubt. If I had little chance of winning his favor before, I have no chance now." He dragged in a breath then let it out on a huge sigh. "But, I'm not about to give you up. No woman will ever match you or take your place in my heart."

"Nor you mine, Remy. I think I love you." Sara lowered her gaze as her cheeks went hot. When she glanced up, longing and surprise filled his dark eyes.

"Only think?" he asked huskily, enfolding her in his arms and kissing the tip of her nose.

"Well, I have no knowledge of how I should feel. I miss you when you aren't near." Sara gazed up at him and admitted, "I dream of you most nights. Not the sort of dreams a lady should have." She gave a small self-conscious laugh.

"Sounds like love." He smiled softly. "I dream about you all the time." His expression turned serious. A chill crept up Sara's spine when he kissed her tenderly, and then moved away, turning his back.

"I'm going away, Sara," he said in a low voice.

"No! Where will you go, and why?" she cried, going around him until she could look fully into his face.

He spread his hands. "I can't stay here, don't you see? Bella is absolutely stunned by Aggie's death. She would never openly blame me, but who else is there to blame, I ask you? The atmosphere in the house is so thick you can feel it. Tiger didn't say I had to marry the girl, and I know they were both against the idea of forcing us to wed. But this will always be there between us, souring our lives."

"But what about me?" Sara scrubbed at her cheek where a stray tear dribbled. "What of your declaration of undying love for me?" She felt like screaming at the unfairness of the situation.

"Sara, you must see that I have to go away. There can be no future for us while I'm serving my term. Your father wouldn't allow it as long as he lives and breathes. I love you more than life itself, but look at me. I'm a bloody con, beholden to Tiger and Bella for the clothes I wear, the food I eat, everything. I love my sister only slightly less than I love you, and I see how she looks at me now. I can't bear to be the source of her unhappiness."

"But you're a convict. You'll have to go to a new master." Sara couldn't seem to focus her thoughts. All she could think was that Rem was going away. And it was likely she would never see him again. Anger replaced her misery. "How can you do this?"

"With a heavy heart, believe me." He caught her by the shoulders, his eyes grave as he vowed, "I promise you this, I'll come back when my term is served. When I'm a free man I'll come back and ask you to marry me. Will you wait for me?"

"That will be years from now. How will I stand it here without you?" Sara flounced away from him. Then a sudden idea hit her. "Let me come with you," she pleaded.

"Don't talk daft. I'm a convict, and you're a well-bred girl of quality. Your father might be the worst kind of bigot, but at least he's raised you in the style befitting a woman of society."

"But it could be years till I see you again, Remy." Tears clogged her throat, and she threw herself into his arms. An idea hit her: he hadn't married Agnes, even though she carried his child, because he didn't love her. But he loved her, Sara, and had sworn she would be the only one he would ever love. "Make love to me before you go." She pressed herself against him.

With a jerk that startled her, he pushed her away from him. "Are you mad?" He looked really angry.

"What's mad about that?" Now she was confused. "You said you would always love me. Well, I love you, and want to be with you forever. If you must go away, then at least let me have something to remember you by."

"What, such as a baby inside you? Christ, Sara, don't you think I've ruined enough lives with my stupidity? That would be just about the daftest thing I could possibly do."

"Daft? How can you say that making love with me could be stupid?" she yelled, pushing at his hands when he tried to pull her into his embrace again.

"I didn't say that would be stupid. I said it would be the daftest thing I could do. Supposing you got yourself with child, eh? Supposing you ended up in the same mess as Aggie. How do you think that would make me feel?"

"But then my father would have to let us wed, don't you see? How could he refuse if I carried your baby?"

"Easy, that's how. Sweet heavens, woman, he barely puts up with me now. He'd have an apoplectic fit if you went to him and told him you're having my baby. No, Sara, listen to me." He shook her gently. "I love you more than life itself and want nothing more than to wed you one day, but we must do this my way. I have to go away. It's for the best. I'll come and claim you when I'm free, and all this mess is far behind us. It'll be a struggle to convince your father even then, for he thinks me beneath you, and truth is I am."

"Don't talk that way. You're a bigger man than he'll ever be," she cried, throwing herself against him and clinging in desperation.

"So promise you'll wait for me?"

"Forever," she vowed. They sealed their pledge with a long kiss fueled by longing, but tinged with a sadness she felt deep within her soul.

Chapter Nine

Sara dismounted, sighing as she put her head against the warm sweat-streaked neck of her mare. The wind was cold on her ride, but she'd welcomed its bite on her cheeks, relished its sting as she galloped heedlessly over the windswept landscape as if a demon rode at her heels.

How would she survive without the meetings with Rem? Life looked bleak already.

"Thank you, Dick," she said when the boy took the reins and led her mare away. She lingered in the yard, staring across the paddocks as if she could see Remy over there, preparing to leave her, perhaps for years.

"So, lover boy's leaving, eh?"

She gave a startled gasp as Luxton lumbered from the stable and moved to stand within a foot of her. Her lip curled as she tossed her head, refusing to answer him.

"Proves he don't care much for you if he can up and leave at the first sign of trouble." The vile man grinned evilly. How she despised him.

"What he does is no concern of yours," Sara snapped.

"Perhaps not. But you'll be missing his kisses and the secret meetings you had with him now, won't you?" He licked his thick lips, his lecherous eyes glinting as they wandered over her before settling on her bosom.

"What do you know of such things?" Sara put a protective arm across her front, gripping her upper arm. "You have no idea what you're talking about."

Luxton sniggered, jabbing a finger over a shoulder to where Dick was filling a bucket from the water trough outside the stable door. Sara followed his gesture and noticed Dick refused to look at her. In fact, the boy looked hunched and guilty.

"Yes, he told all." Luxton sneered Dick's way. "He knows where his loyalties lie."

"More like he knows where punishment will come from if he doesn't obey you," Sara spat. Luxton was renowned for his bullying.

"Don't play the high and mighty missy with me, girlie. Want me to tell your father you've been meeting the half-breed? Want me to tell him about the stolen kisses while Dick was ordered to keep watch and out of earshot?"

Sara began to shake. Although her father had always spoiled her as a child, never stinted on her education or clothing, and allowed her whatever fripperies she asked for, he never showed the slightest sign that a soft heart beat beneath his gruff and overbearing exterior; a heart that would forgive his daughter her indiscretions.

"You don't frighten me," she said softly, turning to walk away before he caught sight of her trembling lips and hands.

Luxton caught her wrist, dragging her about. He pulled her up against his bulky frame. She cringed away from the foul smell of his breath and body as he leaned in close to mutter, "Then why are you shaking like a bird caught in a trap? I scare you all right, milady. But old Luxton would be prepared to keep your secrets safe and sure like, for a small gift in exchange." He licked his thick lips as he bent even closer.

"Gift? You must be mad! Now, take your filthy hands off me. You're hurting me," Sara said with as much menace as she could foster. His rheumy eyes roved over her face and then lower to settle on her breasts again; breasts that were heaving with the exertion of keeping him at a distance. Her heart thumped with fear.

"Only when you give me a nice present for helping you keep your secret safe."

Sara gagged as his mouth swooped, landing over hers, stifling her scream. Dear God! What was she to do? Dick couldn't possibly offer her any assistance; he was as terrified of Luxton as all the other laborers and convicts on the property and had fled. Not only was Luxton cruel, but he could be sadistically triumphant when someone suffered because of him. Sara had heard the cries coming from the convict's compound when he doled out punishment. Her father condoned his mistreatment. She heard him say often it was no more than the scum deserved.

Luxton lifted his head and stepped back a pace, still keeping a hand firmly clamped about one of her wrists. She wiped her gloved hand over her mouth. Then she heard her father's bawl, and Luxton released her. Sara immediately stepped well out of his range, taking out her handkerchief to scrub it across her mouth as she escaped. She would have to be on her guard near Luxton in future.

Oh, Rem, she sighed, as she hurried to her room to change out of her riding outfit. He hadn't left yet and already her life was taking a downhill slide. How would she survive in a house filled with people who had no inclination to offer her aid or were too cowardly?

* * *

Rem felt like a thief, sneaking away in the night like this, but his shame ate at him. He couldn't face Bella's sorrow any more, couldn't abide her disgust. No matter how she tried to hide it, her disappointment was like a lance in his side, catching him with unbearable pain each time he looked on her.

Tiger more or less told him, as politely as he could, that Rem would be better off going back to Sydney. And Rem had little doubt this was the best option open to him. A party from the barracks was leaving at dawn. He would join them; Tiger had arranged his passage. Now all Rem had to do was leave a place that had brought him such happiness when he and his sister re-united, and then such pain. Leaving Sara was the hardest thing ever done in his life. And he had done some gruesome things.

Propping the note on the lamp in the middle of the kitchen table, he took one last look around the homely room, and walked out purposefully.

A pale sun sent its weak rays streaking across the landscape as the wagons began to roll. This small party consisted of six soldiers and four government officials who had been over here on some sort of survey. Rem was one of four convicts, one little more than a boy, one an old man crippled with rheumatism, and the other destined for the gibbet for going at an officer with a blade. His name was Rex. But everyone called him Big Ox for obvious reasons. Built like a giant tree, he towered over everyone by at least a foot. His face bore many scars and the teeth that remained in his mouth were rotten.

Rem decided straight on he would keep well out of this man's way. Evil sparked from his eyes and the stink of decay clung to him.

The first few days and nights passed uneventfully. They tethered Big Ox at night like an animal, and during the day tied his feet to the wagon and bound his hands in front of him. One of the soldiers was given the unenviable task of accompanying him on his trips to attend to his bodily functions. Big Ox seemed to enjoy humiliating his guard and on one occasion pissed all over the soldier's trouser legs. Another time as he was squatting, he suddenly swung round, knocked the guard off balance, and shit on his boots. From then onwards they tied him up a distance from the camp and left him to stew in his own mess.

That didn't seem to bother Big Ox. He was little more than an animal anyway.

By the time they were well into the mountains, they had worked out a routine. Rem and the boy took care of the cooking and cleaning up afterwards, and the old man was in charge of collecting wood and keeping the fire going. Everyone was usually too tired by sundown to do much more than sit for a while chatting over a pipe before they sought their bedrolls. One soldier kept watch each night, waking another so they took four hourly shifts. Rem thought this a useless precaution. They were so far from town it was unlikely they would meet up with bushrangers.

How wrong he was.

One night when the moon sat high, Rem lay rolled into his blanket as near to the fire as he could get when he heard the scuffling of feet. The old man snored a foot away, and the officials all appeared to be sleeping. Lifting his head, Rem peered into the darkness.

Dark shapes loomed over the sleeping soldiers; then he heard Big Ox whisper, "What kep' yer?" One of these shapes bent to untie his tethers, cursing softly, presumably at the stench surrounding him.

"What the hell?" One of the officials sat up, but a whack over the head with a rifle butt silenced him.

"Come on, Big Ox, let's get out 'a here afore the rest of 'em begins to stir," one of his rescuers muttered.

The boy, who had been near Rem's feet, jumped up, asking, "Can I come with you?"

Big Ox slapped him around the ear, knocking him sideways. "Course yer can, lad," he rumbled.

The old man with arthritis feigned sleep. Rem guessed he had no desire to go romping around the mountains with a bunch of renegades.

Rem hoped to go unnoticed. He pulled the blanket over his face. But the man who freed Big Ox demanded, "Who's this 'un?" bending over Rem and pulling the blanket back as he pressed a pistol to his forehead. Rem went as still as a stick, holding his breath.

"He's going to Sydney to be reassigned. Leave 'im be," Big Ox ordered, preparing for flight.

"Naa, let's take 'im along with us." He stared hard at Rem, who regretted he hadn't feigned sleep like the old man.

"I don't want any trouble," Rem whispered into the man's face.

"What are yer, mad? What yer wanna stay with this lot for?" He waved the pistol about, and the spittle dried in Rem's mouth. Instinctively he knew this man would kill him in cold blood and not turn a hair. If Big Ox had the stink of decay about him, this one reeked of death and menace.

"Who goes there?" one of the soldiers called. Every one of the bush gang went still. Big Ox picked up a stone and aimed it at the head of the soldier. His cry of pain and the thump as he keeled over woke everyone else.

Pandemonium broke out as the officials and soldiers rose hastily, some wielding weapons, some empty-handed as they jostled each other in their haste to retrieve weapons left idly by their sides.

"Let's get out 'a here," Big Ox yelled as someone fired at them, the bullet singing past Rem's ear before hitting a tree. Someone groaned and another yelped as the soldiers began firing indiscriminately.

The stink of gunpowder filled his nostrils as Rem suddenly found himself held tightly against Big Ox's chest in a bear hold. "Let me go, for God's sake," he shouted, pushing ineffectually at the great arms.

"Not bloody likely," the big man growled. By now he'd backed away, using Rem for a shield as he stumbled and groped his way through the trees, surrounded by his rescuers. Rem fought him every inch of the way, but it was like a cat fighting a lion. Big Ox's fists were the size of mutton legs, and he was intent on keeping Rem in his embrace until they were well out of the range of the bullets whizzing through the trees. To his dying day Rem would wonder how he didn't take one of those stray bullets in the chest. He tasted blood and realized he had bitten into his lip.

Rem had no idea what direction they took as they stumbled and half-ran, over rocks and into gullies. Big Ox never once loosened his hold, until Rem felt as if he was being strangled by a giant boa constrictor he read about once, capable of crushing a mule.

"This way," someone hissed. After careening and lurching past trees and over fallen branches they came to a small clearing where horses stood tethered. At a rough count Rem thought there were fifteen. Big Ox finally let him go, and Rem stumbled backward, catching his breath as he bent over, hands on knees. He thought of running, but forsook that idea when everyone milled about him. They would have no reason to spare his life; he meant nothing to them now.

"Who's that?" a strange voice demanded.

The ugliest person Rem had ever encountered confronted him. The man's face would instil fear in the hardiest of souls, would give a maiden nightmares. The scars running across his face were raised, as if they had been patched by an unwieldy hand—which they probably had. It was unlikely this renegade would seek practiced medical assistance. A two-inch square of vivid red skin on his right cheek looked as if it had been burned at some stage. As he neared, Rem forced himself not to cringe with repulsion.

Prodding Rem with his whip the man demanded again, "Who the bloody hell have we here? And what did you fetch that kid for? You gone mad? Kill 'im."

Rem shuddered.

Big Ox slapped Ugly on the shoulder, saying in a voice that proved he wasn't intimidated by this ugly brute; doubtless the gang's boss, "He's all right, Craddock." He let out a roar of laughter. "He made a good shield. And the boy wanted to ride along with us. He's a good 'un."

Rem thought of making a run for it. He had little doubt this Craddock intended to kill him. Might as well make a bid for freedom; what had he to lose? Just his life, which had no value to this crowd.

Big Ox foiled any attempt at escape by latching onto his arm. As he pushed Rem before him, they all began to mount up. The others seemed uninterested in what was going on.

"Let me go," Rem pleaded as the big man took hold of the reins of a giant roan.

"Listen, kid, Craddock would shoot you in a flash. Do you wanna die, eh?" When Rem shook his head, he grinned evilly. "Didn't think so. He won't let you go now you've seen him; don't you see? You could tell the scum who rescued old Ox. Craddock likes to see men die, so don't think on doing anything foolish." He spat near Rem's boots. "No, better make the best of it and ride along with us. You might decide you like being part of our gang. The ladies all swoon over tales of us bushrangers." His laughter rang through the trees, and the others all chuckled. Rem felt goose bumps rise all over him. He had no choice; he was likely a dead man whatever road he chose.

"You double up with 'im," Craddock told one of the younger men, and Big Ox roughly pushed Rem to that horse and helped him mount. The boy was hauled up in front of one of the others.

They rode silently for about two hours, deeper into the forested mountains. Craddock led. It was apparent he knew these mountains as well as most men knew their back yards.

When they finally stopped and dismounted, still silent, they led their mounts in single file through a tangle of shrubs into a clearing beneath an overhang of rock. Two of the men took the horses to a rough enclosure made of saplings and rope and unsaddled them, a chore done swiftly. Big Ox gestured for Rem to follow him, and they entered a large cave in the rock face. One of the men put a spark to a fire a few feet inside the opening. It soon began to blaze.

"Got any rum?" Big Ox asked, looking about as if he expected it to jump up at him. "I'm gasping for a swig." He rubbed his mighty paws together and then motioned for Rem to sit.

Rem sat in the dust, his knees bent. God, he'd never get out of this alive, he knew it.

Someone produced a flagon, and Big Ox proceeded to guzzle. "Jesus, I thought you was never gonna make it," he grumbled when Craddock entered the cave and sat on his haunches near Rem.

"I said to give us a day or two in the note I sent, didn't I?" Craddock took out a pouch of tobacco and began to fill a pipe languidly, while watching Rem thoughtfully. "So, what's your sentence?"

Rem shrugged. "Seven."

Craddock grunted. "Seven, eh? What did you do? Steal a lady's purse?"

Big Ox guffawed. "Leave the bloke alone."

Craddock gave him a look that would terrify most men. "We don't have no one here we don't know about, Big Ox. Let him tell us a thing or two about himself." He nodded Rem's way.

"I was transported in '24." Rem shrugged. "Caught stealing, nothing much. Did a stretch in Sydney Town, and was about to be sent north to Newcastle when I was sent over to Bathurst instead." Rem wasn't about to disclose how Tiger rescued him from the treadmill and took him over.

"What's your tag?"

"O'Shea."

"Right, O'Shea, pull your weight, keep out of my way, and do as you're told, and you'll live. See this ugly mug." He jabbed a finger at his disfigured face. Rem nodded. "The bloke who did this to me died an 'orrible death, didn't he, Big Ox?" He lit his pipe with a twig from the fire and took a few drags.

Big Ox roared with laughter as he slapped a knee and belched. "Depends if you reckon being left dangling head-down over a cliff, to wait for the rising tide with a hole in yer gut, 'orrible enough for what he did, Craddock."

"No, I don't think it was. Matter of fact I should have cut his balls off too." He ruminated for a bit, adding, "Yeah, should have gutted him as well."

Rem winced. This man might be exaggerating to put fear into him, but something told Rem his heart was as rotten and ugly as his features.

The man he had shared a horse with handed Rem a filthy scrap of blanket. "Get some shuteye." He rolled himself in it as best he could and pretended to sleep.

There were twelve men in the gang. Adding Big Ox, the boy they tagged Scab because of his marked face, and Rem, the count was now fifteen. Rem hadn't a doubt Craddock would drop him in a flash if he made any attempt to flee. How the bloody hell had he gotten himself into this mess? He trembled and sweated, despite the cold. To push it from his mind, he pictured Sara. How was she faring without him? No doubt by now her father had heard Rem had gone and was gloating.

All the gang settled down eventually. Most snored abominably, the sounds reverberating off the den walls. Rem tried to work out a plan, failing miserably. Big Ox could break him in two with his bare hands. Craddock would take delight in doing him in, in the worst possible way. Most of the others looked as if they would relish killing him. The authorities would no doubt accuse him of going with the bushrangers voluntarily, and he had no idea how to get back to Bathurst even if he did manage to escape.

Cursing silently, he decided to wait it out. Surely, at some stage there would be a chance to escape.

* * *

A week later, Rem reached the conclusion he was destined to remain with this unsavory bunch forever. Scab took to gang life like a fish to water, and eagerly helped with the chores. The gang planned a hold-up for the Sunday after Big Ox's escape and rescue. The night before the proposed hold-up, Rem lay awake planning how he would sneak away while they were off.

"Give him the cobby gelding," Craddock ordered as the sun came up, pointing Rem's way, and his hopes faded. Apparently, he was going along with them. Still, perhaps he would get a chance to take off during the hold-up. There was more chance of that away from here where someone watched him constantly. He didn't hold a lot of hope, but if the opportunity arose he would take it.

Eight of them rode out and left Big Ox and Scab behind. "You're too hot at the moment," Craddock told the big man. "You lay low for a while until the chase cools down."

"Why did I have to come?" Rem asked as they took a treacherous track skirting a mountainside. "I'll be more hindrance than help. I know nothing about holding up wagons." With his heart in his mouth, he watched a small rock kicked up by his horse tumble over the precipice. It fell endlessly into a seemingly bottomless canyon.

Craddock, riding behind Rem, was silent for so long Rem thought he wouldn't reply. But then he said, "The Big Ox has the brain of a flea. For some reason he's taken a liking to you. I'm not taking chances that he might feel sorry for you. This way I can keep an eye on you."

Rem doubted that was the real reason, for Big Ox knew quite well Craddock would show no mercy for anyone who defied him.

Rem breathed a huge sigh when they reached the bottom of the trail, and Craddock motioned for them to dismount. They tethered and concealed the horses in a gully, and then climbed a small hill and settled down to wait amid a stand of trees. Rem was pushed onto his haunches, and the others crouched low. Craddock filled his pipe, poked it in his mouth, but didn't light it.

The creak of wagon wheels and the shouts of the drivers urging their horses on signaled the arrival of wagons. Rem's insides dropped as the sounds grew louder. Was he really about to take part in a bushrangers' hold-up? This was like some odd dream. His limbs felt heavy, as if his mind had left his body and watched the bizarre scene from above the trail. The dream-like feeling intensified.

Craddock pulled his filthy kerchief over the bottom half of his face and gestured for the others to do the same. "Get up."

"No." Rem wasn't about to go out there and get himself filled with gunshot. He wondered at his calmness in the face of the ugly man's ferocious glare.

"I said get up and move out, or I'll shoot you where you sit," Craddock barked.

The driver of the first of three wagons coming over a ridge let out a shout and reined in his team. Craddock shot him in the chest. The poor sod threw up his arms and toppled sideways, falling heavily onto the track. His mate, a look of terror on his face, jumped sideways, missing the second shot.

98

Shouts echoed as the other drivers tried to stop their horses careening into the wagon in front of them.

Craddock's menacing yell echoed through the trees as Rem ran into the brush, and the other gang members crouched low, firing at random.

"Get back here," Craddock hollered, but Rem wasn't about to slow down. A bullet whistled by his ear; then he fell. His last thought was that he had dropped off the face of the earth.

Chapter Ten

Rem blinked his eyes open. It was dark and wet. The eerie shapes of overhanging branches told him he lay beneath a tree, and a small creature scuttled around in the undergrowth nearby. Raindrops spattered onto his face, and he wiped at them with his sleeve. Had he been unconscious hours or minutes?

There was a movement nearby. He struggled to rise, expecting to see a kangaroo or larger animal, but a female said, "You are awake?"

She had a strange accent to her speech, and Rem racked his brain to recall where he had heard that singsong way of speaking before. At that moment, it hit him that his left leg was bound. Jesus! She had tied him up. He tried to move and a shaft of pain shot up from his ankle. Rem guessed then he had broken his leg and there was a splint on it.

"Where are you? And who are you?" he called. "Did you do this?" Rem pointed to his lower leg. She hadn't done a bad job of her doctoring. It was bound securely but not so tight it cut off his circulation.

His rescuer moved stealthily toward him. Rem couldn't make out her features, but she was tiny and had hair as black as coal, for she blended into the shadows like a creature of the night.

"I am called Oyyou," she said low, moving with extreme caution. Like a fawn prepared for flight, she hovered just out of reach.

"Don't be afraid." He rolled onto his elbows, wincing in agony. "I can't harm you even if I felt inclined to, for I can't stand. Did you bind my leg? If so, thank you. It hurts like crazy. Have I broken something?"

"I think you have broken your ankle bone, but cannot be sure," she said. Her voice was melodious, like water trickling over rocks, and it reminded him of a cool stream on a hot day. He grunted at his fanciful thoughts. Perhaps he was hallucinating.

Glancing about into the dense shadows, he could make out the dark shapes of trees and shrubs, but he lay in a small hollow, a carpet of leaves beneath him. "Where are we?"

"You fell when the men began to shout and shoot their guns," she said softly, looking behind her furtively. "I hid, then when they had gone I came to see what had happened to you."

"Thank you for that. How long ago was this?"

She shrugged. "You have been asleep for a long time."

"Long enough for you to bind my leg. That was very kind of you." Rem tried to raise himself again, but sweat broke out on his back, despite the cool rain that had soaked his clothes. With a groan of impatience, he flopped back onto his soggy bed of leaves. "Where do you live? Surely you can't live out here in the middle of nowhere. Or were you on one of the wagons they were going to rob?"

"I live not far from here." She seemed reluctant to tell him more as she glanced about, looking as if she expected a dangerous animal to jump out on her.

"But not alone?"

She shook her head.

"What happened to the others? Did you see where they went?" He couldn't believe he'd escaped from Craddock and his mob so easily. They would have chased him. Unless they thought the fall killed him.

"The man with the ugly face was shot. I heard them talking, wondering what to do with his body. Then two of them lifted him onto a horse. They rode away and the other robbers followed, after waving their weapons. The wagon drivers picked up the man who fell then also went. I hid for a long time."

"Craddock was killed? Well, I'll be blowed! Look, do you think we can get out of this rain?" He was shivering as if he had an ague. She'd probably rescued him only to have him die of a fever.

She looked about again, still wary. "I cannot take you with me. You must go alone."

"Go alone? Blimey, I can't walk." After a few useless struggles to rise, Rem fell back with a groan of frustration. "Do you live with your parents? Have you brothers and sisters? What on earth were you doing out here alone anyway?"

"I live with my...my husband. He is looking for gold. I heard the shooting while I was outside the house and feared men were coming to rob him, so I hid." She locked her hands together nervously. "I cannot take you home."

"Surely your husband wouldn't turn away a traveler in need." This was ridiculous. She had taken the trouble to help him, now intended to desert him. His shudders grew stronger, and he felt dizzy, sure he was about to vomit.

"You are not a traveler. You were with the gang about to rob the wagons," she said bluntly.

"I'm not a robber, believe me. I was with them under duress." Rem swallowed, closing his eyes when his head whirled. His ankle throbbed as if a ten-ton hammer was banging on it. "It's a long story. I'll tell it some time when I feel more up to it. For now would you please get me somewhere dry before I pass out again?" She came closer by degrees and through the haze of pain he saw that her eyes were filled with sympathy. "You can trust me."

A small grunt showed her doubt. "I trust no man!"

"Maybe so, but I'll do you no harm. Just help me up. You bound my leg. How can you think of deserting me now? You might as well stab me and leave me here for the wild animals. Go on, hit me over the head with a rock, then go."

She sucked in a sharp breath. "Do not speak so. You know I cannot kill you. I saved you."

"Exactly, so how can you think to leave me here to perish?"

"Can you get up?" She knelt at his side. "I cannot lift you, I am too small."

She certainly was. Rem couldn't remember seeing such a tiny, fragile woman. She would probably double over when she tried to lift him. Sweat beaded his body as he struggled onto his side then pushed himself into a sitting position. It seemed to take an hour to get onto his good knee.

She rummaged about in the undergrowth, coming back with a branch. After stripping its leaves, she handed it to him, and he agonizingly pushed himself upright. When he put weight on his injured leg Rem thought he would pass out. Like a hot poker, pain shot up his calf to his thigh. He groaned, and she muttered what sounded like a prayer as she took some of his weight on her slender shoulders.

"I don't want to hurt you," he mumbled as they began a slow shuddering progress.

She ignored that and said, "I will put you in the mule's stable."

"Sounds like heaven," he mumbled, not caring now if she let him drop and left him to die. The pain was horrendous.

Through a haze of agony, Rem saw a couple of buildings loom out of the shadows. She halted, a small hand on his chest as she stopped him from stumbling forward. "We must be quiet," she whispered urgently. "My husband is not...he is not a good man."

"Is he Chinese like you?" Rem asked. During their short acquaintance he worked out where he'd heard that accent before. He still couldn't make out her features, but with hair as dark as night and such slight build it was obvious what part of the world she hailed from.

"No, he is from here."

"Is he really your husband? Or are you his…?"

"My parents sold me to him," she blurted. "We never went through a marriage ceremony."

"What!"

"Now, you must be silent, please?" Rem shut his mouth at her pleading tone. "Stay here." Propping him against a tree, she slid into the darkness.

Rem pressed his back against the trunk and dragged some much needed air into his lungs. Her slight frame was silhouetted against the light as she opened the door of the largest hut and went inside.

Within moments she returned, a bundle under one arm and a lamp swinging from a hand.

"He is asleep." With her free hand, she assisted him across the few paces it took to get them to the small shed a few yards from the other hut. "He will sleep until morning. He has finished a flagon of ale."

"Ah, he's drunk. Is he often this way?" Rem asked, feeling immeasurably sorry for this tiny woman.

"Mostly every night." She shrugged gracefully. "It is best."

Rem understood that reasoning. While drunk he left her alone; something she obviously preferred.

"Come," she insisted as she closed the door. In the light thrown by the single lamp Rem saw one small stall where a mule stood, eyeing them indignantly. He wondered how she was going to keep his presence secret from her drunken husband in this confined space.

"You can rest here until morning, and then you must leave," she whispered. "Please go before dawn." She passed him a piece of tattered blanket that smelt like the mule had been lying on it, and then turned to go.

Rem hoped that by first light he felt more able to get away. Right now he wouldn't be able to walk a few paces unaided, but wasn't about to tell her that. Best wait to see what the new day brought. Perhaps he would make a miraculous recovery. Huh, and ducks couldn't swim!

"Oyyou," Rem said quietly. She stopped, facing him, her fingers playing with the belt of rope securing her coarse, ragged garment. "Is that your real name? It sounds very strange, like no name I've heard before. Is it Chinese?"

"It is what he calls me. He shouts Oy You, and I must do his bidding or be beaten," she muttered.

"The bastard! I'll call you Lulu. What he shouts is no name, but a rude insult. Lulu's much better, don't you think?"

"Lulu." She nodded. "It is strange, but, yes, I like it." A ghost of a smile flitted over her mouth.

"I must rest." Rem knew that if he didn't lie down he'd fall down. His knees gave way beneath him, and sagging sideways, he fell awkwardly. As consciousness faded, he was dimly aware of being covered by the scrap of blanket. Then he knew no more.

* * *

A loud noise, like a saw cutting through rough wood, brought Rem half-awake. Shaking his head in an effort to clear it, he peered up at the weak shaft of light drifting in through a crack in the bark slats of the wall.

His mouth felt as if a family of mice nested there. Putting a hand to his head, he cursed. Even after a heavy night of boozing with the laborers, it never ached so much. A searing pain in his leg brought the truth back with a jolt. He peered down at the makeshift splint the Chinese woman had fixed there. Lulu! Where was she, he wondered, trying to move and falling back with a groan of pain. Then he remembered she'd asked him to be on his way before daybreak. There was more chance of the stupid mule flying than him walking. Perhaps aware he had called it stupid the mule began to make his awful braying noise again and Rem realized that's what had awakened him.

"Shush!" he hissed. As if it understood, the animal went quiet, staring at him balefully over the rope separating them, while a hoof batted at the ground.

"Get yer bloody yeller arse moving!" The guttural shout echoed across the clearing, and Rem winced at the brutal tones.

The poor wench. How could parents give a daughter to such a man? Still, it was a fact some people would do anything for cash, especially if they were starving. More shouts were followed by a lull. Likely he was eating. Rem's stomach grumbled, and he realized he hadn't eaten for many hours.

A thought hit him. What if her husband came to fetch his mule? Glancing about for something to cover himself, all he could spot was the tattered blanket and some loose hay. Shuffling about as best he could, wincing and cursing with the pain movement brought on, he finally managed to conceal himself. It was a patchy job and wouldn't pass muster if the brute decided to shift some hay. By the looks of the humble dwelling, not much tidying had been done in a long time. Bullies were renowned for laziness. They usually forced someone else to do their dirty work.

The door opened, and light streamed in. Rem held his breath, but the soft whisper, "Man, where are you?" signaled the arrival of Lulu.

Rem pushed hay out of his face and whispered, "Over here. I thought it best to try and hide when I heard your husband. Is he likely to come in?"

"No, he is too lazy." She confirmed his suspicions. "I must fetch the mule. Why are you still here?" Desperation darkened her voice.

"I've only just woken. And, truth is, I've little chance of walking, or even dragging myself."

"I see." Her eyes skimmed over him, and her bottom lip took punishment as she chewed on it. "Very well. He will go soon, then I will fetch you food. But you must go before he returns from his mine." While talking, she took down the harness from nails, expertly put a bridle and saddle on the mule, and led it out.

A lot more shouting ensued. Then Rem heard the man heading off, his insults echoing through the trees as he urged the mule along.

A small hand shaking his shoulder brought Rem awake with a jolt, and he realized he must have dozed.

"Eat." She offered him a tin plate. It held a slice of grainy bread and a lump of dark roasted meat he guessed was kangaroo. Ravenously he ate and took a swig from the mug she passed to him. It was weak, sweet tea, and tasted like ambrosia to his parched throat.

"Where does he go for supplies?" he asked as she set his empty plate aside.

She'd been watching him silently, and shrugged. "He has things sent up with the passing travelers. Once we went into town, but he doesn't like going there."

"Only once? In how long? How long have you been up here with him?" he asked when she looked at him mutely.

"Two summers have passed."

"Over two years. Good God, and you've only been back to town once. How do you stand it up here, so isolated?"

Her dainty shoulders lifted again. Rem had taken a good look at her for the first time. She was lovely. She didn't have Sara's radiance or beauty, but with her slanted eyes and exquisitely formed nose she reminded him of a fragile doll. The sleek dark hair framed her face and fell to her shoulders, straight as a waterfall.

"How old are you, Lulu?" She looked about fifteen, until you looked into her eyes. They held the look of an old woman. One who had seen and experienced too much anguish.

"Twenty. I think. My parents never told me of my birthday."

Rem spat out a curse. "They are no better than your husband. To sell a girl of eighteen or maybe less to such a man is not Christian."

"They are not Christians," she assured him as she took his mug and placed it on the plate by their side. She had tiny delicate hands, but the nails were broken and dirty. His heart swelled with pity for her. Such a delicate beauty should he pampered like a hothouse plant, not forced into slavery with a brutish man.

"Does he beat you?" he blurted; then wished he'd kept quiet when her face paled even more, making her look ethereal in the dim light where dust motes danced in the shafts of sun.

"He says I am lazy and stupid." A shudder ran through her slight frame. "He beats me if I don't do things as he expects them to be done, then is never satisfied when I try to please him."

"Why don't you run away?" Without thinking, Rem took one of her hands, clasping it firmly when she made to jerk it away.

"Where would I go? I am lost out here. I would die if I walked into the bush." With a movement that was so wistful Rem could have cried for her, she looked over a shoulder, her eyes dreamy. "Sometimes I think I will do that. Just walk away until I can walk no more."

"Don't talk like that," he scolded as thoughts of Aggie returned in force. Had she done that? Walked into the river and not looked back? He shuddered.

"You are cold?" With one more jerk, she released herself from his clasp.

"No, but I do have to go outside, and I don't know how I'll manage it." Struggling onto his side he started to push himself onto his hands, sweat trickling down his face as the pain intensified.

"I will help." Hastily she got to her feet and with her thin arms about his waist helped him to rise. Rem hobbled outside, leaning on her heavily until he thought she might tumble over. Like a pair of drunks after a binge, they reached a group of bushes. "I will wait here," she said, blushing as she turned her head to watch a few chickens scrabbling about.

After Rem saw to his needs, she helped him back to the shed. Then she went off and fetched him a bowl of warm water and a piece of rag. He felt better after a wash.

But she looked very worried, a frown marring her pale brow as she watched his struggles. "You have not the strength to walk today. It will be better if you stay one more day." Wringing her hands, she added, "But you must leave tomorrow."

"Thank you. I doubt I could make it past the clearing on my own." Rem felt exhausted after the small task of washing and drying himself. In truth, he couldn't see himself walking unaided for days. "My ankle's throbbing like blazes. Do you have something for the pain? Perhaps some of your husband's spirits." Hopefully he looked up at her; she stood near him, the bowl she had emptied tucked under an arm.

"I dare not touch his spirits. He measures how much is in the jug each morning." She seemed to ponder something. "I will fetch you some of the thing he chews. It makes him sleepy, and brings a smile to his lips."

"Chews?" Rem frowned as he tried to think what she meant. Then it hit him. "Ah, you mean opium?"

She shrugged. "I do not know its name. But I think it comes from the juice of the flower called a poppy."

Rem nodded. "Yes, that'd be opium. Where the hell did he get that from?"

"I guess he bought it from one of the travelers along the road. He meets up with them and they give him this potion along with supplies, and he pays in gold."

When she was gone Rem dozed again.

"I found this," he heard her say, and Rem blinked as he stared up at his angel of mercy.

She held a small bottle aloft. "What is it?"

"I cannot read what is written on it, but I think he took some once when he came home with a terrible cut on his arm. He said it eased the pain. He hid it, but I found it. I thought it might be better for you than the poppy juice." She knelt at his side.

Rem took the bottle and read the label. "It's laudanum. Same thing, I think, as poppy juice. I have no idea how much I should take." To err on the side of caution Rem took a sip. As he handed the bottle back to her she went to rise. Rem stopped her with a hand.

"Don't go. Stay and talk with me."

"I have many chores to do before he returns." Despite her words she seemed reluctant to leave.

"There can't be that much up here to keep you occupied for a whole day. What time does he usually come back?"

"At sundown mostly. But sometimes he returns during the afternoon. When he wishes to..." Her cheeks colored as she fiddled with the hem of her pathetically thin torn and creased garment.

"When he wishes to bed you?" Rem touched her fidgeting hand, and she stilled, nodding.

"Ah, Lulu." Rem had no idea what to say. Why should anyone endure such a life? Stuck up here in the back of beyond with no company but a brutal husband who treated her no better than a whore. Worse than a whore, for she had to live with his insults and beatings.

"Think about coming with me when I go. I'll see you get a position in a fine house or somewhere. Anywhere would be a step above the life you have now. I can't promise anything, I'm still a convict and will have to accept my punishment when I get to town. But I know one thing, you'll be better off away from this." He jerked his head, giving their surroundings a scornful glance.

"I do not think so." Her acceptance made him see red. With a jolt he realized the throbbing in his ankle had eased, and he felt very drowsy.

"Think about it," he murmured as he drifted off to sleep.

Rem floated in and out of sleep, his rest interspersed with dreams of ugly faces, shots being fired, falling through space, and being rescued by a maiden with hollow eyes with the hands of an angel.

Lulu brought him another meal at midday, more tea, and more of the laudanum. It certainly lulled the pain and made him drowsy. She helped him outside again then left him to sleep some more. As the sun set and the shack grew dim he heard the shout of her husband. Her sweet lilting voice drifted across to him as she offered words of welcome.

All she got in return was insults. Rem huddled beneath the tattered blanket when the door opened. But it was Lulu who entered. She took the harness from the mule, roped him into his stall, and then offered the animal a bucket with a small amount of grain in it. The mule began to munch happily.

"I will be back later," Lulu whispered, going out again.

110

No doubt when her husband was drunk.

He was right. About an hour later, she crept in, kneeling beside him. "I brought you the…what you called opium, this time," she said. "I thought it best—in case he needed the other potion and noticed it was less than before."

"That was a good idea."

"What is your name?" she asked shyly.

"It's Jeremy O'Shea. But most call me Rem or Remy," he said.

"What shall I call you?"

"Rem, of course. You're my friend aren't you? All my friends call me that."

"I would very much like to be your friend."

"You're more than that, Lulu, you're my savior. You likely saved my life."

For the first time since he'd met her she smiled. It transformed her face, lit up her eyes, made her appear almost childlike. But Rem had a feeling she had never been a child.

"Rem. It is an odd name, but I like it."

While they talked, Rem chewed on the opium powder. He began to feel light-headed and extraordinarily carefree. With a sigh, he leant back, taking her hand. She allowed him to cradle it in his.

"Odd name for an odd fellow," he muttered, running his thumb over her tiny wrist. "You're as frail as a little bird." Not plump like Aggie, or strong and well-formed like his Sara. Sighing his love's name, he tried to force his eyes open, but they drifted shut.

Chapter Eleven

A week later Rem was stronger, but suffered from cabin fever after his confinement to this dingy space. Lulu made a concoction from green ants to substitute the opium. She was justifiably terrified her husband would notice the laudanum and powder had diminished. She also made a poultice from ground roots and leaves she applied regularly to the break in his bone. Rem had no idea what the plant was, and neither did she, but somewhere in her past she had seen a woman use it to knit bones. Most of the bruising had disappeared.

Lulu's tormentor—funny, but Rem hadn't found out if he had a name—was apparently onto a strike of gold. He was away most of the daylight hours, but Rem ventured outside rarely. Lulu was terrified the brute would return early and find Rem there. One day he came back before sundown and yelled for her. Rem lay shivering while he imagined what the man did to the fragile woman Rem had come to really like. An hour later, she crept into the stable, her demeanor shouting humiliation. Rem didn't query her, not wanting to add to her shame.

The next morning, her husband left later than usual, and Lulu came in with Rem's food and a mug of tea. When she helped him outside, he saw that half her face was bruised purple.

"What did that monster do to you?" he demanded, balancing on the branch he now used to make his slow progress to a place of privacy.

For a minute, she kept her head bowed, her hair hiding her face. Rem reached out to lift her chin. "Did he bash you? The coward."

"It is nothing." She shrugged.

Rem cursed violently. "The man's no better than a wild animal. What did you do to deserve such treatment?"

"I did not cook his meat to his liking. Do not worry for me. I am used to this." She pressed a palm to the cheek, now beginning to swell.

"Nobody gets used to being treated like he treats you, Lulu! Come away with me. I'm getting stronger by the day. As soon as I can put a little weight on this bloody foot, I'll be able to start out. But I can't leave you here."

With a wistful little smile, she shook her head. "I cannot go with you. He would find me and kill me."

"How would he find you? Good God, he's drunk most of the time. If he's onto a strike of gold he won't think about deserting his claim, I can tell you that."

Rem went behind a tree to relieve himself and was adjusting his breeches when she whispered urgently, "Stay hidden!"

Rem ducked back behind the trunk of the gum tree. Just in time, for he heard a rough shout. Her husband had returned.

"What yer doing over there?" he yelled. Rem heard Lulu scuffling through the leaves as she went over to him. "You lazy little doxie!" A sharp crack followed. Rem froze. The bastard had walloped her again. With an indrawn breath, he sought to control the urge to go to her aid. It wouldn't help her one bit if he was to show himself.

"Get inside and get yer clothes off!"

Rem clenched his jaw so tightly it ached. Lulu began to whimper, and Rem heard the sound of ripping cloth. Sweet heavens, the brute was tearing her clothes. Easing over so he could see beyond the tree trunk, he saw the bastard toss her to the ground, while struggling with his trouser buttons.

"Take your hands off her," Rem shouted. It seemed that every bird for miles went silent. The man stopped unfastening his breeches, and his face wore such a look of shock Rem would have laughed had it all not been so tragic.

113

"Who the bloody hell are you? And what's it to you what I do with her? She's mine to do with as I please." He glanced about, as if expecting other company, demanding, "Where the fucking hell did you spring from?"

By now, Rem was beginning to regret his hasty move, but he'd acted completely by instinct. No woman deserved to be treated like a common doxie. "I sprang from hell. I'm the devil's disciple and you're a dead man if you don't leave that woman alone."

"What?" He looked genuinely puzzled. "This woman happens to be my property, and what's more it has nothing to do with you or anybody how I treat her. Now bugger off. I don't know where you came from, but you can carry on with your journey and get off my land."

"This ain't your land. This land belongs to no one, except maybe the government."

"Piss off!"

Lulu had taken the opportunity to crawl out of his reach. With a growled curse, the man made a grab for her, wrenching one arm up and twisting it. She screamed.

"If you don't release that woman now, you're dead." Rem hobbled toward him and his eyes widened at Rem's bound leg.

"You ain't no traveler. You can't even walk." He pulled a knife from his belt, wielding it.

"How observant of you."

Lulu began to cry.

"Keep quiet," he yelled, kicking her in the side. "Shut your trap."

"I told you to leave her alone," Rem said through bared teeth.

The brute's guttural laugh echoed through the trees. "What are you gonna do about it if I don't?" The knife slashed through the air, and Rem knew a moment's sheer panic. If he threw the knife and his aim was good, Rem would be the dead one.

"I have a pistol," Rem said levelly. "Before the knife you hold can be on its way toward me you'll be shot in the chest."

114

While Rem pondered on what would happen if the man realized he was bluffing, Lulu threw herself at his legs. He ground out a string of oaths as he toppled forward. Grabbing a stout branch from the ground, she bashed him over the head with it. His language was vitriolic as he twisted away, putting a hand to his temple. He went purple with rage when he saw blood on his fingers.

"You whore! I'll kill you." He lunged at her with the knife.

Rem moved as swiftly as he could, his pain forgotten as he brought the branch he used as a crutch up and bashed her attacker over the head. The man was stronger than he looked, for the blow only temporarily winded him. He dropped to his knees and fished around in the leaves for the knife.

Rem knew he would use the knife without compunction. This was the only chance he had. With a shout, he raised the branch once more, bringing it down on the man's back, and then his head with as much might as he could muster. Lulu's tormentor fell forward, grunted, and then lay still.

Lulu crawled on her hands and knees until she could touch the inert body. With a finger, she timidly felt for a pulse in his neck.

"Is he dead?" Rem shuddered violently with reaction now it was all over. It had happened so quickly. Although he'd threatened the man with death he really hadn't intended to do away with him.

"I think so. I cannot feel his heartbeat." She sank back onto her bent legs. Rem saw a matching shudder run through her.

"I couldn't have killed him with a blow from this." He waved the branch. "He must be unconscious." Rem awkwardly eased himself down beside her. Taking a shuddering breath, he pushed the man over onto his back. There was no doubt his life was over; the knife protruded from his chest, right where the heart sits. His filthy shirt grew redder by the second as his life's blood spurted from the wound.

"Christ! The blade went into him." With a shudder of revulsion, Rem scraped his hands down the front of his shirt, as if that would wipe him clean of guilt. "Now what'll we do?" He twisted his head to gaze at her. Shock and something else was etched on her features. Was it relief?

She shook her head. "I do not know. You should not feel guilty." It was clear she read his face well and saw he blamed himself. "He died by his own hand. You were trying to protect me. I am glad he is dead." Her vehemence brought on more shudders. Truth be known, Rem was glad too. The brute didn't deserve to live after the way he'd treated her.

"We'll have to move him, but how?" Rem didn't have the strength to lift himself, let alone a lifeless body.

She nibbled on her lip as she pressed her fingers to her temple. "I know," she said at last, getting up and running to the shack. She returned with a quilt, obviously stripped from the bed. "If we can push him onto this, then perhaps we can drag him along." She flapped it out, spreading it on the ground beside the body. "Help me roll him onto it."

Rem dragged in a ragged breath and got down as best he could again. His ankle throbbed like crazy. But they had to get rid of the corpse as soon as possible. There'd been no visitors since Rem's arrival, but if someone happened to pass through now he would be for the gibbet for certain. And Lord alone knew what would happen to Lulu then. No one would believe it was accidental death.

Sweat dripped from Rem as they pushed and pulled the lifeless form until they had him on the quilt. Her strength amazed him. When they had the job finished, she ran off again, coming back with a length of rope.

"We must tie it up," she said. Rem nodded. It was another tedious task to get the rope beneath the body, then to secure it. Rem's strength was running out, as the body seemed to grow heavier.

"Now what?" he asked, panting and dizzy with the exertion. She brought him the laudanum, and as he waited for it to take effect and ease his pain, she sat thoughtfully.

"I think we should put him down his mine," she decided. "No one knows where it is. He was very secretive and greedy."

"So how do you know where to find it?"

She grimaced. "I followed him one day. He beat me, threatening me with death if I told anyone where it was. Yes, that would be a good resting place for him."

"I agree. But how do we get him there? Is it far?" Rem licked his lips. The pain had ebbed, but he still felt faint.

"We will use the mule." She jumped up and went to fetch the animal that had been grazing nearby. They secured the rope about the body's ankles then tied one end of it to each of the stirrups. "Can you mount the animal?" she asked.

It proved a struggle, but Rem managed it. The mule kicked up a fuss and it took a while to pacify it. But once they started to move, with Lulu urging it on from the front and Rem kicking its ribs, they made a slow progress up the track her husband had made on his daily journey to the mine. It took a good half hour to reach their destination.

When both Lulu and the mule stopped, Rem asked, "Where's the mine?"

She looked about furtively. "It is here somewhere. He must have concealed the entrance. I will find it while you undo the ropes. It is not far away." She carefully paced away while Rem slid off the mule and undid the bindings. Now the body was covered, he didn't feel so bad. His trembling had died down, but he probably owed the feeling of tranquility to the potion he'd taken for the pain.

"I have found it," she called from about ten paces away. "He covered it with branches."

Together they dragged the body the short distance. Rem stared down into the pit her husband had dug. It must have taken months of grueling work.

"Do you suppose he brought up much gold?"

"I do not know. He hid it well somewhere." She shrugged. "We will find it."

"Let's do this." Rem wished to get this awful deed over as quickly as possible.

She looked at him searchingly for a drawn-out moment; then together they heaved the trussed-up bundle into the dark hole. It made a dull thumping noise as it hit the bottom. Rem's heart thudded noisily in his head. Dear God! What had he done now? There would be no place in God's heaven for him.

"Come, I will pull the branches back over the hole to conceal it, then cover our tracks."

"Wait, he must have a ladder secured somewhere." Rem glanced about, and she ran to the nearest tree.

"I forgot. Yes, you are right. It is here, tied to this tree, and there was a thing…" Her thin arms waved about in the shape of an arc. "I do not know the name of it. He pulled the dirt up in a bucket with a rope tied to it."

Rem slapped at his head. "Of course. I have no idea what it's called either, but it's a sort of frame he would have used. God, the man certainly hid everything well."

She picked up a branch and began to scrabble about in the leaves and undergrowth. "It is here," she said after a few moments, and together they dragged the makeshift frame to the hole.

Once they had hurtled everything down and she'd made sure the tracks were all covered, she pulled the limbs into place. Together they stood side by side, staring at the spot, both heaving with exertion. The piles of dirt brought up would soon be covered by undergrowth, Rem knew, for most of the small mounds in the area were already half concealed.

"Come, we must go." She touched his arm, and then helped Rem onto the mule.

She followed the plodding mule down the track, brushing fallen leaves and debris over their trail. Rem stopped at the bottom of the incline, looking back. She had covered their tracks well. Soon there would be no evidence anyone had used this track daily. The mine was so isolated Rem doubted he would find it if he retraced their steps in a week or so.

But he would always know! He'd killed a man and thrown the body down a mineshaft. Another sin to add to his growing list.

"You must take off your shirt so I can wash it," Lulu said when they returned to the clearing and the mule had been stabled. Rem looked at his front where blood had dried. Revulsion filled him as he whipped it off and tossed it to the ground.

An hour later, he was dressed in one of her husband's clean shirts. She also changed her dress. The inside of the shack was as neat as she could make it, considering the lack of amenities. The bed was made of sacking roped to legs fashioned from branches tied with rope, and there were two stools also made from tree stumps. Another stump served for a table.

"I will burn these." She took the small assortment of clothing from hooks behind the door.

Rem followed her outside carrying a pair of boots and a hat. Together they destroyed all evidence of the man who had no name. It took a while until all that was left in the bush grate were ashes. Only then did they face each other.

It was a while before Rem spoke. "When he collected supplies from the wagons passing along the road, did you go with him?"

"No, he never let me accompany him. No one has seen me. I don't think he had any friends or family in Sydney. When we left town he spoke to no one."

"What about your parents? They knew you came out here with him." Rem felt sure someone somewhere would know eventually her husband was dead. But the colony was full of such people. Many men and women fled England seeking riches or anonymity in New South Wales, or were transported and lost track of their families.

"After they took the gold in payment I never saw them again. They would not know where we went or what we did. They did not care." She bent her head.

Rem swore vividly. What unfeeling bastards. It was useless suggesting she go back to find them; they wouldn't want her anyway, unless they thought to sell her to the next bidder.

"I'll look after you," he said, wondering how he would do that. They couldn't stay here indefinitely. "I have to go back to town—you know that, don't you, Lulu?"

She nodded silently.

"I need to serve out my term, and then be a free man." He wasn't about to tell her once that was attained he intended to marry Sara. "The longer I stay here, the harder it will be to convince the authorities I didn't abscond but was taken by Craddock's gang."

"I understand." A wealth of understanding filled her eyes. This woman was used to facing anything life threw her way. "But you cannot travel until your leg has healed. So, until then we can share peace."

How could he deny her a respite? Besides, she was right, he couldn't go anywhere until he could walk. Then they could make their way to the road and hope to catch up with a wagon going to Sydney. Or perhaps one going to Bathurst. Either way it made little difference. He would end up being escorted back to town.

She went inside and dragged out the bedding. After burning it, they made up a new mattress using dried grasses. She brought the tattered blanket Rem had used and they spread it over the straw. Then she found a clean scrap of linen to use as a sheet.

Lulu prepared a meal. They ate in silence; then she cleared away the dishes and washed them in a tin bowl. By the time she fed the mule and settled it for the night, the sun had gone down. During all this time, she barely met his gaze, and Rem had no idea what she was thinking. Did she expect him to share the bed they prepared?

When there was no reason to linger, he said, "I can sleep in the stable."

Rem couldn't read her expression as she stood before him, fingering her tattered dress. "Do you not desire me?" she asked softly.

"I..." Stunned, Rem swallowed. How could he not desire her? "You're a beautiful woman, Lulu. Of course I desire you. But…" He looked toward the door. "I thought perhaps you didn't want me touching you, after the way your husband treated you. I thought you didn't like men too much. And I wouldn't blame you. Sweet heavens, the man was a brute."

"But you are not. You are a kind man. I know you would never hurt me. I wish to know what it is like to be touched by a gentle man, one who cares about my feelings and not his own lust. Would you give me that, Remy? That is all I ask."

Rem ran a finger down her pale cheek. "How can I refuse such a plea?" Deep inside he knew he should refuse, but at that moment all he could think about was giving this woman a touch of kindness and gentleness—so far lacking in her life.

Considering this life she had been forced to lead, her skin was like silk. Would the rest of her feel like that? A pulse began to thrum in his temple. "Come, lie with me and let me touch you."

"You must show me what to do," she said as they both knelt facing each other on the rough pallet. "I have never given myself; always I have been taken." A small smile played about her mouth, and Rem leaned to place a kiss there.

"First we have to learn each other's shape," he said, also smiling when she jumped as he ran a finger over one of her nipples. Rem helped her draw her garment over her head, then, her eyes averted she helped him remove his clothing. Her every move proclaimed her shyness—clearly she had never done such a simple task before.

When they faced each other again on the bed, he said in a hushed voice, "You have such lovely breasts." They were up-tilted and small, but so nicely rounded. Rem held one in a palm, and for the first time she looked down at his dark hand on her pale flesh.

"Such a difference," she whispered. "I have never had a man touch me so gently."

"All you'll ever get from me is gentleness, Lulu. We're so different in all ways. Touch me, and you'll learn that I'm hard while you're soft. I'm hairy while your skin is smooth as silk beneath my fingertips." With a thumb, he incited the proud little nipple to a hardness that made her gasp.

"That sent a shiver to my toes," she whispered, and he knew for certain she had never known the wonderful pleasure that comes from a simple touch.

"I'll make you tremble all over," he vowed, intent on making this as pleasurable for her as he was able. Already he was hard and wanting. And her eyes showed a slight misgiving as she looked down to where he throbbed. "And I'll never hurt you, I promise. Touch me; watch what it does to me to have your tiny hands on me."

With a slight hesitance, she obeyed, and Rem nearly jumped out of his skin. "You feel so hard yet so soft all at the same time." Her eyes were now cloudy with desire.

Gently Rem laid her back and with equal care, half covered her body, letting her learn his weight, learn that despite his strength he could be tender and caring.

"You're beautiful," he said above her mouth as he explored her body and shivered with delight as tentatively she did the same to his.

In a soft voice she told him how he made her feel, and Rem told her that she was the loveliest creature he'd ever known. It was a lie, of course, and for a moment Sara's image appeared behind his closed eyelids. Sara was unobtainable right now—perhaps would always be—but this woman in his arms was so pliable, so soft, so warm, that he forced the image away and gave all he was capable of giving to someone who had known nothing but pain and anguish in her short life.

"You are a loving man," she said when they lay quiet and spent, wrapped in each other's arms, their sweat drying on their cooling bodies.

"And you are a generous woman."

"Thank you." She pressed a kiss to his shoulder and tightened her small arms about him.

"You have nothing to thank me for, Lulu."

"Yes, I have," she insisted. "If not for you I would never have known there is delight to be had in coupling.

Without you I would have died thinking all men are pigs and treat women no better than their animals, worse at times."

Playing with his chest hairs, she went silent for a while, and then declared, "I am happy he is dead." She placed a finger over Rem's mouth when he made to speak. "I am sinful I know. But it was his own fault. My soul may never rest in peace for having such awful thoughts, but he deserved to die. And you must never blame yourself. He died by his own hand, remember that. And it was a fitting end to such a man."

Rem knew she was right but suspected he would be haunted by his death, as well as Aggie's, forever.

Chapter Twelve

"No, I cannot believe it!" Sara stared at Bella, her eyes burning with tears. As if a fist clutched at her heart, a pain filled her chest, threatening to choke her. Perhaps she was having a heart attack. Was it possible in one so young?

"We found it hard to accept at first," Bella said.

"No, Remy can't be dead. There has to be some mistake." Sara knew that must be the case. Surely if Rem's life had come to an end she would feel it in her heart. "What happened?"

"We heard that the wagons were attacked and this man, a convict on the way to be hanged, was rescued by his cohorts. It seems Rem went with them when they made off."

Sara watched, stunned, as Bella wiped away tears. "Rem wouldn't have gone willingly. They must have forced him."

"Exactly what I said. Tiger was told that a young convict boy made off with them too. One story is that Rem was used as a shield by this convict." She sniffed back a sob. "I'm inclined to believe that story."

"But how did Rem come to be killed? I don't understand." It was too awful to contemplate. No, she didn't believe it. They must have the wrong man—it couldn't be Remy.

"It seems the same gang, led by this man identified as Craddock, an awful character who has been terrorizing people on the mountain road for months, attacked a group of wagons. He killed one of the drivers, and then was shot. There were lots of shots fired. Apparently Rem was last seen falling over a precipice." She choked on her words.

"But surely they looked for him. How could they leave him out there, not knowing if he was alive or dead?" Sara paced about, her distress blinding her.

"You know what it's like in the mountains, Sara. Anyone who falls from the mountain road usually ends up in impenetrable scrub." Bella tucked her hands beneath her arms, as if she tried to hold herself together. "They had injured people and couldn't spare the manpower to search, probably fruitlessly, for someone who was doubtless dead anyway," she finished on a despairing sigh.

"There you are then," Sara persisted in desperation. "Rem is likely lost out there. We have to believe that. He'll turn up, you'll see," she cried. "I don't believe for a moment he willingly took part in a robbery."

"I don't either." Bella's shoulders hunched as she rubbed absently at her crossed arms. "And no one wants to believe he might turn up more than I, Sara. But we must face the awful truth. Rem is gone from us forever." Her face crumpled as she gave way to heart wrenching sobs. Sara put her arms about her, trying to console, when her own heart cried out for consolation.

Rem dead! No, it could not be true.

But two weeks later, when teamsters brought in their laden wagons, the truth was forced on her. If Rem was injured he would have made his way back to the road, she knew it. Passing teamsters would have picked him up. Wagons bound for Sydney had no news of an injured man being picked up along their route over the mountains.

Sara's sobs frightened her mother and angered her father.

* * *

A month later, as October drew to a close, her father brought a stranger to the house. "This is Clive Ravenbrook."

They entered the sitting room. While her mother and Josie worked on their sewing, Sara stared into space and ignored both men. She had no interest in strangers or visitors. Had no interest in anything anymore. Her life had lost all meaning.

"Sara, where are your manners," her mother scolded, when introductions had been made. Sara hadn't replied, let alone spared the newcomer a thought.

"Oh, I'm sorry." She looked up. The newcomer was taller than Remy, and broad of shoulder. He looked to be nearing middle age, with a full head of very fair hair, almost white. His cravat was knotted immaculately over a shirt of fine linen. His jacket and trousers, obviously fashioned by a master tailor, fitted him well. He bore the stamp of a gentleman, down to his highly polished boots. Sara's first thought was how out of place he looked this far from town. Most of the men hereabouts didn't dress like dandies.

He stood over Sara and bowed, watching her from pale eyes that gave no hint of his thoughts. "I can't tell you what a pleasure it is to meet you," he said urbanely, and then turned to bow to her mother, who set her sewing aside.

"Josie, go and order tea," Edmund barked, and the stupid woman scuttled off to do his bidding.

"Please take a seat." Eleanor gave him a sickly smile. Clive Ravenbrook settled on the sofa beside Sara, too close for her comfort. "And what is your business in the district?" she asked timidly. Sara was stunned to see a slight blush on her mother's usually pallid cheeks.

"That's his concern," Edmund interrupted abruptly. Then, waving a hand the visitor's way, he barked, "He's going back to town in a couple of weeks, isn't that so, Ravenbrook?"

"True." He eyed Sara with a look that made her feel oddly uneasy. Shifting to put more space between them, she stiffened when he also shifted slightly. He gave the impression he was intent on her father's words, but she sensed his interest was solely on her.

The maid came in and conversation dwelt on the mundane while she served tea and cakes. Once she left, Sara's father got right down to the reason for Clive Ravenbrook's visit.

126

"Clive here is looking for a wife, ain't that so?" Edmund gave the visitor a smile that made Sara's insides churn. Her father never smiled. It was crystal clear what was on his mind.

No! A silent scream rolled round her head.

When all small talk ended and the tea finished, Edmund ordered, "Take Clive out and show him around the garden, Sara."

Sara had remained sullenly silent while the conversation flowed about her. She desperately wanted to refuse but knew it would be useless. Her father's weak excuse to push them together was ludicrous. Rising, she protested, "There's not a lot to see."

"No matter," he boomed, waving a hand her way. "A breath of fresh air will do you good. You've been mooning around the house for days."

That was true. She hadn't the heart for riding since hearing about Rem. Hadn't the heart for anything.

"You'll need a wrap," Eleanor advised in a silly voice that grated. "It's still cool."

What on earth had come over her mother, she'd never been so concerned. It was embarrassing how she simpered over this stranger.

The maid was sent off to fetch the wrap, and Sara almost cringed when Clive looped it about her shoulders. She led the way outside. As they walked between the few trees planted on their arrival, now struggling for survival, she said, "I wasn't lying, there's really nothing worth looking at in our gardens."

"On the contrary, there's you. I find I could easily spend all my days looking at you, Sara. You're extremely beautiful. But I suppose you've been told that a hundred times or more."

Sara smiled for the first time in his company. "As it happens, I've been told it a few times. But outward beauty means little, don't you think, Mr. Ravenbrook?"

"Please call me Clive. Yes, I believe you're right, but something tells me your beauty is not merely skin deep."

He put his hand on her elbow, and she resisted the impulse to shake it off. He was merely being gentlemanly after all.

"Pray tell me how you can decipher my character at such a short acquaintance? Most beautiful women are spoilt and pampered to such an extent they are usually rather self-centered creatures." Perhaps she was one of those women; she'd never given it a lot of thought.

"Ah, but I'll wager you haven't been spoiled in that way." His pale eyes swept over her; assessing. "Certainly not by your father. Am I right?"

Sara pulled a face and shrugged. "That's very astute of you...Clive. Have you known my father long, to have worked out his nature so well?"

"We knew each other in town, yes." He paused, running a long-fingered hand over his chin. Her eyes were drawn to that hand. Without a doubt, he didn't know what it was to labor on the land; his skin was as white and smooth as a woman's. "That's why he asked me to call when he heard I was over here on business."

"You never did say precisely what that business was, did you?" Sara halted, staring at him in an effort to gauge his reaction to her query. Not a flicker of expression entered his eyes. Never had Sara known a person whose thoughts were hidden so well.

"I had business with the commandant. Nothing that would interest a lady. Tell me, have you a beau? Is there some lucky gentleman seeking your hand?" Was it imagination or did his grip tighten as he waited on her reply?

Sara held back a cry of dismay. The realization Remy was never coming back as he'd promised had slowly taken hold. He was never going to gain his freedom and make his fortune, so he could prove to her father he was worth something. He would never meet her out riding again. Was never going to kiss her, make her feel cherished and desired ever again.

"There was someone." She gazed toward the mountains in the distance. "But he's missing." She paused. "It's been presumed that he's dead."

Clive didn't seem surprised. How much had her father disclosed? It was probable he had told this stranger about Remy, how he supposedly died, how presumptuous he was in daring to think he stood a chance at gaining Sara's hand in marriage.

"I'm sorry—for him. But very glad for myself." He stared at her thoughtfully then said, "I leave for Sydney a week from Monday. I would be honored if you would allow me to call on you in the time I have left here. Perhaps you would ride with me tomorrow."

She did, and every following day. Clive's easy way of laughing at himself, and the world in general was a balm to her battered spirit. He surprised her by having a quick wit, an inquiring mind and a loathing for country life.

He divulged that he was forty. Sara had to admit he seemed to have the stamina of a young man in his prime. He regaled her with stories of his early days in London, his exploits as a solicitor, his dealings with the gentry.

Sara admitted to herself, although it amazed her, that she began to enjoy his company. Admitted she'd be sad to see him leave, for he brought a smidgen of interest back into her dreary life. No man would ever take the place of Remy in her heart, but Clive Ravenbrook eased the pain somewhat, pushed the despair to a recess of her heart.

This temporary respite shattered when, on their final ride before he was due to leave, he said, "I've spoken to your father, my sweet. He's agreed to give me your hand in marriage."

"He's what?" Dumbfounded, she stared at him while anger flared. How dare her father do such a thing? Her mare began to prance when she wheeled to a halt and faced him. "I'm sorry, Clive, I have no idea where he got the notion from that I'm ready for marriage, but he's wrong. I can't marry you."

"Can't or don't wish to, my dear?" His tone was altogether too blasé as he stopped his horse and moved in close to put a hand on her reins.

"Both," she told him bluntly. If her father chose to make a fool of himself, that was his lookout, but she was not about to be coerced.

"Think about this more thoroughly before you refuse me out of hand," he urged, with relaxed charm. A way of behaving that seemed to come easily to him.

"I don't need to think about it," Sara said. "I won't marry you, Clive. I'm sorry, but my heart is elsewhere." She refused to meet his eyes. "I simply…cannot be convinced that…that the man I care for is dead. I know he'll come back some day. He promised, and for that reason I can't possibly think of marrying you."

Clive sighed, patting her hand as if she were a child. "The man you speak of is dead. Nobody could survive a fall such as he had. And he was injured. One of the travelers saw him go down, and then saw him fall. Face up to it, he's never going to keep that promise of his."

Sara rubbed a gloved hand over her face. How did Clive know so much about Remy's disappearance? But, of course, her father would have disclosed all the details. The thought made her sick at heart. Deep in that heart she knew Remy wasn't coming back, but even so the thought of marrying someone else sickened her.

"Are you happy in your father's house?" Clive suddenly asked. The question didn't surprise her; a fool could tell that her family wasn't a normal, contented circle. Always there were undercurrents when they were together. Ten minutes in their company, and it was clear to anyone her father was a bigot and her mother a useless weakling.

Why hide the truth? "I hate it here," she said dully. "I hate living out here in isolation." Remy helped dissolve some of that dislike, now it had returned, with double strength, until Sara felt stifled at times. How she pined for city living. "I despise having to wait months for supplies to be brought from town. Even the most trifling item such as embroidery thread or a book has to be ordered and waited on. It doesn't occur to my father that a young woman needs friends of her own age."

Sara sighed. How she despised her father's dictatorial and heavy-handed ways, her mother's simpering weakness. Often she wanted to flee from the angry outbursts that flared up when Edmund was displeased, which was often. Bella Carstairs coped with life out here for she had a loving husband who doted on her and their children.

"I've a fine house on Pitt Street," Clive said. "My servants would tend to your every need. I need a wife, Sara, one who will oversee my household. And I want you to be that wife. Something tells me you'll go to great lengths to get away from your father." He waved his riding crop to encompass the surrounding area, grimacing. "And to get away from this God-awful sheep country. You weren't meant to be out here away from all respectable society any more than a man such as I. Wouldn't you like to return to town living and the refinements it offers? Return to the company of your female acquaintances? I'm a wealthy man; you'd want for nothing." His tone grew cajoling.

"I would like to return to town, but I don't think I could marry you, Clive."

He stared at her, the expression in his pale eyes never changing. "We could even visit England at a later date if you felt so inclined. I still have quite a share of business involvement over there."

Sara shook her head. "Could I at least have the chance to think on it?" she asked as they turned their horses for home.

"By all means," he quickly agreed. "Your father asked me to dine with you this evening. As you know, I leave early tomorrow. My life would be complete if you are by my side on the journey and for the rest of our lives. I wish I could give you more time in which to grow to know me better. Time to assess and evaluate my many charms." He smiled at this bit of whimsy, and she couldn't help thinking how handsome he was.

"I will give you my answer then," Sara said, knowing her answer would be no.

* * *

Sara watched Clive as he rode off, tall in the saddle, his manner assured. If she knew for certain Remy was dead, had seen him lifeless before her, and had to choose a husband, Clive was likely the one she would pick.

A man of the world, he knew how to treat a woman, knew how to impress her without being overpowering in his attentions. He'd hinted on the way back that he wasn't a man who would make great demands on his wife. He wanted a son to inherit his wealth and name, but gave the impression he wouldn't expect more than she was willing to give in the marital bed. The thought of coupling with him to produce his heir made her go cold, but she would dearly love a child. She'd dreamed of seeing her and Remy's sons, their chestnut curls shining in the sun, romping in the garden of the house she and Remy would have owned one day.

With a shuddering sigh, she dismounted, giving the reins over to Dick. With a small nod, he led the mare away. The boy barely spoke to her these days—probably eaten up with guilt at his cowardice. Mind you, how could she blame him? Luxton would likely whip him if he didn't do his bidding. Had probably beaten him into submission many times.

"So, the old man's picked out a fool for you to wed, has he?" Startled, she jumped as she faced her father's manager. Luxton's wide grin was evil, as always. The vile smell surrounding him seemed worse than ever today and Sara wondered if he ever bathed, or perhaps evil had a stink of decay attached to it.

"Don't you ever wash?" she snapped, and his grin fled, replaced by a snarl.

"Not fancy enough for Miss Snobby, eh? Mark my words, your fine suitor may smell a mite sweeter than old Luxton, but 'e's not as fine as 'e appears." He clamped his sweaty hand about her wrist.

"Take your filthy hands off me!" Sara reeled back as his sour breath floated across her face, sickening her.

132

"You said that before, missy, and I warn you, I don't like it." His grip tightened, his eyes narrowed to menacing slits.

"I don't care what you like or dislike, Luxton, but you'd best do as I say, now..." Sara turned her head to the side in revulsion.

"Or what?" His cackle made her shudder. He spat in the dirt near his feet, barely missing the hem of her riding skirt, and she flinched. "Now, we have some unfinished business to conclude." His grip firm on her arm, he began to drag her toward the stable. Sara screamed, struggling.

Luxton was trying to cover her mouth with a filthy paw when her father bellowed, "You're back."

Never had she been so relieved to hear her father's bark. Luxton released her instantly, and leaning close whispered hoarsely, "Saved again, but my time'll come, madam, don't fret. If you're going off with the fancy gent, then Luxton'll make 'is move soon." He strode off, disappearing into the barn.

Sara shook so uncontrollably she felt sure her father would notice but should have known better. He was too insensitive to her feelings and likely wouldn't have cared if he had seen her distress.

"Luxton's making indecent suggestions to me," she said on a choked sigh, walking at his side on shaky legs.

Waving his crop he made a harrumphing noise in his throat and bellowed, "Don't talk nonsense, girl. Luxton knows which side his bread is buttered. He wouldn't dare step over the line with you."

"But he did, father, and it's not the first time. I hate him!"

"Well, he's not the most likeable person around, I admit." He laughed as if he'd said something highly amusing, and in that moment she truly despised him. "But, he keeps the trash in line, and that's all that counts out here. You have to have an overseer who knows how to handle the convict rubbish or you'll get nowhere."

Sara knew she might as well have saved her breath. Tiger Carstairs never seemed to have any bother with his convict labor, and he treated them like men, not animals, gaining their respect.

"Did you agree to Clive's proposal?" he demanded as they neared the door to the house.

"No, I told him I had no wish to wed anyone, certainly not a man I barely know," she retorted, her head high as she glared at him.

He stopped, waving a fat finger under her nose. "You'll not get as good an offer this side of the mountains, Princess." For a moment, his face softened as he used the endearment left over from her childhood. "I know you had your heart set on that young half-breed, but there was no way you could have married him, even with the slim chance I might have relented and allowed the match. Why not be sensible about this. Ravenbrook's a man of substance with a fine house in Sydney, property back in England, a clutch of servants at his beck and call, and a sound income. There's not a lot more a woman can expect or ask out of life."

"Isn't there, Father? What of love? Doesn't that enter the equation at all?" she cried.

"Love? Piffle." He grunted, and then scoffed, "You women are all full of romantic notions. It don't exist in real life, and whatever you might think is seldom part of any arrangement. Best put silly notions of romance out of your head and take my advice."

"And what if I don't?" Sara stared into his bloodshot eyes.

"Don't you get all high-handed with me, my girl! You will." With what she knew were his final words on the subject, he marched away, mumbling about women and their nonsense.

Sara removed her riding habit and boots and sank onto her bed. A deep and soul-destroying lethargy encompassed her. What was she to do? If she stayed here, she would be at Luxton's mercy, always fearing his attentions. Her father made it clear he would offer her no assistance. It was wicked, she knew, but she was reaching the point when she despised him with a fervor that was frightening. There was

134

no one she could turn to for help, comfort, or advice. Bella Carstairs was her only close friend in these parts, but how could Bella assist her in this predicament? If Sara fled to Bella's home for sanctuary, her father would only drag her back here.

Clive was attentive, gentle, and obviously wise in the ways of women. Perhaps her father was right and romance and dreams were only for fools and children. At least if she went with Clive she would be out of her father's jurisdiction and would be back in town where she had female friends, especially Meg, to turn to for advice.

And so, without careful thought, her decision was made.

* * *

"Goodbye, take care." Sara thought she saw a tear in her mother's eye as she made her farewell. Josie nodded once, and then turned away, her lips compressed. There had been no liking between her and the taciturn woman, and Sara would be glad to see the back of her. The thought that she wouldn't miss her mother saddened her.

"Clive here'll make you a fine husband," her father announced with surety. Sara wondered what gave him such confidence. He'd known the man in Sydney, but they had never been close friends.

The marriage ceremony took place in the early hours of the morning when the sun was barely above the horizon. As if in a dream she repeated the reverend's words, and the sense of unreality still clung to her. Why did she agree to this farce of a marriage? Because the alternative was unthinkable—a life here with her father's constant badgering, Luxton's ever-present threats, and emptiness that filled her soul until she felt she would go mad. She was making her escape, plain and simple.

Glancing back at the group on the veranda as Clive clicked the horses on, Sara was struck by how arid her life had been to date. Except for those few short weeks with

Remy when she'd blossomed and known love, there was nothing to regret in leaving this place.

* * *

Sara stared into the darkness. The wind howled about the tent and the man who had claimed his marital rights lay snoring at her side.

Dear God, what had she done? In her fevered dreams of her wedding night, it had been Remy lying beside her sated and as fulfilled as she. What had taken place resembled nothing akin to any romantic dreams she might have cherished. She felt unclean, used, and ready to die. Despite her pleas that he wait until they were in his home before he exerted his rights, Clive stripped her of her clothes along with her pride. The only saving grace about the whole awful episode was the speed with which he satisfied himself and rolled off her to fall immediately into a sound sleep. Sore and aching in her lower body she bit into her knuckle until she tasted blood.

As soundlessly as she could in the confines of the tent, she pulled her chemise and petticoats on to lie sleepless for hours. Sometime in the pre-dawn darkness he awakened, and when he found her half-clothed, uttered a curse her father used often enough.

"What's this?" he muttered, easily stripping her again. "I have no use for a nincompoop in my life." He tossed her undergarments aside. "I told you I want an heir, and pretty soon at that. You'll be compliant or know the strength of my wrath."

Sara clenched her teeth, holding back a scream as he violated her again, tearing at her innocence and pride, stripping her of all hope that this marriage would be a redemption and an escape. She had left one prison only to fall headlong into a loveless trap.

Chapter Thirteen

October 1827

Rem looked down at his palm where a nugget of gold lay dull against his skin. "'Tis strange that a piece of ordinary-looking rock can cause such strife in life." He turned to give Lulu a smile.

"But it can bring happiness to some," she said.

"Right. I'll put it back." He placed the rock back in the heavy sack. They found it in a hole beneath a piece of bark in a corner of the shack, concealed beneath a chest. Not a perfect hiding place, but her husband likely guessed Lulu wouldn't know what to do with the gold had she found it. Even if she got as far as the road, her escape would have been curtailed by the first travelers who came across her. A Chinese woman alone on the trail would instantly arouse suspicions.

Rem poked the sack into the hole beneath a banksia bush; then covered it with dirt and a few rocks. It was within ten strides of the shack. A passing traveler might search the house and inadvertently come across that hiding place, but without a map, no one would have a clue where to search away from the shack.

"I'll begin the meal," Lulu said as Rem went to the washing bowl and began to rinse the dirt from his arms and hands.

"Just a minute." He caught at her wrist and pulled her into his arms. It still amazed him that she was so tiny, as fragile as a bird, yet so strong. To have withstood all those tribulations, she had to be as strong as an oak.

"Yes? You wanted something?" With sparkling eyes, she gazed innocently up at him, her hands resting on his shoulders as she stood on tiptoe.

"As a matter of fact I did," he drawled, kissing the end of her small, perfect nose. "How's about a kiss for starters?"

"Just a kiss? Why, Remy O'Shea, that's not a great demand to make." With a chuckle, she stretched up and planted a kiss on his lips. "There, will that do."

"No, it certainly won't." Making a soft growling sound he dragged her full up against him and covered her mouth in a demandingly erotic kiss that left them both trembling.

"You won't get your meal for a long while if you keep that up," she said in a husky whisper when they finally pulled apart, both panting.

"Bugger dinner." Bending to lift her slight frame into his arms, he joked, "Crikey, Lulu, you putting on weight?" He carried her inside and then set her down on the low cot he fashioned from tree limbs and rope. As soon as he could, he had tossed out most of the makeshift furniture her husband made.

As she stripped her garment over her head, she said, "I think I am. It must be happiness. Look, my stomach is getting fat." With a small frown, she ran a palm over the slight mound.

Rem went on his knees beside her and reverently laid a hand on her tummy. "I do believe you are putting a lot of fat on around this part. Have you had your monthly flow lately?" They'd made love practically every night and day since that first time, and not once had she turned him away.

Her frown grew deeper. "No, I haven't. But sometimes I have been a long time without seeing blood," she confessed. "I have never known when to expect my bleeding."

"Could you be with child?" Rem went hot and cold at the thought. God, he had not given it a thought while reveling in their playful frolics, serious lovemaking, and sensual mating. How could he have been such a fool? Aggie had gotten with child after one coupling, and he and Lulu had been together for weeks.

"I could be," she said, hesitatingly stroking her belly, a look of wonder replacing her frown. "But if I was carrying your child, Remy, I would not be getting big yet. You have not been here long enough."

Of course, she was right. His leg had only just healed and he tossed off the splint two weeks ago. He didn't know a lot about women and babies, but knew enough from Bella's carrying them that at two months a woman's stomach was still flat.

"It is happiness for sure that makes me fat and contented," she said with a soft laugh.

"Must be. It sure is making me fat and complacent," he agreed, coming down beside her and covering her mouth with his. "Oh, Lulu," he said on a sigh as she wrapped him in her slim limbs and pulled him over her. Sinking into her welcoming warmth, he thought fleetingly of the dark-haired beauty who held his heart. But then, he lost himself in the splendor of the moment, and Sara was pushed to the back of his mind.

* * *

"Remy!"

It was so dark he thought momentarily that he was still asleep as he rubbed at his eyes. Then he heard a moan from beside him and knew he was awake. Lulu was rolling about, groaning his name.

"What is it?" Rem put a hand over her arm and felt tremors beneath his palm. "Lulu? Wake up. Are you dreaming? You're having a nightmare."

"No, no nightmare," she said on another long moan. "I hurt bad."

"Hurt? Where? Tell me where you hurt. Your head? Your back? Did I do something?" Dread filled him. Perhaps he had been too violent in his lovemaking. She was so tiny he often worried he might hurt her accidentally. Pressing a hand to her chest he realized she was very wet. "I'll be right back." Jumping up, he lit the lamp. When he knelt beside her he saw the blood soaking the thin piece of cloth beneath her. Rem's head spun.

139

"You're bleeding! God, did I do that? Lulu, where do you hurt? Please say I didn't hurt you in my sleep." She didn't open her eyes so he gently shook her.

With lips pressed tightly together, she pointed to her stomach.

"Down there. Your belly hurts?" Frantically Rem looked about. He grabbed up a piece of rag she used as a towel and ordered, "Sit up so I can see where it's all coming from." Shakily he eased her head up. Only then did she open her eyes.

"I am losing the baby," she whispered.

Rem could have hit himself for being such a fool. "Put this beneath you." He helped to raise her hips then pushed the cloth beneath her. "I'm sorry, love," he crooned as she began to cry.

"Don't be," she murmured. "It is not your child. I have no wish to bear that monster's baby. Please do not fret. It is the way of things. He was evil and his child should not live."

"Dear God, Lulu, don't say such things." Rem felt like vomiting. She was right, of course, but coming from her it sounded like blasphemy to wish a child dead. "It was part of you too."

"When I bear a child, my love, I want it to be yours. Only yours," she whispered, before more pains racked her. She began to groan again. Then she screamed, and Rem's heart stopped beating for a moment. Never had he been so scared.

"Lulu, don't you dare die on me," he ordered as she writhed, her knees bent to her chest.

It seemed an eternity before she ceased bleeding. Rem went outside to fill the tub with water and put the soiled cloths in to soak. By the time he heated water to bathe her, she had fallen into a deep slumber that frightened him more than her writhing in agony. He felt hopeless, helpless, a man in a woman's private world.

Once he had her cleaned up and lying on fresh bedding, he settled down gingerly at her side, cradling her.

Holding her through the long hours of the night, Rem silently prayed for her recovery.

* * *

"This can't go on." Rem brushed Lulu's hair back from her alabaster brow. "I'm sorry, love, but we have to go to Sydney. You need help; medical assistance I can't give you."

It was three weeks since her miscarriage, and she could still barely walk a few paces without having to cling to something for support. Rem had never been so scared or worried in his life. He might not adore Lulu as he cherished Sara, but the tiny woman had become so dear to him he couldn't contemplate life without her.

"You worry too much, my Remy, I will be fine." She cupped his jaw, and Rem felt the trembling in her fingers. She was like a fragile sparrow, and Rem feared her bones would break as there was little flesh covering them. "I need a little more time, and I will be back to how I was before. You'll see."

But she wasn't. Two days later Rem returned from hunting to find her prone outside the door of the hut. Tossing the dead wallaby down, he knelt at her side.

Trembling, he pressed a finger to the pulse point in her neck. A faint heartbeat assured him she was still alive. Picking her up, he tenderly carried her inside and placed her on their pallet. She didn't stir. Sweat beaded his face as he poured water into a mug.

"Lulu. Wake up. Drink this," he said softly, as he put an arm behind her neck to ease her forward. He pressed the mug to her gray lips. His heart pumped faster when she suddenly opened her eyes to smile weakly.

"Why am I on the bed?" she asked, her eyelids fluttering, then closing.

"Because you passed out. I found you outside, on the ground." Rem picked up one of her hands and wrapped it in his. She was so cold. Pulling a blanket over her, he tucked it around her, saying, "That settles it, Lulu. No arguments please, we're going to the road tomorrow. We'll hope to catch a lift on a passing wagon. There's lots more traffic on the road now, and we shouldn't have to wait more than a few days."

"But, Remy," she whispered, licking her lips as she tried earnestly to raise herself on her elbows. "You will be captured and perhaps sent to the treadmill again." Fear contorted her dainty features.

"No I won't," he said with a confidence he was far from feeling. "I intend to give myself up, and tell the truth. I'll tell the authorities exactly what happened and the worst they can do is send me to Newcastle or elsewhere to work out my term."

Clutching weakly at his arm, she cried, "They won't believe you. If they send you to Newcastle I will never see you again."

"Now, don't talk nonsense." He smiled in an effort to reassure her. He was the one talking nonsense. Who knew what would happen to them once he was back in custody. "I'll make sure they find you a nice place of employment once you're well. Then I'll come back for you when my term is served. It's only a few years."

His insides tightened at the lie. That was two women he had made the same promise to. And he knew without a doubt which promise would be fulfilled.

But she was so sick. Rem was no expert but knew instinctively Lulu would die if she didn't get medical aid soon. She'd faded before his eyes since losing the baby. If possible, she was paler than before; her skin, like parchment, looked as if it would crack beneath his touch. They hadn't made love since she'd bled, and he wouldn't have brought himself to touch her even if she'd been well enough. The thought that she might get with child again was enough to curb his desires. Whenever he held her, he worried he might break her bones.

"I won't ever see you again," she repeated on a sob, and Rem took her gently in his arms as he lay at her side.

"We'll go in a day or two," he said firmly. "I must do this for you."

Rem packed the last of their meager possessions into a roll and tied the bundle to the front of the saddle. "Remember, if anything happens to me, you find someone to accompany you back here for the rest of the gold."

"I can't see why we can't take it all with us," Lulu said with a touch of unusual impatience.

"I explained," he said patiently. "If I produced a stack of gold the authorities would accuse me of being in with the bush gang I escaped from. The last thing I want them to do is have doubts about my story of being forced to join the gang. And how the hell do you think you can carry a sack of gold about with you when you're on your own? Someone would bash you on the head at the first opportunity and run off with it. No, my way's best, you have just enough to buy some decent clothes and food to keep you going until you get placed in employment once you're well enough."

Rem had no idea if any household would accept her. A gut feeling told him she wouldn't find employment easily. She looked sick, her frame having shrunk to skeletal proportions, her once shiny hair now lusterless. His first priority was to seek medical aid for her. After that—well, it was in the hands of whatever god she prayed to. It was likely his God wouldn't do him any favors.

"Come on, up you get." Gently he lifted her atop the mule. It had grown fat and lazy since not having to work, spending its days foraging about wherever Rem tethered it. "All right?" He gave her a reassuring smile as she nodded. She wasn't all right, and they both knew it.

With a last longing glance at the hut, she pressed her lips together as Rem tugged on the halter and urged the mule on. Perhaps they would never come back. Was he right to leave the stash of gold? Perhaps he should try to reach Tiger and Bella's property. But that idea was silly. Lulu could barely sit upright as it was. Days in the saddle would deplete her already meager strength.

No, best wait for a wagon to pass along the road. Within a week perhaps they could be in Sydney where she could get the help he couldn't give her.

By the time they reached the road she was bent over the mule's neck, clutching at its mane. For the last mile Rem had trusted his instincts, for Lulu was too weak to offer even a perfunctory word of advice as to whether they were heading in the right direction or not. Rem hoped the barely definable track he followed led to the road. He used the sun to give him guidance, stopping now and then to mark a tree or leave a pile of stones in case they were going round in circles.

His spirits soared when he rounded a rocky outcrop and found himself on the road.

"We're here." He touched her arm. Lulu moaned as he lifted her down and set her gently on a patch of moss near the roadside. Rem tethered the mule and untied their bundle; then quickly unrolling the strip of canvas he brought, set about erecting a small shelter. He looked to the sky. God, he hoped it didn't rain. The cover would protect them from a drizzle but would be useless against a downpour. Lulu was in no state to get drenched. He took her to relieve herself; then wrapped her in a blanket and sat down, his back to a tree trunk, her nestled in his arms.

"Are you hungry?" he asked a while later, when she stirred. She shook her head, asking for water. After taking a mouthful from the bottle, she dozed again.

Rem prayed a wagon would pass soon. He didn't fancy spending more than one night out here. Although it turned warm during the afternoon, once the sun went down it began to get chilly. Wrapping his blanket about them both, he lay back and tried to sleep, Lulu held tightly in his arms. She slept soundly—too soundly. Rem wondered if she'd slipped into a stupor and fretted so much sleep eluded him.

Near dawn, she stirred, opening her eyes to look at him, saying, "You did not sleep."

"Of course I did," he lied. "How do you feel?" Pulling the blanket up to her chin, he smiled.

"Better." That was also a lie. A small frown crinkled her brow.

"I'll build a fire, and make us a warm drink," he said.

He was pleased when Lulu managed to amble behind a bush to see to her toilet. She ate sparingly of their supply of cooked meat, took a few mouthfuls of rum and hot water, and was soon dozing again.

Rem went off to find some stringy bark to reinforce their shelter in case a storm brewed, and they were forced to spend another night out here. Once he had done the best he could with their shelter he took her in his arms again, settling back against the tree.

A shout roused him from a doze, and Rem blinked a few times before he realized what that meant. Someone was nearby. Then he heard the creak of wheels and the bellow of an ox. Travelers were on the road! Now all he had to do was pray they were heading to Sydney.

They were heading east. Elation filled him as he set Lulu gently down, shaking her shoulder, urging softly, "Wake up, sleepyhead. We're on our way." She opened bleary eyes to gaze up at him. While Rem felt joyful, the emotion clouding her eyes was sadness.

As the cavalcade neared, he waved his arms and shouted. There were two ox-drawn drays loaded with wool and two covered wagons, each drawn by six horses with a spare horse tied behind each. A man rode a giant sorrel gelding, his eyes narrowing on Rem in a speculative manner.

The dray drivers looked surprised to see a man on foot so far out, but in their usual fashion said naught as they waved back.

"What the bloody hell are you doing out here alone?" the man on horseback said as he pulled the sorrel up a few feet from Rem. His hair was almost silver, his eyes so light they appeared to be colorless. "Surely you didn't come all the way from town with only a mule for transport."

"My woman's sick. I was taking her to town to get medical help," Rem explained. "Would there be room on one of the wagons for her. She's very weak."

"Of course, we can find room for her." The rider nodded to the covered wagon just pulling up behind a dray. "My wife will be only too pleased to take her under her wing." With another strange glance at Rem, he waved his crop toward the wagon and shouted, "Sara, darling, this man's wife is sick. You won't mind if she shares your wagon, will you?"

A ringing in his ears made Rem wobble, and his world spun as he stared in disbelief. This couldn't be happening. But it was. His Sara, his beloved, beautiful Sara sat staring at him as if mesmerized, her eyes reflecting the horror, the magnitude of what was happening.

"Sara," Rem whispered, unsure whether he called her name out loud.

"Yes, Sara," the fair man said, and for the first time Rem noticed a malicious glint in his strange opaque eyes. "Do you know my darling wife by any chance? But no, that's impossible," he answered his own question. "Come, bring your wife and belongings over and we'll get them settled. Tie the mule behind one of the wagons. Jenkins," he shouted, "fetch a saddle and untie the roan for our fellow traveler here."

As if stunned by a head blow Rem did as bid, his eyes settling on Sara as he gently set Lulu down in the narrow space behind the bench seat. All he saw in Sara's eyes now as they watched him cover Lulu with the threadbare blanket was disillusionment and despair.

"She's not my wife," he whispered as he jumped down and stood staring up at her.

"But he's my husband," she said in a hollow voice. And Rem's dreams crumpled, blown away like dust.

Chapter Fourteen

How would he bear it? Sara married to Clive Ravenbrook! The reproach in her eyes when she looked at him was unbearable.

Lulu slept for hours, only waking when they stopped for the night. The leader of the group, a taciturn Scotsman, gave Rem a tent to share with Lulu. Once she ate sparingly from the offered stew, Rem carried her into the tent. She soon fell asleep once more.

Rem was relieved. He wanted a chance to talk to Sara. But when he went back to the fire her husband was seated at her side.

"My wife tells me she knew you in Bathurst," Ravenbrook said tersely, eyeing Rem belligerently. Rem hated his guts, not simply because Ravenbrook had wed Rem's love, but there was something sinister about the man. He couldn't say why, but knew he wasn't to be trusted.

"Yes, we knew each other quite well." That was an understatement if ever there was one.

"We thought you dead," Sara said in a husky little voice. She played with a fold of her skirt, her eyes skittish.

"Lulu saved my life." Rem stared at her as if he could will her to look at him, to see the truth in his eyes.

"Oh, how so?" Ravenbrook brought a flask from his pocket and took a swallow. Rem guessed it contained rum.

"I was forced to take part in a hold-up. The leader of the gang was killed, and I took off. I fell and broke my leg. Lulu found me and tended me, then helped me back to her bush camp where I stayed until well enough to travel."

"And what was a slip of a wench doing out in a bush camp alone?" There was a cynical twist to his mouth.

Sara's fingers twisted the fabric of her skirt in agitation. When at last she looked up the pain in her eyes sliced through Rem like a knife in the gut.

"She wasn't alone." Rem wondered how much to tell this man, but an explanation had to be made. Why not start the lie now? "She lived with her husband. He was a miner."

"Was?" Ravenbrook's gaze never wavered.

"Yes, was." Rem nodded and then stared at Sara. "He had a mine. One day he never came back. His mule returned alone. We searched for the mine-shaft, but couldn't find it." Rem shrugged. "You know how it is out in the bush; a man can disappear as easily as that." He clicked his fingers. "We searched extensively, but found no trace of him or his mine, and presumed he must have fallen down his own mine-shaft."

"How long ago was this?" At last Sara spoke, asking the question in a whisper.

"Some weeks. I couldn't walk, so we were forced to wait until my leg healed sufficiently to allow me to walk out." Rem wanted desperately to get Sara alone. To explain so she would understand fully. He sighed. What did it matter anyway? She was married, beyond his reach. "How long have you been married?"

Sara flinched and Ravenbrook gave a funny sort of laugh as he said, "We were wed the morning we began our journey. Sara made me the happiest man alive when she accepted my proposal."

Of course she did. Any man on this earth would be glad to have her for his bride. "How're my sister and her family?" Rem felt empty and numb.

"Bella is heartbroken. She thinks you dead." Sara's voice had a catch in it. "We heard you were dead. Heard you were shot then fell over a precipice."

"I wasn't shot, but can well understand why it was thought I was. There was a lot of shooting going on around me. I ran when the chance presented itself, and by the time I came to, the wagons had gone on."

"You must send word to Bella that you're alive," Sara urged. "She will be absolutely delighted. She was stricken when we heard the news." Sara looked stricken too. How could she have allowed herself to be pushed into a marriage with this man? It eased the pain in Rem's heart to believe she hadn't gone into it willingly.

"I will, just as soon as we meet up with another wagon train on the trail going back to Bathurst." Rem shrugged as his eyes met Sara's. There was nothing in Bathurst for him now. "If not, I will the minute we reach Sydney."

"You don't wish to return to Bathurst?" Sara's voice conveyed as much misery as he felt. It was so great he wondered how he was managing to stay upright. He wanted to curl into a ball and die.

"If I did before, I certainly have no desire to now. There's nothing there for me anymore." Rem searched her eyes; eyes misty with longing, anguish and pain. "I'll present myself to the authorities as soon as we reach town. It will be up to them where I go next."

"And what of your woman?" Ravenbrook suddenly demanded.

"Lulu's sick. She needs care and attention. I aim to see she gets it."

"You'll hardly be in a position once you give yourself over to the authorities to offer her aid. She seems impoverished." Rem hated the belligerence the man showed. Had Sara attached herself to a replica of her father?

"Lulu has a little gold." Rem watched a glint of interest light the man's strangely opaque eyes.

"Would that be from the husband's claim?" he queried, too blandly.

"There's not much. The man must have hidden his gold well. We couldn't find it." Rem stared into the fire. "We searched, but found only a small stash. Enough to secure Lulu medical attention and a few necessities."

Ravenbrook was pensive for a moment; then said, "Come, my love, let's retire." Rem felt sure Sara flinched. But that was probably his over-active imagination forcing him to believe what he wanted to.

"You go ahead; I'll be with you in a moment." Sara rose, nodding at the surrounding bushes. Her husband hesitated, looked from her to Rem, and gave a small nod.

"Right, don't go far from the fire, my dear. Are you sure you wouldn't like me to accompany you?" he asked silkily.

"No, no, I'll be fine," she assured him hurriedly. Short of arguing in front of the others, he was forced to walk off.

Sara turned to whisper to Rem the moment he was out of hearing, "Sweet heavens, Remy, I cannot believe you're alive."

"You didn't wait too long before wedding that idiot," he snapped, not caring who heard him. The other members of the group were all paying them scant attention while they prepared for bed.

"My father forced me into it." Sara put a hand over her mouth as if to stifle a sob. "I thought there was little hope of your returning. Luxton made improper advances to me, and my father was intent on marrying me off as soon as possible."

"God, what a mess!" Rem wiped a hand over his face. "Surely you can't have any feelings for this Ravenbrook."

"I can't abide him!"

"Is he treating you unkindly, Sara? I'll kill him." Rem clenched his fists.

"No, please don't harm him, Remy." She reached out as if to touch him then drew back sharply. "What good would it do? You would then be up on a charge of murder. It's too late for us." She let out a sob. "You must face up to the facts. We were never meant to be together. There's no way we can change things now. You must forget me—as I will try to forget you. Fate has deemed we go separate paths. I must go," she said sharply as Ravenbrook appeared in the circle of firelight, obviously having seen to his needs.

"We must talk again," Rem whispered as she turned to hurry off.

Ravenbrook strolled toward Rem, menace clear in his eyes. "You will leave my wife alone," he grated. "If I catch you so much as talking to her again, I'll tell the magistrate you're a murderer. That you murdered this Chinese woman's husband and stole his gold. Do I make myself clear?"

"Perfectly." Rem turned and strode off in the opposite direction to Sara.

* * *

"So, the half-breed didn't die after all," her husband said mockingly, releasing the tent flap and coming down on his knees beside Sara.

Sara put a fist to her mouth and dragged in a choked breath. How was she going to bear this pain? Refusing to answer Clive, she pulled the blanket up to her chin. In the light from the lamp, he looked like a demon kneeling over her. How had she ever thought him handsome.

"What's this?" He pulled the blanket from her hand and slapped at her fingers as she tried to retrieve it. "Tut-tut, how many times must I chide you about your modesty, my dear? You cannot sleep in your clothes. Come now, take the garments off."

Sara lay rigidly staring at the ceiling of the tent, her fists clenched at her sides. If he wanted her undressed, he would have to do it himself. Never again would she willingly allow him access to her body.

He began to undo the fastenings of her bodice, as she should have guessed he would. It was useless to fight him. If she screamed and drew attention to her predicament Remy would come to her aid and that was exactly what Clive wanted. He would then have a perfect excuse to ensure Remy received punishment.

The anguish she suffered deadened her senses, which in a way was a blessing, allowing her to lie like a lifeless thing while he abused her body, stripped her of every last vestige of self-respect.

Long after he slept, she lay with silent tears streaming down her face, dampening the pillow beneath her head. She wanted to die. If her life held little happiness before Remy entered it, it stretched before her now like a barren

151

wasteland. Remy was alive, but might as well be dead to her—he was forever out of her reach.

* * *

If there was a place called purgatory on this earth, Rem dwelt there. Lulu was constantly sick in the following days, too weak to see to the smallest tasks. Rem even had to help her when she went to relieve herself; something he knew shamed her immeasurably. The rough road was hard enough on everyone, but it seemed to jolt her frail bones. At the end of the day's traveling she would lapse into a deep slumber that frightened him. Once or twice each night he bent over her to make sure she still breathed, for she lay so still.

Clive Ravenbrook watched Sara like a cat watches a mouse, and Rem felt torn to shreds as he imagined what he and Sara were doing each night in the tent they shared. One thing was positive; she wasn't in love with the man. Each morning she appeared, listless and pale and ignored her new husband most of the time.

He felt helpless. Sara was right; their paths were headed in opposing directions, his dreams were shattered. It was too late to do anything. She was wed, and he was still a convict, whatever way you viewed it. His life revolved around seeing to Lulu's needs and morosely contemplating a bleak future. He had no doubts Ravenbrook would and could see him hanging from the gibbet if he so wanted. There was little doubt also Ravenbrook would delight in shooting him down if given an excuse.

As far as Rem could tell his only hope was to see out his term. Beyond that, he knew not what to do.

* * *

"What do you mean, there's no hope?" Rem clenched his fists and stared at the doctor, whose face was lined, almost haggard. Overworked and faced with unqualified assistance it was clear the man cared not one way or the

152

other if Lulu lived or died. "Surely there's more you can do. She lost a baby, for God's sake, she didn't suffer some dreadful disease."

The doctor laid a hand on Rem's arm and compassion fleetingly clouded his eyes. "If your...wife had been here when she suffered her miscarriage we could possibly have done something for her, could have treated the infection that has laid her low. But...." He lifted his hands and shrugged. "Seemingly healthy women still die during childbirth or after losing an infant early in the pregnancy. And your wife is so frail. In fact I can't remember seeing a female in such a fragile condition." He rubbed his chin as he stared at the tiny woman whose body barely made a lump under the blanket.

Rem never felt so useless. Leaving the wagons as soon as they arrived in town, Rem left Sara to stare after him as he carried Lulu's feather-light body to the hospital, where she had lain motionless for the last twelve hours. Rem had a feeling she'd given up on life—could have fought if she felt there was something worth fighting for. Her last whispered words to him before lapsing into a deep sleep were fraught with worry for her future once he was taken back into custody.

"You must be able to do something." He clutched at the sleeve of the doctor's coat. "I have a small amount of gold. I'll pay you well."

A footfall behind him brought his head round to see a constable standing there. Rem gently placed Lulu's limp hand on the bed-sheet.

The policeman's face was grim. "Are you Jeremy O'Shea?" he asked.

Rem nodded, his insides clenching.

"Then it is my duty to take you into custody." The constable appeared to be shamefaced. He shuffled his feet.

"Custody?" Rem asked stupidly. "How did you know I was here?" Then it dawned on him. "Ravenbrook? He told you that you'd find me here, didn't he?"

The man now looked sheepish.

"There was no need to search me out," Rem said on a sigh. "I would have given myself up. I intended to front up before the authorities as soon as I sorted things out here. My woman is sick. Did Ravenbrook tell you I was about to abscond?"

"No such thing, me lad." The constable looked even more uncomfortable.

The doctor put a hand on Rem's arm. "Best go along with him," he advised. "There's little you can do here. She'll sleep for a while now. I'll send word if her condition improves in the next few hours. Perhaps they'll allow you to come back to visit your wife."

"And what if she doesn't improve? What then?" Rem shivered convulsively, rubbing his neck where a pain lodged, like a hammer bludgeoning him. He felt as if he hadn't slept in a month.

The doctor blew out a tired breath. "Well, then, there's little either of us can do."

Rem knew that was the truth, but hated leaving Lulu here with strangers. "Supposing she wakes up. She'll be scared when she finds me gone. Can't you possibly let me stay?" He turned pleading eyes on the policeman. "I'm not going anywhere."

"Can't be done, lad." The constable turned to signal to an associate who stood just outside the door. The man strode over and clamped a hand on Rem's arm. Rem began to struggle but realized there was little to gain by fighting these men. "Come along quiet like now, and we'll see if we can't arrange a chance for you to come and see your woman tomorrow."

Rem had to be satisfied with that.

"All that can be done will be done," the doctor said as Rem shrugged out of the policeman's grasp.

With one last look at Lulu's pale face, he walked away with them.

* * *

The gold that was to have paid for Lulu's treatment paid for her burial instead. Rem stared down into the grave, his mind numb, and his body feeling as if it had been battered with a ramrod.

With a last silent farewell to the woman who saved his life, likely saved his sanity, he turned away. This was his punishment for the way he treated Aggie.

Chapter Fifteen

March 1828

Rem tipped his head and swallowed from the water bottle. "Christ, I don't think I'll ever get used to this heat." He swore violently, but it didn't help.

"Unlikely." The man at his side grunted as he lifted another bag of grain onto the cart. "One thing's for sure though, O'Shea, we'll be well prepared for hell when we get there."

Rem was already in hell. Even if it was a hell of his own making. Haunted by thoughts of Sara living with that bastard of a husband, memories of Lulu's death, and Aggie's drowning, he doubted he would even be allowed in the lower regions. Probably purgatory would be too good for him.

At least with Tiger and Bella he had never been made to feel like a convict, but now he was humiliated and reminded of his status every hour of every day.

The guards allowed Rem to write to Bella, so she knew of his survival. Her answering letter cheered him no end. How Rem wished he was back on Tiger's property, working alongside his brother-in-law before his life took a downhill slide after that night when the silly chit threw herself at him. If only he could turn back the hands of time.

Ah, poor Aggie loved him foolishly. God rest her sweet soul. What had she done to deserve such treatment? He didn't merit any woman's love. His darling Sara was probably better off where she was, with Ravenbrook. That thought brought him nothing but anguish; kept him awake at nights, invaded his sleep when he was able to doze off. How he wished he could set eyes on his beautiful love one more time. But that was a fanciful dream now.

Tiger knew all there was to know about sheep and farming his land, but the man Rem was now assigned to had about as much knowledge of husbandry as Rem. And that was precious little.

This farm on the Hawkesbury River would be successful in Tiger's hands, but Rem wondered daily if the owner knew what he was doing. Not that it was any concern of his.

* * *

Sara tied the strings of her bonnet beneath her chin and gave herself a perfunctory glance in the mirror above the hallstand. "If I'm not back by lunchtime don't worry, Maisie. That means I'll be lunching with Mrs. Howe."

"Right you are, ma'am." Sara's maid nodded. If Sara had cause to hate everything about her new life, at least there was one consolation; Josie's replacement as maid was a lot more jovial and eager to please. Clive brought the girl to her on their arrival at his Sydney home, and she was the one ray of sunlight in a house filled with nothing else one could find pleasure in, or like. The housekeeper took an instant dislike to her new mistress, and it seemed her influence over the other staff was supreme.

Clive's driver, Brace, waited with the carriage. Sara settled back and watched the bustle as they traveled the two blocks to her friend's house. Sydney had grown since Sara lived here with her parents. The population was cosmopolitan, with people from all parts of the world now visiting and settling here. Languages from Spain, Italy, Germany, and France mingled with the local dialects at most of the meeting places. If Sara's life weren't so unhappy, she would have enjoyed being a part of the ever-changing scene. As it was, there was little joy for her.

Meg's house was far from splendid, with vines festooning the balcony posts and a tiny front garden, but Sara would willingly swap Clive's splendid residence with Meg's any day to gain a fraction of her friend's contentment.

The servant answered the door as chirpy as a London sparrow, relieved Sara of her bonnet, and led her straight to the rear of the house. "Mistress Ravenbrook," she announced, bobbing a curtsy before darting off to the kitchen.

"Sara, come and sit out here," Meg called. "There's a small breeze blowing today. At least the brickfielder has died, and we can enjoy some sunshine without our heads getting blown off and our ears filled with dust."

"Meg, how are you? And how are those darling girls of yours?" Sara joined her in the small gazebo at the far end of the garden. If Meg's house was smaller in scale than Ravenbrook's, it was certainly cozier and generated the contentment and happiness of its inhabitants. The garden boasted a riot of plants, all growing haphazardly. Meg's gardener came in once a week, and Sara sometimes wondered why Meg's husband paid him, for Meg refused to have order brought to the chaos.

"The little horrors are having a nap—at last." Meg wrinkled her turned-up nose. She was petite with hair the color of ripened corn, pulled back into a bun. Strands were forever flying free of its confines. She looked onto her world with interested appraisal. As she spoke of her babies, her eyes went dewy with love. "They were yelling their precious heads off at midnight. Hungry again."

At three months Meg's twin babies, although small for their age, were extremely lusty and healthy. Sara's heart ached when she saw how Meg's husband doted on them and the wife he cherished. If only her own life was different. She sighed and shrugged that thought aside. Chances were her father would have put any obstacle in her and Rem's path to keep them apart, even if the course of events hadn't taken such a tragic diversion to slant fate to her father's side.

"You look peaky, love. Is this weather getting you down?" Meg eyed Sara with concern in her doe-soft eyes.

"If only the weather was all I had to worry about." Settling herself on one of the wicker chairs, Sara accepted a glass of lemonade from Meg's maid and waited until the girl left them alone. "I hate to burden you with my problems, Meg, but I have no one else to turn to."

"Nonsense, it's no burden." Meg reached across and squeezed Sara's hand. "I love you like a sister, my dear. After a shaky start we've become such good friends I hope you feel you can trust me with any confidence."

"Oh, Meg, I don't know what I'd do without you." Sara sighed. "My husband finally admitted to all the evil actions he hitherto denied and makes no bones of his infidelities. I'm cold, he claims, so why shouldn't he seek the comfort his mistress can offer him?" Even while she rejoiced that he didn't want her in his bed any more, she was still filled with humiliation and shame at the way he had used her. Separation from Rem would have been so easier to bear if she had a loving husband. Or even one who treated her with respect.

"Sara, no!" Meg put her palms to her cheeks, horror clear in her eyes. "The brute. I could kill him."

Sara rubbed her temples. "Have no fear, I've thought of doing away with him myself. At least now he's openly claimed to have a mistress; perhaps he'll leave me in peace. He hasn't come to my bed in a week, so I'm hoping he never will again." Sara shrugged away her shame. "He is often well into his cups when he comes home, and I have taken to locking my door." She stared down into her glass, chewing on her lower lip. How long that state of affairs would last she had no idea. Clive wanted an heir and would see she bore him one in due course.

Meg made a distressed little sound in her throat. "You lock the door against your husband? I don't blame you, but he won't stand for that. He has the law on his side."

"Don't I know it? But I don't care." Sara swallowed and then blurted, "He hit me, Meg. That was the final humiliation."

She nodded when her friend gasped in outrage. "Yes, he'd been at his gambling club two nights ago, and likely at his mistress's before or after. He lost a considerable amount it seems, so had to take it out on someone. Clive hates to lose. I argued with him, something else he hates. To my folly, I allowed him to enter my bedroom. Well, in truth he forced himself in there. And when he began to rant and rave I told him to go back to his mistress and tell her his problems for I had no desire to listen to him. I thought for a moment he was about to have a fit, for his pale features turned a livid red and his eyes bulged. But alas, instead of dying he brought his fist up and punched me."

"No! Where did he hit you, Sara? You have no bruise to show for it." Meg bent to peer at her face.

"Of course I don't. He's far too clever for that. No, he left a mark on my side, here, and one on my upper arm." She gingerly touched her ribs then rubbed her still sore arm. The blow to her side caused such pain Sara thought at first that perhaps ribs were broken.

"Poor Sara." Tears misted Meg's soft eyes.

Poor Sara, indeed! Sara even thought of taking her own life. What had she to live for? At times, she pictured the empty, desolate years stretching ahead of her. Rem was forever out of her reach. Where was he now? If only she could see him—if only for a moment—so she could be sure he was well and not suffering.

Meg's brow furrowed and she said quietly, "You could leave Clive."

Sara made a small sound of dismay. "If only it were that easy, Meg. Where would I go? I thought of going home, but my father would disown me."

"Surely not, he wouldn't be that heartless, would he?"

Sara laughed, but there was little mirth in the sound. "You don't know my father. He was too eager for me to marry Clive; he wouldn't sanction me leaving him. I have no money of my own now. Clive handles my bank account and allocates me enough funds to keep me in outfits and personal requirements." Sara shrugged, sighing. "Besides, even if I had independent means where can a young woman make a life for herself here in the colony, except as a courtesan."

Meg gasped. The maid reappeared, and they changed the subject while she put their used glasses on a tray then bustled out.

After a morose pause while they both stared into space, deep in thought, Sara asked, "Can I see your little darlings?"

"Of course." Meg's face shone again as she jumped up, pushing at her wayward hair. She dragged Sara up by the arm. "Come along, we'll take a peep at my beloved pets." They went inside and along to the nursery where the two babes slept side by side in separate cots.

"They're so beautiful, Meg. You are truly the luckiest woman alive," Sara whispered.

"I know." Meg kissed Sara's cheek. "You need a child, Sara. Everything will be brighter when you have an infant of your own to love. Once Clive gets his heir, perhaps he will leave you in peace."

Sara shook her head. Yes, she would dearly love a baby, but the thought of having to put up with Clive's brutish attentions to fulfil that wish made her feel ill with apprehension.

An hour later, Sara took her leave of Meg. As the carriage bounced along the street Sara's thoughts dwelt longingly on Meg's two infants. How lucky her friend was. And what had she, Sara, done that she should be denied such a life?

Suddenly, she jerked upright, staring at a group of convicts idly talking. The four men were obviously waiting on their master. One head covered in dark red hair caught her attention. Not many men had hair of that rich shade of chestnut; in fact, she knew only one. The sun glinted on it and even from this distance she saw its sheen of cleanliness, unlike the scruffy heads of the other convicts in the group.

The man turned, his face breaking out into a grin at something one of his companions said. He shoved his mate in the arm.

"Rem!" Sara breathed his name disbelievingly. "Stop." The word left her mouth before she had a chance to think about it.

Clive's driver, a surly man, usually ignored her orders, following only his master's dictates. But for some inexplicable reason, today Brace obeyed, pulling the horses to a halt about twenty paces past the group.

Sara leaned over and waved, calling, "Remy."

At her cry, the man who haunted her every dream looked her way. The smile died on his lips, and she saw him mouth her name.

He loped across to the vehicle. "Sara?" His eyes glowed with surprise and pleasure. "How are you?" He put his fists on the door and looked up at her.

"I'm fine," she lied, taking in every detail, from his leanness to the lines on his face that had never been there before. The reckless, careless man she'd known at Bathurst had disappeared. She knew him to be twenty-five, but he looked at least ten years older.

"You look like a dream. How's married life treating you? Or more to the point how's that husband of yours treating you?" he asked, ignoring the driver, who Sara knew heard every word, would likely report to his master. Sara cared not a whit. What more could Clive do to her?

"I have no complaints." Another lie—and such a big one. Her list of complaints would fill a ledger.

Rem's eyes wandered over her face, piercingly, as if he could see into her head, read every lie for what it was.

"Well, then that's good." He didn't look at all pleased with that news.

"What are you doing in town?" Sara asked.

He shrugged, and she noted that his shoulders didn't seem as wide. In fact, he didn't look robust. "My...." A short pause was followed by a soft grunt. "My master is collecting supplies. We helped him shift it. One of them cons had to have medical attention." He jerked his head at the group he'd just left, who now watched him with interest. "Another wants permission to marry. I'm here because I'm in charge of the others." Another grunt. "Their overseer, so to speak."

"Oh." Sara wanted to ask a thousand questions. "Are you going back tonight, or staying in town?"

"Actually we're staying overnight." He ran a hand over his hair, and Sara wanted to grab that hand, press her lips to it. "The boss wants to visit his mistress, I reckon."

"Could you get away?" Sara lowered her voice, hoping the driver couldn't hear her question.

Rem looked puzzled. "Get away? You mean can I pay you a call? What of your husband?" The word oozed contempt, and his beautiful mouth twisted.

"Clive is seldom home at nights. He has other...interests that keep him away." Sara knew she was flirting with fire, but was past caring. Now she'd seen Remy again all she wanted was to spend a few moments alone with him. It might be the only chance they would ever get to be together. "Do you think you can come?"

"Where should I come if I can get away?" he whispered, glancing at Brace's stiff back.

She smiled. "Please try. The house is on Pitt Street, on the left going toward the cove, just after Park Street. You can't miss it; it has iron gates with a shield in the center of each. Perhaps you could come after dark. I'll tell my maid to expect you. She'll watch out for you."

"Should I come to the kitchen door?" Rem looked about uneasily.

Sara shook her head. "No, don't do that, use the main entrance. The cook and butler aren't the friendliest of people." What an understatement that was.

"I'll try my hardest to get there. The boss is pretty lax. He doesn't care half the time if his convicts abscond." For a moment, she thought he would reach out to touch her, but he must have thought better of it with so many eyes on them. "While he's otherwise engaged I'll try to get away."

"Please try, Remy," she pleaded, not caring that all her desires must have been evident in that small plea.

The driver was now giving Remy strange looks. Sara thought it prudent not to dally any longer. "Drive on," she called, and as they pulled away she kept eye contact with Remy until they turned the corner and he was out of sight. She spent the rest of the afternoon in a fever of anticipation.

Would he come? Surely, the fates wouldn't be so cruel to deny her one more chance to see him, to touch him.

* * *

Rem ran a hand through his hair. God, if only he had some decent clothes to change into. He looked like the convict he was in the drab trousers of twill and the shirt borrowed from one of the other men in his group because his own got torn while loading supplies onto the wagon.

He easily found the address. He'd learnt to be stealthy. His boss wouldn't be worrying what he was doing tonight; was probably already ensconced in his mistress's bed. Rem couldn't blame him for seeking the warmth and comfort of a harlot. His boss' wife was lacking in a shred of warmth, and probably didn't allow the poor wretch anywhere near her bed.

So, this was Clive Ravenbrook's residence? Rem thought. It was grand by Sydney standards, with a portico, vines trailing from an upper balcony, and an impressive facade. He glanced about before letting himself in through one of the iron gates. There were a few carriages on the road, but fortunately nobody on foot to notice him. Going up the three steps leading to the front door he was about to knock when it opened.

A cheerful face peeped round its edge, and the owner of it asked, "Yes, sir?" blushing scarlet as she bobbed a curtsy that made Rem smile. No one had shown him such deference before.

"Your mistress is expecting me, I believe," Rem said.

"And what might your name be?" She gave him a grin as she opened the door wider, looking over a shoulder as if expecting someone to jump out at her any moment.

"Rem's the name. Is that the one your mistress told you to expect?"

"It is that." She put a finger over her lips. "Best be quiet. Cook and the tyrant who has the cheek to call 'imself a butler are likely tippling in the kitchen with the housekeeper, so they're all too busy to mind what's going

164

on up here. Still, best not give them something to gossip about. The poor little mistress has enough on her plate without them stirring up trouble."

"And what exactly does your mistress have to contend with?" Rem asked as he looked about the large entrance hall. Clive Ravenbrook must be wealthy to own such a property. A door was open on what looked like a sitting room, and a master craftsman had obviously made the furniture he glimpsed. At least Sara would be living in comfort. Rem cringed when he thought of what he could ever offer her in contrast.

"Ain't for me to say, sir. Come on, and be as quiet as you can." She seemed to be delighting in this small subterfuge as she closed the door and gestured for him to follow her. Creeping up the stairs after her Rem felt like a felon. "Here we are, sir." She stopped, tapping softly on a door. Sara opened it instantly, smiling when she saw the two of them standing there.

"You came," she whispered, opening the door wider. "Thank you, Maisie," she said to the girl, who nodded. "You'll keep your ears open, won't you?"

"Yes, ma'am, of course." Maisie nodded vigorously before darting off.

"Come in." Sara ushered Rem inside then locked the door after him. "A precaution," she said as he watched her put the key on a small table.

Rem studied her as she gestured for him to sit opposite her in one of the two easy chairs. It was a comfortably furnished room, with patterned carpet, a dressing table, chest and tall wardrobe. But the wide, high four-poster bed drew his eyes, making his stomach lurch as he imagined her sharing that bed with Ravenbrook.

"Where's your husband?" he blurted, uneasily looking about.

Sara shrugged, pulling her mouth down at the corners. "My husband doesn't share my room or my bed. He has other interests." Her long fingers folded a pleat into her skirt. "His gambling takes up his evenings, and his harlot takes care of his nights. If I'm lucky he doesn't turn up until breakfast-time most days."

"God, Sara, I'm sorry," Rem said, knowing a deep glow of satisfaction at the news Ravenbrook didn't share her bed any more. "How did things reach this state?" He raked his fingers through his hair.

"'Tis for the best. My father would never have let you and me be together, Remy. He thought Clive would make a good husband as he had this nice town house and property elsewhere." She looked immeasurably sad as she glanced about. Rem noticed lines at the sides of her beautiful mouth, most likely wrought by unhappiness. "To my father possessions are all. I hate him for forcing me into this marriage," she said vehemently. "And I hate Clive!" The way she uttered her husband's name convinced Rem that what she said was the truth.

What a mess they had gotten themselves into.

"I made a promise to you, Sara, love. I'll claim you for my own one day, and that's one promise I intend keeping. When I gain my freedom, I'll come back and one way or another we'll be together." Rem found it hard to keep his hands off her. He thrust them in the pockets of his trousers.

"If only it was that simple," she said on a small sob. "Oh, Remy, too many obstacles stand in our path now. I've resigned myself to a life without love. You must forget me."

"Never!" Rem knelt in front of her, placing his hands on her knees. "Listen to me, Sara. You have as much right to happiness as anyone, and I intend to see you get your share of it. But I have to serve my term." Helplessly he looked up at her.

When she put a hand to his cheek, Rem jumped as if scalded. Her touch could still ignite a flame within him. "If only words could be deeds, Remy. But you must forget about me. What of your Chinese woman? Wouldn't she be rather annoyed with me taking you away from her?"

"Lulu's dead," he said starkly, shaking his head as memories surfaced.

"I'm so sorry." She gave a shuddery sigh. "Would you like something to eat?" she asked as she looked to the covered dish on a small table beside her chair.

"No, I don't feel hungry...certainly not for food." Rem stroked his hands over her thighs and watched her eyes grow misty. With desire? "I'm hungry for you, Sara. Always will be. I doubt this hunger I feel for you will ever be satisfied."

"I feel the same. I wanted you that time I offered myself to you, and you refused me. And I want you still. Take me to bed, Remy," she whispered. "If we only have this one moment in time for ourselves, let's make it a perfect one. Love me."

"Always. You're the only woman I'll ever love, Sara. With all my heart and soul, I love you." Rem brought her hands to his lips and lavished each knuckle with his attention. She stroked the fingers of one hand down his cheek as he moved closer and buried his face against her breast.

"And I love you. I want you with a passion that frightens me."

"Don't be frightened, love. Never be scared of me or anything I do. I'll never hurt you. Not intentionally anyway." Rem wasn't sure of that at all; he'd made a habit of hurting those who loved him.

"I know that." There was a tremor in the fingers she used to unbutton his coarse shirt.

"I wish I didn't look like a convict." He watched her white fingers as she fumbled over her task.

"You'll always look handsome to me, Remy, no matter what clothes you wear. Anyway, there's one sure way to remedy that. Take off your clothes, and then you'll be no worse than any other man and certainly better."

Rem let a small smile turn up the corners of his mouth. "That's my Sara. Always saying something to surprise me. You're like no other woman I've known or ever will know."

"What of the Chinese woman?" she asked softly as she drew his shirt over his shoulders and pulled it from the waistband of his trousers.

"Lulu was the kindest person I've ever known, Sara. But you should never be jealous of her; she couldn't replace you in my heart. Lulu saved my life—if not for her I would have lain to rot in the mountains. Fate sent her to save me, and in a way I saved her. She knew a short space of happiness before she died. She was expecting her brute of a husband's baby, and doubtless she would have died out there, for he wouldn't have aided her. Now, let's forget about her and your husband. Tonight there's just you and me, love."

"Yes," she agreed as they both stood. They undressed, each showering the other with endless kisses until they were side by side on the bed, their eyes and hands adoring.

"I've never known desire like this," Rem said on a groan as she took him in her fingers and brought him to the brink of ecstasy with her touch. "If you don't stop that right now, this'll be over too soon. I want this first time with you to be perfect. And it won't be that while you continue to torment me with your touch."

"Just having you here with me makes it perfect, Remy. I never dreamed this moment would ever come. I feared our paths would never cross again. If this is all we're destined to have together, I'll cherish these moments and keep them in my memories forever."

Rem caressed her until she trembled in his arms. Every part of her was beautiful, from her straight neat toes to her hair that shone as black as midnight against the white pillow. Her pink-tipped breasts were perfect, fitting his palm as if designed specifically for them.

Rem kissed each rosy peak, and then she flinched as he ran his fingers down her sides. He drew back sharply and frowned. "What is it? Did I hurt you, love?"

"No, no, you could never hurt me, Remy. It's…" She touched her side where he now noticed discoloration.

"God, it's a bruise! Where did you get that?" Rem stared in horror, and after studying her for a moment, noticed she also had a bruise on her upper arm. "He did this to you, didn't he?" he demanded, going back on his haunches to examine her more closely. "I'll kill him for sure!"

"I fell, Remy," she said softly, pulling him over her. "Please, I beg of you, don't even think of attacking Clive. I tripped over a rug. One of the stupid maids left a corner turned and I caught my side and arm on a table as I went down." She touched his face, her eyes filled with tenderness as she reached up to kiss him. "Let's not waste time on that—we have so little time together. Please love me, now," she begged.

How could he resist such a plea?

Her limbs were strong, the legs she wound around him as she drew him inside her, long and perfectly shaped. Together they flew to the brink of ecstasy, and Rem felt as if he'd scaled a mountain, reached another plane. Truly, she was his soul mate. He told her so as they lay sated, arms about each other, staring into each other's eyes.

"You're crying." Rem stroked the teardrops off her cheeks with trembling fingers.

"Tears of happiness." She sniffed and tried for a small smile, but it went awry as she ran a hand over his chest. Rem shuddered anew.

"That's good. I hoped they weren't tears of disappointment."

"Never that." She placed a kiss on his chin. "That was the most wonderful experience of my life."

"Even better than it is with your husband?" Rem hated himself for having to ask.

The small deprecating sound she made confirmed his suspicion. Her husband never satisfied her.

"Clive has never treated me with tenderness. He showed no gentleness the first time, and soon grew tired of me." She bit into her bottom lip with her small white teeth and then admitted, "The only reason he comes to my bed is because he seeks to have a son. That's why he married me, I presume, because he decided I had the attributes he wished to pass on to his heir."

Rem kissed her deeply. "You realize I could have given you a child tonight, don't you, Sara."

She laughed, and the sound lifted his spirits until they soared. "I hope you have. I want your baby, not his. The thought of carrying his child sickened me, but if I've conceived this night then the child will be loved and cherished."

"Oh, Sara, come here." Rem pulled her close and covered her mouth with his again. Desire rose up, strong and potent. Would he ever get enough of her? He doubted it. "If I live to be a hundred you'll always have this effect on me," he said as he caressed her silken body. Rising up and over her, his weight on his elbows, Rem watched her eyes glaze with desire.

A mighty crash from the floor below startled them. "What the hell was that?" Rem cocked his head to listen.

"Mistress," cried Maisie from the other side of the door. "He's back." She knocked a few times as the thump of footsteps on the stairs grew louder.

Rem groaned.

"No!" Sara pushed at his shoulders. "It's Clive. Why did he decide to return early tonight of all nights? Don't worry, he sounds drunk." The foul language coming from the corridor outside her room proved he was far from sober. His shouted curses were slurred.

"Get out of the way, woman." They heard Maisie cry out. Ravenbrook bellowed, "Open up, you whore!"

Sara cringed as he pounded on the door. Rem swore; he leapt from the bed and hastily began to dress. "Go away," Sara shouted. She reached for a wrap and slipped into it, a finger to her lips as Rem pulled on his boots and buttoned his shirt.

"Not likely," Ravenbrook hollered. "Open this door. I know you have the convict mongrel in there, so you might as well open this door now." Rem thought the door would splinter at any moment as he continued with his thumping.

Sara gestured to the window. "You can climb down the tree outside," she whispered. "Go now, Remy, please."

"No. I won't leave you to face him alone." He grasped her hand, but she pushed him away and with frantic urgency turned him to face the window.

"I'm used to his threats. Please go now." She hustled him across the carpet. "He has no proof you're here. I'd say his housekeeper sent word that you were with me. Or his driver told him we spoke to each other earlier. They are all on his side, except Maisie. If you flee now he'll simply rant and rave for a while until he passes out. Believe me, I know him."

Undecided, Rem looked to the window, then back to the door. "I hate to leave you."

"Please, it's the only way," she insisted, shoving him.

Rem pressed a kiss to her lips; then he turned. "I'll try and get back, Sara."

"It's no use." Her voice cracked with anguish. "Now he suspects you of being here he'll make them watch me even closer. Look after yourself." She clutched at his arm as tears ran down her lovely cheeks. "Thank you for this night. Whatever happens I want you to know it was beautiful and worth any pain that might follow."

"I love you," Rem kissed her and opened the window, putting his foot over the sill as Ravenbrook turned the key in the lock. The last thing he saw was Ravenbrook's face, livid with anger, as Sara walked toward him, a placating hand held out. A man, obviously the butler who imparted the news of Rem's visit, stood at his side, a sneer of satisfaction on his pasty face.

Rem reached across and swung himself easily into the wide-branched tree and then lowered himself to the garden, heedless of the scratch of bark on his arms. As his feet hit the earth two shapes loomed up before him, one brandishing a club. Rem barely had time to bring a hand up in defense before the weapon crashed over his head. Sara's name burst from his lips as the ground came up to meet him.

Chapter Sixteen

June 1828

"Fetch the chamber pot, Maisie." Sara rolled onto her stomach on her bed, a hand to her mouth.

"Oh, mistress, 'tis the third time this week you've been sick. Shall I tell that old crone who calls 'erself the housekeeper to let me fetch the doctor?" Maisie patted Sara's back as Sara brought up the toast and tea swallowed only minutes before.

"No point, Maisie." Sara groaned. "We both know the problem. No use trying to hide it from you. I'm pregnant, and that's what the doctor will confirm." When Maisie came back from putting the chamber pot by the door, she handed Sara a dampened cloth. "Don't tell anyone downstairs, will you? I don't want my husband to know about this." Sara wiped her mouth on the cloth.

"Don't want 'im to know, ma'am?" Maisie frowned. "But 'e'll 'ave to know." The poor girl's fingers twisted in agitation.

"I'll tell him in my own time." Only when she was forced to. This was a secret she wanted to hug to her breast for as long as possible. "I'll be going out as soon as I've bathed. I'll wear my blue woolen dress. Tell Brace I'm going to Mrs. Howe's."

"Yes, ma'am." Maisie fetched warm water. After Sara washed her hands, face and arms, Maisie helped her dress. By the time she was ready to go out she felt better, but still weak.

Not long later, she was let into Meg's house. Her friend's home had become her only refuge. If Clive could stop her coming here he would, but until now seemed to

172

have decided no harm could be done by her visiting her only friend. Brace always brought her, and the driver could be relied on to report back to his master.

"I'm sorry, Meg," Sara said as she entered the nursery. Meg sat playing with her babies on a rug laid out on the floor. "I'll be wearing my welcome out soon if I keep coming to see you like this."

Meg waved a hand. "Nonsense, come down here and join us. We love your company. Don't we my pets?" She bent to plant wet loud kisses on her babies' cheeks. "You can go and have a cup of tea," she told her nursemaid.

Sara knelt on the floor beside Meg, and one of the babies put out a fist. She let her capture her finger, her heart filling with sudden joy. "I'm going to have a baby," she blurted.

Meg's face lit with surprise and gladness. "Oh, Sara, that's absolutely splendid news. When do you think it will arrive? This is so good, just what you need to drag you out of the doldrums."

"I can't tell you how happy I am, Meg." Happier than she had the right to be under the circumstances. Sara rubbed the belly of the baby gripping her finger. "It's not Clive's baby," she divulged. And, oh, how delighted she was it wasn't her husband's seed that produced this new life growing inside her.

"Not your husband's!" Puzzlement and a certain shock shaded Meg's tone as she stared at Sara.

"No."

"But what will he do when he finds out?" Poor Meg looked so taken aback Sara almost laughed. But this was no laughing matter. "Do you think he'll believe it to be his?"

"The answer to both those questions is I don't know. I have no idea what he'll think about it, or what he's likely to do. He's not stupid, just insensitive." Sara settled her skirt about her legs and pulled the baby onto her lap. "Only my maid knows at the moment, and that's how I would like to keep it."

"That will be an impossibility, Sara, and you know it."

Yes, she knew that. "He hasn't touched me since the night Remy and I made love, and hadn't been in my bed for a few weeks before that." Sara shrugged. "I'm hoping he'll think it born before its time. I will have to see his physician; I doubt he'll let me pick one of my own." Uncertainty clouded her mind.

The other infant made a face as if about to cry, and Meg picked her up. "I know what you can do." Meg put a finger to her baby's nose and tweaked it gently, encouraging a smile. "What say you go to see my doctor? Perhaps Clive will accept that. After all, he knows I have my twins, doesn't he?"

"I'm not sure." Clive paid no heed to Meg's life. Once it was established that Sara visited a respectable married woman he lost interest in all else. "If I see your doctor there might be a chance Clive won't find out when the baby was conceived. I don't fear for myself, Meg, but I would fear for my child if Clive found out it was Rem's." She bounced the gurgling baby girl on her knee. "He managed to arrange Rem's transfer to Moreton Bay and delights in telling me how dreadful the conditions are up there."

Sara's nights were filled with horrific nightmares since her husband brutally described what fate awaited Rem in the new settlement up north where men lived like rats in the heat and died of numerous tropical diseases. Her heart told her she would never see Rem again. Only the babe growing inside her gave her the strength to go on.

"Surely he isn't such an ogre he would harm a baby." Sara could see that Meg was shocked to her core.

"Clive's capable of anything." How could she explain the depths of her husband's jealousy and hatred of Rem? "The man's half insane." This was not a figment of her imagination but the truth. He ordered his servants to watch over her as if she were a felon. Sara knew Brace and the housekeeper reported all her movements to their master. The two of them would do anything to keep their positions. They were too well off to consider the alternative; both stashed nest eggs by stealing from their master. And the awful truth was that Clive would rather believe them than his own wife, so she would gain nothing by exposing their tricks.

"I don't know how I can keep a visit to your doctor secret." Sara nibbled on her lower lip. "Brace will surely report back to him."

"So let him." Meg wrinkled her nose. "You make excuses. A woman carrying a baby is often accused of reckless and unusual behavior. Tell him you don't desire his doctor treating you in such a personal way. I will arrange an appointment for you when I visit my doctor tomorrow."

It was all so simple for Meg. Loved and cherished by her husband, she had no inkling of what it was like to be married to someone eaten up with jealousy, not because of his love for you, but merely because he considered you his possession.

Chapter Seventeen

September 1828

Death would be a blessing. In an effort to take his mind off the excruciating pain, Rem tried to focus on his memories of Sara, loving and sated in his arms, in the precious shared moments before Ravenbrook interrupted them. However, her face kept disappearing as the agony engulfed him. Lord knows what happened after the flogging but his back felt as if it was on fire. Perhaps he was in hell and his body was being engulfed in flames.

"Perhaps now you'll keep yer 'ead out of trouble and mind yer Ps and Qs, O'Shea," a gravelly voice said from his side.

Rem blinked, striving to open his eyes, which felt as if someone had thrown hot water into them. He lay on his stomach, his head turned to one side. The rough blanket that was his only bedding scratched at his cheek and chest. It stank of sweat and blood, and he tried not to inhale; tried not to bring up the bile hovering halfway up his throat. His mouth tasted like last week's garbage rested in it.

"A man don't need to do much up here to get hisself in strife," he croaked from a throat that felt as if he'd swallowed a bucket of sand.

"That's fact," his mess-mate said. "You least of all of us."

"How long have I been out?"

"Long enough. You was taken to the 'ospital, but they told me to bring you 'ere this morning."

The hospital, if that's what it could be termed, was not meant to accommodate convicts, more to see to the needs of the military. Convicts were considered scum: the horses were treated better up here where life was cheap.

"'Ere, take a drop of this." Rem's mate held a spoon to his lips and dripped some warm, vile tasting water on Rem's lips.

Rem's tongue came out to sup them up. The few drops made his stomach roil. "I'm gonna die," he groaned.

"No you ain't. Not yet awhile at any rate. If you was gonna die you'd 'a carked it afore they finished yer flogging."

Regardless of what Salty said, Rem knew he was going to die. No man could feel this awful and live. Like hot knives, pain seared his back. Even a slight breeze brought him fresh agony.

After another few drops of water passed his lips, he turned his head to hang his face over the end of the pallet. The water was impure and vile.

"Did you boil that?" he demanded, retching from an empty stomach, which brought him more pain. Dysentery killed many men in the last few months. On the captain's orders, a tank was erected in the brickfields and hand pumps and wooden pipes now distributed water, but it was still putrid.

"Huh!" Salty's grunt told nothing. "Why the bloody 'ell didn't yer keep yer ugly mug out of the sergeant's way?" he grumbled. "If I told yer once I told yer a 'undred times, it don't pay to get noticed up here."

Rem mumbled a vile oath. The old man everyone called Salty had been among the first group of thirty convicts to arrive at Moreton Bay, in '24, with about twenty military under the command of Lieutenant Henry Miller. The old fellow hoped to win an early ticket of leave, but he'd been one of the first to try to escape, so his original sentence of seven years set down in London had grown to fourteen. Salty managed to get as far south as Port Macquarie before being captured and brought back, emaciated and sick. So far, no one had gotten further than that. Moreton Bay fulfilled all the Governor's predictions of being an ideal prison, too isolated for successful escapes.

Two separate floggings convinced Salty it was safer to keep quiet and obey orders. The only ones who successfully escaped this hell so far were those who had blessedly died. And plenty had gone to meet their maker, if not from the effects of disease, but because of floggings by the present captain, known to all the cons as 'The Ogre'.

The bastard put the settlement on half rations, as if they weren't starving already, and even ordered some men's turds be examined for undigested kernels of corn they were accused of stealing.

Even so, it was still better than when those first few arrived. Salty was lucky to be alive; the tales he'd told Rem of the first months here! When the crops all died, most men got scurvy because they couldn't get anything to grow; seeds died in the ground, and the place was infested with ticks, flies, scorpions, not to mention deadly snakes.

Rem shifted, groaning as pain knifed through him. "How many lashes did I end up getting?"

With a sorrowful sigh, Salty said, "Fifty. Good job you never got more. You've been out cold for two days. Which was a blessing. Gave them time to treat yer wounds without you feeling it. An' think yerself lucky they stopped when they did. That bastard of a captain has been known to go as far as five hundred without blinking an eye." He spat in the dirt. "I got an 'undred me first time!"

Rem wondered how a man could survive such brutality. He'd seen one fellow stumble his way across the yard after a flogging with blood running from his lacerated flesh and squashing out of his shoes with every step. His sinews, white and ragged, had protruded from his mutilated back. With a defiant oath at the scourger who inflicted this agony on him, he'd walked past the scavenging dogs quarreling over a lump of his flesh that had gone flying during the flogging. His hundred lashes took over an hour to inflict, with the sun beating mercilessly on him. That man died the next day; whether from the actual lashing or from the dysentery plaguing him, no one knew. What difference did it make anyway?

Rem drifted into a nightmare-invaded sleep and when he awoke yelling obscenities, it was dark outside the hut.

"Here, take some of this in." The boy called Scab offered him a mug. "It's stew. Salty says you need to get something inside yer."

"Thanks." Stifling a moan, Rem propped himself on his elbows as best he could and took a sip. "That's good. Beats water any day. Where's Salty?" He looked about, wincing.

"He's having a kip. They got him working in the brickfields today. The captain wants his new barracks finished in a hurry." Scab uttered one of the foul words he often used to punctuate every sentence.

Rem met up with the lad again four months ago on the vessel bringing him north, after Ravenbrook saw to it that Rem was sent as far away from Sara as possible. It was stunning how quickly he'd accomplished this. Rem vowed to kill her husband once he gained his freedom. If he wasn't dead before then. The way he felt now he wasn't banking on surviving to see Sara's lovely face again.

Scab was taken into custody after that failed hold-up and informed Rem that most of the gang were killed. Big Ox was sent to Norfolk Island, and another two gang members were at Newcastle.

Scab and Salty were the only two out of the four hundred or so convicts living in this hell on earth Rem could vaguely term as mates. He knew if it came to it they would likely have no qualms about saving their own skins before his. Who could blame them?

No friendships formed in a place where it was a struggle to survive amidst deplorable conditions. Dog eat dog was the by-word amongst men considered lower than rats by the men charged with guarding them. They flogged men to death here, and worked them in chains until they dropped. Rem had seen men slung into shallow graves as if they were of less importance than the dogs who fought over the scraps of flesh the lash scattered around the triangle during a flogging. The first flogging he witnessed sickened him. But eventually a man learned to accept most things.

"Did I scream?" Rem had to know.

"Nah," Scab said, chuckling. "You ain't made of sandstone, mate. You're an iron man."

That was some consolation. An iron man was one able to stand up to the pain without blubbering or crumbling like sandstone.

"You even spat at the feet of the bastard who gave yer the red shirt."

Red shirt! God, he'd seen what a man looked like after thirty lashes of the cat. How disfigured would he be after fifty? What did it matter? He was destined to die up here. If the flogging didn't kill him disease would. Already mosquitoes gave men a strange fever; someone told him they called it malaria in foreign parts. What had he to live for anyway? There was no future with Sara, not while Clive Ravenbrook lived. And if he ever got back he'd kill that bastard; then be strung up for the murder anyway.

"Here, take some more of this stew. If you don't eat it, I'll have it."

Rem knew Scab would have no qualms about stealing his share of the food. A man didn't survive up here by being generous and thoughtful. Although Rem felt sure he had little chance of surviving in the long run, his sense of self-preservation was strong. Gritting his teeth against the agony of pushing himself up, he finished the stew.

Three days later, he was back at work helping build the captain's barracks and roasting beneath the relentless sun.

Chapter Eighteen

January 1829

"Oh, ma'am, the master's gonna kill yer," Maisie wailed. She stood by the bed, cradling the newborn baby in her arms, her eyes stricken as she looked from Sara to the swaddled babe.

With a sniff, she passed the infant to Sara, who pressed a weary kiss to her son's downy head. Soft tufts of almost chestnut-colored hair testified to his father's identity as nothing else could.

"I doubt it, Maisie." Sara sighed tiredly. "He'll likely want to." Clive wouldn't do anything that might put his head in a noose. He was far too artful for that. She ran two fingers across the fluff on her baby's crown. "Perhaps he'll think the baby inherited his darkness from me and my parents." And pigs might fly!

"Oh, ma'am." Maisie's expression said she doubted that about as much as Sara did. "What with his own hair being so light, and most babes take after their pa more than their ma." Maisie helped Sara put the baby to her breast. After a few false starts, the infant was soon sucking happily. She said disgustedly, "Anyways, 'e's off at his gambling club right now and probably won't be home for a good while. He was cringing something awful when you were screaming." She chuckled.

"I did make rather a fuss bringing this little man into the world, didn't I?" Sara smiled down, as her baby curled a fist around her little finger. "But it was worth all the pain." Would be worth all the heartache she knew would stay with her always without Rem to share this precious arrival. "Now I have him I can endure anything my husband deems to toss my way."

"What you going to call 'im?" Maisie asked as she began tidying up the mess left by the doctor, a gentle man who had been only too glad to be of assistance throughout the pregnancy and birth. Meg made the appointment, as promised, and when the doctor visited the house Sara was vague about the time of the baby's conception. It might be that Clive could be convinced the child was his, for it was large, and the doctor inclined to believe it had been overdue. But that was a fickle notion for there was no way Clive would be convinced it was his child once he got a look at the dark hair.

"I'll call him William," she said, as she transferred her son gently to the other breast.

"That's a nice name. Was it your papa's?" Maisie asked. Sara let out a burst of laughter. If it was her papa's name she would never have used it on her precious baby.

"No, it's just a name I've always liked." She would love to call him Jeremy, but that was out of the question. "Did you take the letter I gave you to the coaching station?" She had written to her parents advising them of the birth, but the last thing she expected was for either of them to be the slightest bit interested in her offspring. One letter had come from her mother since arriving in Sydney and none from her father. Out of sight out of mind, she guessed. It was sad, but it didn't surprise her in the least that they had put her out of their minds.

Her child might never know the love of his father, but he would have no doubt that his mother worshipped and cherished him.

Once the baby was satisfied and sleeping Sara let Maisie settle him in his crib beside her bed. There would be no nursemaid for her baby. Months ago, she decided she would nurse her own child. Apart from the pleasure gained, it would give her something to offset the stifling boredom. At last, her life had something of worth in it. From now on, her existence would revolve around her son.

Sara awoke from a doze to hear a commotion erupting downstairs. Maisie came rushing into the room, but no sooner had she warned her mistress the master had returned and was inquiring after his heir than Clive burst in, slamming the door on its hinges. His hair was unkempt and his usually pale face flushed so he looked like a pomegranate. With his cravat twisted and jacket undone, Sara guessed he'd left his latest mistress in a hurry.

Sara struggled to sit up as he shouted, "Where's my son?"

The baby wakened with a wail. "Keep your voice down," Sara hissed. "You've upset the babe."

Maisie picked William up and placed him in her arms. A smile that had begun to curve Clive's mouth abruptly disappeared and shock blanked his features. For a moment, he stood like a statue. Then his shaking fist shot out as he stood over the bed. Sara put a protective hand over her baby's head, cringing from the wrath that threatened to erupt from him at any moment.

"That child isn't my heir!"

"What makes you presume that?" Sara dared to ask.

Clive brought his face down until he was within a hand's span of hers. His spittle hit her cheek as he raged, "We both know where it's inherited that repulsive hair from. Do you take me for a fool? How dare you insult me in this way? It's that half-breed's child."

For a moment Sara thought, and hoped, that her husband might collapse with his rage. Arms akimbo, he shook his fists. Still protectively shielding her son Sara stared at the lunatic raging over her.

What could she say? Would he turn her and her child out of his house, she wondered, as he paced back and force, such obscenities flying from his mouth that Maisie flinched. She stood huddled in a corner of the room, her apron twisted so tightly in her fingers Sara thought she would rip it. Sara had seen Clive angry many times, but never filled with such demonic rage. If capable, she would have fled from his sight.

"Whore! How dare you bring disrepute on me?" He stalked from the room, slamming the door so forcefully everything moveable in the room rattled.

Sara laughed, she couldn't contain it. He'd paraded his whores under her nose from the first day they arrived back in town, yet had the audacity to accuse her of whoring. He was just about as disreputable as a man could be, with his gambling, gallivanting, and mistresses.

"Lawd, ma'am, I ain't ever seen him that wild before. What'll you do if he throws you out?" Maisie wailed. Forgetting her status she sat on the side of the bed to stare at Sara from terrified eyes.

Sara shrugged, feeling immeasurably weary. "I'll go home to my parent's farm if he decides we can't stay here."

"You won't leave me behind if you go, will you, ma'am?" Maisie begged.

Sara put William to her breast. They watched him suckle greedily, and Sara promised, "I'll take you wherever I go, Maisie. I would never leave you here with that man and his awful skivvies, don't worry."

Sound advice. At this moment, Sara had never been so worried about her welfare. Clive was angry enough to turn her out tonight. She could hear him knocking furniture about in his room, sounding like a wild bull let loose. China crashed and something heavy thumped against the wall. The man was definitely insane.

Then a sense of resignation settled over her. She had Rem's son, a child to love as she loved his father. She smiled down on his beloved face, pressing the tiny bundle to her breast.

Her parents' home had never been inviting, and her eagerness to flee from it had brought her to this sorry situation, but right now it shone as a haven of peace.

* * *

Rem dragged the scrap of rag from around his neck and wiped the sweat from his brow, squinting up at the sky. Not a single cloud marred the blue, and the sun beat down mercilessly on their heads.

With the captain's barracks completed, Rem was among the gang of convicts working on his new

Commissariat store near the riverbank. Salty had died a month back, just on Christmas. Just one of the dozens who succumbed to malaria and violent dysentery in the past year and were now in the cemetery along the river. The old man was so sick near the end, death came as a blessing.

"This bloody heat is gonna kill us if the mosquitoes and bloody vile water and grub don't first," Scab muttered at Rem's side.

"Too true." Rem was resigned to his fate now. It was likely none of them in this disease-ridden place would ever mix with polite society again. Likely, they would never know what it was to eat a decent meal, drink pure water, and wear anything but rags.

"You gonna meet yer doxie later?" Scab licked his dry and cracked lips as he grinned, showing decayed brown teeth.

Rem clipped him round the ear, and the lad yelped. "Tilly isn't a doxie, and don't ever call her that," he scolded. "She's a decent lass."

"Oh, yeah. So what's she doing in this rat haven if she's so pure and nice?" Scab rubbed at his ear, a rude noise erupting from his mouth.

Rem wiped a fist across his brow then retied the rag round his neck. "She's doing what we're all doing here. Surviving."

"I got meself a lady of me own," Scab boasted, tapping his skinny chest with a thumb.

"Now that's something I really want to see, you with a lady." Rem laughed. "No decent woman would spare you the time of day."

The lad used one or two of his customary swear words then bent his back to digging when the overseer walked nearby, his whip tapping on his thigh.

For a while, they continued with their digging. Rem let his thoughts wander to Tilly, the lass he met a week back. The factory built on a rise north of the barracks housed the women who had begun to arrive last year. Tilly wasn't like any of the others, mostly doxies as Scab noted. She was tall, as skinny as a broomstick, and held herself aloof.

185

Perhaps this trait drew Rem to her, for he took scant notice of any of the other females, even though a few had eyed him with interest.

The overseer blew his whistle as the sun neared the horizon. The convicts washed the sweat and grime from their bodies in the river; then the guards escorted them back to the barracks. Once locked in for the night, Rem joined the others for their main meal of the day. Most ate like hogs at the trough, and the food disappeared in less than three minutes.

Too exhausted even to play cards or sit and talk, most hit their pallets straight away. Rem lay back and waited for the snoring to reach a crescendo. How these men could sleep in this heat he didn't know. Night after night went by when he barely closed his eyes. Sometimes exhaustion caught up with him and he managed to doze for an hour or two, but then the nightmares returned; he could feel the cat biting into his flesh, could hear the whistle of the whip, reliving the agony as the leather bit into his flesh. Then he would jerk awake, a silent scream echoing round his head.

"I'm off." Scab sat on the side of his pallet, pulling on his boots. He spat on his hands then ran them over his scraggly hair.

"I'll come with you." Rem hadn't bothered to remove his boots. Turning sideways, he stood. One or two of their companions began to grumble.

"Shut yer gob!" Scab hissed at the man nearest him as he and Rem made for the door leading to the yard. The guard was busy with one of the doxies, his grunting loud in the stillness of the night. With little trouble, they pinched his keys and unlocked the outer door.

As soon as they were clear of the barracks, Scab went on to the factory. Rem headed left toward Wheat Creek. "Tilly," he whispered as he neared the tree they had arranged to meet under.

She stood up, a shadowy figure in the night, tall and ethereal looking against the mottled sky. A cloud crossed over the moon and then he saw her clearly.

"Hello lass, been waiting long?" he asked as he neared.

She shook her head. "Not long. I had trouble getting out tonight. So many of them are skipping off, they're keeping a closer watch on us."

Rem wondered why they bothered to erect a fence around the factory. The military were willing to turn a blind eye to the comings and goings of the women. Why should they enforce stiffer rules when they were using the doxies for their own enjoyment?

"Let's sit here." Rem went down by the tree and she sat at his side, her arms looped about her knees. "How was your day?"

"Same as all the others, just plain rotten." She pressed her nose on her skirt and sighed. "I was pulling vegetables, so that was better than scrubbing or sewing."

"Don't you like to sew? I thought all women were handy with a needle." Rem thought of Sara and wondered if she ever stitched. He hadn't a clue. There were a lot of things he never learned about her.

"Not all of us. Some, like me, never had the chance to learn."

"Tell me more about your life in Devon." Rem leaned back against the tree, crossing his legs at the ankles.

"Not much to tell." She tucked her skirt in tighter.

"Tell me anyway," he urged. "I like to hear about England. It seems like those days were dreamed, don't it?"

Tilly never volunteered information freely. She kept it well corked, like her emotions. Just like a still dark pool was Tilly.

She pulled a face and then began quietly, "Ma and me and my two little sisters worked for this gent in his grand house overlooking the sea." She looked out over the creek, and Rem thought she wasn't about to say more, but then she went on, "It was a lovely spot, but could get rough and rugged when the wind howled about the roof in winter."

"How long were you there?" Rem waited patiently. "You told me your dad worked in the gardens until he died."

"I was a littl'un when we went there." Her skinny shoulders lifted a fraction. "Two, I suppose. Mum had the

187

other two a year apart, the first when I was five. I was thirteen when Pa died." She dragged in a deep breath and stared off into the past.

"So, did the master keep you on?"

For a long time she didn't answer. Then she said flatly, "Oh, yes. I was just the age he liked his girls."

Rem cursed in disgust. "Why couldn't your ma step in and help you. Couldn't she stop him touching you?"

"Huh! You know how it works. She would've got thrown out without a farthing. How could she do that with the other two to care for? He told me if I didn't let him have his way he would take Jane. What else could I do?"

"Oh, Tilly. I'm sorry." Rem put a hand on her arm, and she stiffened beneath his touch.

A strange little laugh erupted from her throat. "It was all in vain, for he had both of them anyway within the next couple of years. The shame killed Ma. When I began to kick up a fuss and even went as far as telling the local constable, he accused me of stealing his wife's necklace, didn't he?"

"And that's how you came to be sent here?" She gave a small nod. "What happened to your sisters?"

After sighing, she whispered, "They're still there for all I know. Perhaps they got lucky and died."

"Don't say that." Although he argued, Rem could understand her reasoning. Sometimes death was a blessing. "Did you get any word from them after you were arrested?"

"No. They were too young to understand what was going on through the trial and everything. Too young to attend the court, but not too young for...." Her voice cracked as she broke off. "Bess was fourteen the day before I left England," she whispered bleakly.

"Come here." Rem reached out a hand. For a moment she stared at it as if it was about to bite her. Rem sighed. "I won't touch you in that way, Tilly. But we all need someone to hold us now and then. Lord knows I need comforting as much as the next person."

With a hesitant jerk she moved until she was by his side and then tentatively took his hand. Rem passed his other arm behind her back, careful not to put any pressure on her.

"Tell me about your love," she urged. "What's it like to care for someone in that way?"

"Agony, but ecstasy at the same time." Rem swallowed. "Sara's full of fire and spirit. To me the most beautiful creature on this earth."

"That's a lovely name. Do you think you'll ever see her again?" she asked pensively. Rem realized her fingers were stroking the back of his hand.

He hadn't been this close to a woman for a long time, and it had the obvious effect on his senses. He shifted, scared he would frighten her off. As he said, they both needed the comfort of being close to another human, and he would do nothing to squander this chance.

Shrugging, he looked across the creek where he could just make out a couple of kangaroos warily drinking. As if they sensed the humans so near they took off, bounding away toward the wooded area beyond Kangaroo Point Road.

"I doubt it. Chances are I'll die up here." An ache round his heart threatened to choke him.

Her head went up and down, her hair brushing his cheek. The small contact made him shiver. No point in denying it, she knew as well as they all did that their chances of survival were small.

Frogs, insects, and other night creatures filled the long silence with their song before she said, "I once thought I was in love."

"Tell me about him."

Rem could hear a smile in her voice as she said wistfully, "His name was Olaf. What a giant. I was as tall as a tree from the time I was ten, and he was one of the few boys bigger than me. He gave me flowers, a posy of bluebells." She drew in a long breath and let it out on a sigh. "I thought that was the best moment of my life. Now I come to think about it, it probably was."

Rem's heart ached, this time for her. "My best moment was the first time Sara kissed me."

"I've never been kissed," she suddenly admitted, and Rem brought his face round so he could look into her eyes.

"Not even by Olaf? What was he, an idiot?" He grinned.

"No, just an awkward boy of eleven," she said on a small laugh.

"Would you like me to kiss you? No, don't back off." He pressed her shoulder gently. "I wouldn't do anything else, I promise."

For long moments, she fiddled with the stiff fabric of her skirt; then said, "All right."

Rem let his lips touch hers, keeping the contact as light as a feather. Her lips were cracked from working out in the sun, and for a moment Rem compared them to the softness of his Sara's.

With a small moan, she deepened the contact, letting herself relax into his arms. Rem didn't move, leaving it to her to make the next move. She did, looping her hands about his neck. Slowly he brought his tongue out, tracing the line of her mouth.

"Remy," she whispered against his lips, and he wasn't sure if it was a question or a sign that she wanted more.

"I'm here. Don't be afraid." He held his arms wide. "I haven't been this close to a woman in a long time, and you're not stupid; you can obviously feel what effect you're having on me. But not all men are lascivious pigs."

"Oh, Remy, I know that. You're the kindest person I've ever met, aside from my ma." She sat back, pushing at her hair. "Thank you for that."

"Don't thank me. It was all my pleasure."

"I'd better go now."

"Yes." Rem watched as she stood and then watched her as she walked stealthily off. His body thrummed with want. It was a feeling he welcomed. Better by far than the despair and desolation that had filled him for so long and robbed him of all sensitivity.

190

Chapter Nineteen

November 1831

Rem jumped down from the wagon and stood with his feet apart, taking in the scene around him.

Sydney hadn't altered a lot in the time he'd spent at Moreton Bay. There was still a myriad of strange dialects around him, still a hundred and one different smells assailing his nostrils.

"God, it's good to be back 'ere, ain't it?" the man at his side said, and Rem grunted his agreement.

It was good to be anywhere but in the hell where he'd spent the last two and a half years. His only regret was leaving Tilly. Inevitably, they had become lovers weeks after their first kiss. When they had finally lain together, it was a tender meeting of scarred bodies and minds warped by too much violence, anger, and bitterness. Rem hoped his loving had helped ease some of the pain in her heart. There was no telling, for she kept her feelings close to her chest and hadn't even shed a tear at their last meeting.

"See you around," he said to the man as he turned and walked away, absently patting the pocket holding his ticket of leave.

A free man at last. How good that sounded.

He honestly never expected to walk the streets of Sydney again, expected to perish up north where so many others had died. Scab succumbed to the dysentery that afflicted everybody at Moreton Bay; just one of the many diseases and scourges suffered by convicts and the military alike up there in conditions no man should be expected to live in.

First things first.

He had to get back to Bathurst to see Bella and Tiger. On the way, he would go to pick up the stash of gold he and Lulu buried in the mountains. What if he couldn't remember where to look for the hut? What if someone else inhabited the place? Oh, well, he would worry about that if it happened. Life had taught him some harsh lessons; you accepted fate, no sense in fighting it.

But there was one person he had to see before he planned how he would get back to Bathurst. Crossing the road, he made his way along Pitt Street until he came to Ravenbrook's residence. The garden looked unkempt, and briefly he wondered if the house was occupied. It looked uncared for, the shutters in need of paint, the vine trailing from the upper balcony half-dead. His stomach roiled; what would he do if Ravenbrook had moved away and dragged Sara with him? Or worse still, supposing he'd decided to return to England? Rem knew he owned property and held some sort of business investment there.

Settling on a low wall, he watched the house. Two hours went by, and Rem was beginning to think the house was definitely empty, for there were no signs of life from within at all. Then a carriage stopped outside and the coachman got down to open the gates. Rem breathed a sigh of relief as he strolled across the road and peered through a gap in the fence.

There was no mistaking the man who alighted when the carriage pulled up in front of the steps. Ravenbrook's hair was white now, but everything else was the same as before. He reached up, and Rem held his breath. But it wasn't Sara Ravenbrook he assisted from the carriage. It was a girl dressed in plain grey garb, cradling a toddler in her arms. She looked to be about fifteen. No mistaking whose child it was, for the boy's hair was as light as Ravenbrook's. He said something to the driver and then preceded the girl and child up the steps. They disappeared inside the house.

Good God, surely he hadn't taken a child as his mistress! The girl didn't look like mistress material though, more like a nanny by her manner and clothing. Sara must be inside the house. Rem cursed. Had he guessed she was in there alone he would have knocked on the door when he first arrived.

He settled down to wait again. The carriage driver fed and watered the horses but didn't unharness them. When it grew dark Ravenbrook left the house, alone. Rem waited until the carriage was out of sight before crossing the road and opening one of the gates. He lifted the brass knocker and let it fall. After a long pause, someone shuffled to open the door. A woman in a severe black dress stood there.

"Yes?" she demanded, eying him with suspicion. Rem got the idea callers were unusual at this house.

"Can I speak with your mistress?" he asked.

The woman leant close to peer hard at him, making a strange noise in her throat. It sounded like a laugh, but he could be mistaken, for no hint of a smile curved her pinched mouth or lightened her eyes.

"There's no mistress in this establishment," she stunned him by saying.

"But where is Clive Ravenbrook's wife?" Rem demanded. "I take it that's the name of your master."

"Oh, yes, that's the master here. But his wife hasn't been here for…" She seemed to be calculating in her head and finding it a hard task. "Twenty months."

"Twenty…?" Rem reeled back. God, surely Sara wasn't… No, she couldn't be dead. "Where's Sara Ravenbrook?"

"Ravenbrook? Huh! That one don't bear his name. Oh, no, she went back to where she came from and good riddance." Suddenly realizing she might have overstepped the bounds laid down by decent society, she said in a less abrasive manner, "She took the boy and went back to her father's house."

The boy? "What boy? I thought I saw Ravenbrook with his son earlier."

"So you did. With his son. But the woman you called his wife has the other one's son with her. Threw them out on their ear, he did. He has his son, and he's happy as a

193

lark. Didn't want to set eyes on her by-blow, did he?" She cackled.

Rem was too astounded to speak. While he fumbled around in his brain for an explanation, she slammed the door, leaving him staring at the wooden panels in shock. He rapped on the door and after a while, it opened again. The same woman stared at him defiantly.

"What now?"

"You say she has a child with her, and Ravenbrook didn't claim it as his own. In that case who is the father of that child?" he demanded.

She shrugged. "Don't ask me. What would I know of that?" Her mouth puckered. "All I know is she bore the master's child eleven months after the other one and three months later he sent her packing."

A wild sensation was beginning to flutter in Rem's chest. Sensing he would get no more information from this woman, he turned and left, the sound of the slamming door echoing behind him.

Sweet Jesus! Sara must have borne his child. And then Clive Ravenbrook's eleven months later. The implications didn't bear contemplating. Filled with urgency he strode away. The first priority was to find transport across the mountains. Heading for The Rocks, he went to the wharf. As luck would have it, a group of teamsters were idly smoking their pipes while convicts unloaded their wool bales from the drays and carted them into a nearby warehouse.

"You fellows going back over the mountains?" he asked one of them, a wiry man of indeterminate years.

"And who wants to know?" the teamster demanded, eyeing Rem suspiciously.

"O'Shea. I've got family at Bathurst, and I need to get back there."

"You got yer papers?"

Rem brought out his ticket of leave, and the man scrutinized it before handing it back. Expressionlessly he said, "We'll be leaving the day after tomorrow. There's two families traveling along with us, and we'll be toting their

194

belongings. Be at the cattle market at dawn and you can go along with us. Pull your weight and don't cause no trouble and you'll do. We don't take no troublemakers."

"Thanks. The last thing I want is trouble." Wasn't that the truth?

Rem went to three taverns before he found one where the owner was willing to give him food and let him sleep in the stable in exchange for doing menial tasks.

* * *

Well before the first hint of dawn tinted the skies, Rem was halfway up Brickfield Hill on his way to the far end of town. Cattle milled about the yards, causing a racket and churning up dust, when he arrived at the top of Upper Pitt Street. Rem hunkered down to wait, watching the goings-on with mild interest as the market began to stir.

A group of convicts alighted from a wagon; their overseer shouting orders, and Rem glanced briefly at the ten men. Then his eyes shot back to them sharply. One man stood out from the others, not by his clothing, which was just as ragged as the others, but by the mop of unruly hair of a color that looked almost black in the pre-dawn half-light and a profile that was achingly familiar.

"Carlos!" Rem shouted.

Before the man had reacted to his call Rem was on his feet, rushing to meet him.

"Rem? Sweet Jesus, is that you?"

"Aye, 'tis your brother, man. What you doing here? Silly question, eh?" By now they were in each other's arms, and Rem felt as if every breath was being squeezed out of him. Tears filled his eyes, and he pulled back to peer at Carlos closely. "Lord, but it's good to see you."

"Same here. What a stroke of luck, eh?"

"Get over here, O'Shea," the overseer shouted.

Carlos muttered an oath. "Better go. Where you going?"

"Over to Bathurst," Rem said as he followed the group being led to one of the yards.

195

"Well, I'll be blowed." Carlos grinned. "We're off over them mountains too. What you going there for?"

"I can't believe it! I'm off to see our Bella. I've just got my ticket not long ago." Rem patted his pocket. "She don't even know I'm a free man yet. She'll be jumping over the moon to see you."

That was a gross understatement. Carlos was a year younger than Rem, and their sister would likely be so happy to see them both again she'd go barmy with joy.

"How long have you been here?" Rem asked, following Carlos and the others about, ignoring the overseer's occasional reprimand.

"Since twenty seven. I found out where Bella was and sent her a letter. She knows I'm off over there. I'm hoping her husband can arrange for me to work on his farm. What do you reckon?"

"Aye, Tiger will help you. He helped me—until I made a mess of things." Rem ducked his head.

"You? No, you couldn't mess things up," his brother said with rank sarcasm.

Rem didn't want to discuss his many failings right now. The teamsters had arrived and were hitching their oxen to the drays. "I'll see you later. I have to go help load the drays. We'll meet at the first stopover." Rem waved and went off, feeling happier than in a long, long time.

Carlos was here and soon they would be reunited with Bella. And he would be reunited with Sara.

* * *

"So, tell me about how you came to be sent here." Rem sat beside his brother and gave him a nudge on the knee. The convicts had their fire going a distance from the free traveler's camp. Carlos wouldn't have been allowed over there, but the convict's overseer couldn't force Rem away from their campsite. Rem had done his share of work, erecting tents and unloading what would be needed for the night. "How are the others back home?" He couldn't wait to hear about the rest of their family left back in Stepney. "Are they managing all right?"

Carlos nodded, patting Rem on the thigh. It was as if they couldn't stop touching each other, ensuring the other was real, not a figment of the imagination. "The girls managed to find themselves husbands. Emily's bloke's not bad. Lenny has a job with a coachbuilder, so she won't starve. She's got a baby girl."

"A girl, eh? Imagine that? I can just see our Em with a baby. Go on," Rem urged. "What about Cath?"

Carlos pulled a face. "I'm not too sure about Cathy's man. He steals more than is wise and is always out for a lark, but they seem happy enough." He shrugged. "We're used to living on the bread-line so she won't miss much."

"That's a fact." Emily was a year younger than Carlos and Cathy one year younger than her. "And what about young Bob?" Their youngest sibling was two years younger than Cathy. "Is he thieving too?"

"No." Carlos laughed and nudged Rem with an elbow. "You won't believe this, but the sod's got himself employed. He was working at the wharf last time I saw him and promised to come over here on the first ship he could get on after I was sentenced. I've been keeping my ears open, but so far he hasn't been on any of the ships coming in. He has Bella's address, so perhaps we'll see him over the mountains one day, eh?" Carlos put an arm about Rem's shoulders and squeezed. They had always been a demonstrative family, encouraged by their Irish mother and Spanish father to share their feelings.

"That'd be grand." A huge sense of contentment settled over Rem. All he had to do now was see Sara and his son, and life would be complete.

They stared into the fire for a moment, each with his own thoughts, then Carlos asked, "So, what you gonna do when we get over there? You going to stay?"

Rem rubbed his nape. "I haven't thought that far ahead. To be honest, my life's in a bit of a bloody turmoil at the moment."

"So, that's unusual?" Carlos dug him in the ribs and chuckled.

"No, this is a real pickle." Rem chewed on the inside of his mouth. "I've done some things I'm not proud of, Carlos."

"Ain't we all? Life is made up of mistakes and ways of trying to set them right. We haven't exactly been served with a cushy existence, have we? We do what we have to do, and hope the ones we love don't get hurt too much. So, tell me, what you been up to in the past five years then?"

Rem sighed. "It's a long story."

"We've got plenty of time." Carlos looked into the darkness shrouding the mountains. "How long does it take to get over these bloody giant hills anyway?"

"Up to a fortnight, depending on the weather and the animals. The teamsters and their oxen can hold things up or speed along depending on their mood."

"What, the animals' mood or the rough blokes who drive 'em?"

"Both." Rem laughed. It was a fact. The teamsters were a breed unto themselves and answered to no man. But most travelers couldn't manage without their skill and knowledge of the hazardous road.

"Right." Carlos settled back. "I know you met up with Bella after her husband found you in Sydney, but I've sort of lost track of your doings after that."

Rem pondered how much to disclose, but once started he couldn't seem to stop. The words tumbled out. He told Carlos about Aggie and his guilt. Then he told about his love for Sara and the mess he'd made of her life.

"Now I've found out I left her with a babe inside her when her husband had me sent off to Moreton Bay."

"Seems to me her father's the one who made her life what it is, boyo. You've got too much guilt hanging over your head that's not yours to worry over. So, this Sara you love is over where we're going. And what of her husband?"

Rem dragged in a harsh breath. "That's going to be the problem. He's not going to let her go. He don't want her for himself any more it seems, but he ain't likely to give her up. Especially to me."

"Looks like you're going to have a fight on your hands, boyo." Carlos thumped Rem's thigh.

"Looks that way." Morosely Rem stared at a crackling log on the fire.

"So, go on with what happened when you got in with this band of bushrangers," Carlos prompted.

Rem continued with his story. "I'm going back for the gold, Carlos," he said softly, when he reached the part of the story where Lulu died and his life slid further and further down into hell.

"'Course you are. It'd be a foolish man who left gold lying around. Finders keepers—it belongs to you. Can you remember where you've hid it?"

Rem rubbed his chin. "More or less. I only have to look out for certain landmarks when we get near the spot. The hard part is going to be finding my way back to the hut. I reckon the path has overgrown. I left markers, but it's been a long time..."

"How you going to get away from that lot?" Carlos jerked his head to the free travelers gathered about their fire.

"I'll slip off when I get near the spot, and catch up with you further along the trail."

"I'll come with you."

Rem put a hand on his brother's arm. "No you won't. Don't be daft, man. You're a convict. You just stay out of trouble, d'you hear? I've been places no man should be sent and had things happen to me I wouldn't wish my worst enemy to suffer, my lad, so you keep sweet with the authorities and serve your term like a good boy. Hear me?"

Carlos grinned. "All right, I hear you. I ain't bloody deaf. So, carry on with your story. What happened next?"

By the time Rem finished his tale, everyone was asleep and the camps quiet, except for the snores of those nearby.

"Lord man, how's your back now?" All jollity had left Carlos when Rem haltingly relayed his flogging and the conditions up north.

"It's a mess. But the scars up here"—Rem tapped his head—"them's the ones that'll never heal."

"We'll find a way to do this Ravenbrook bloke in, don't fear," Carlos said vehemently. "It'll have to wait awhile until I'm free, of course. There's ways we can do it so's no one will ever know, and this land is so bloody vast we can chuck his body in one of these ravines and no one would be any the wiser."

Rem's blood ran cold. "No! You leave him be, you hear me?" he hissed. "I've made enough mistakes in my life, and I've paid hard for them. Somehow I'll find a way to get even with the bastard that don't involve killing."

Carlos grunted but said no more on that subject. After a lull when Rem thought he dozed, Carlos said, "Hey, I haven't told you the most important news yet, have I?"

"Depends. What else is there you have to say?"

"I found out where Papa hailed from in Spain. And something else."

His grin told Rem there was a lot more to his story to be told. "Oh, yes? Like what? We ain't descended from the King of Spain, are we?" he asked sarcastically.

"Not quite."

"So, go on. I can tell you're just busting to tell me all the details. Where did you find out this about our pa?"

Carlos pushed his hair back. "I met this bloke in Newgate," he said eagerly. "This old geezer was from a ship that had been doing a bit of pirating and smuggling of sorts. Nothing grand, but enough to get the captain and his crew arrested. This bloke shared my cell for a while, and we got to talking. What a bloody windbag. Wouldn't shut up. He was a pain in the arse—at first. But once I heard his tale I was glad he was forever going on about his travels."

Rem's interest was sparked. All tiredness left him as he demanded, "Get on with your bloody story then."

Carlos pulled a face. He was enjoying stretching out the tale. "Apparently he was on this ship in about '74, and there was a lad who'd been brought aboard by the captain." Carlos' enthusiasm grew as he said, "I worked it out. Pa would have been about ten then, and this bloke was almost the same age, that's why he remembered it so well. The kid was Spanish and his pa and ma were killed in some plague that wiped out his family a few years earlier. The captain told everyone at the time they'd been related to the royal family or something, but the crew all laughed it off. This boy couldn't speak their language then so didn't know what was going on."

"That don't prove a single thing." Rem's disappointment grew. "There must have been hundreds of Spanish kids brought to England about that time. How could you think it was our Pa?"

"I don't think, boyo, I know. Remember when Pa used to tell us about the captain and that ship?" Rem nodded, and he went on, "What was it called?"

Rem tipped his head back and closed an eye. "The Lady Mary or some such thing."

"Right, and this was the name of the ship these boys were on. And Pa always said he lived with his parents in a grand house overlooking the sea in a place called Cartagena."

"Yes," Rem said slowly. "But why didn't this captain ever take Pa back to Spain where he rightfully belonged? Pa stayed with the ship for years until the captain died."

"Well, it seems the Spanish declared war against Britain about that time, when the Americas were at war. There were battles going on all over the place in those years, and by the time Spain and the old country were ganging up against the Frenchies the captain of The Lady Mary was sailing nearer home."

"So, that don't alter much." It was all in the past now.

"But it's good to know where Pa came from, don't you reckon?" Carlos seemed disappointed at Rem's lack of interest. "He came from good stock, Remy, my boy, and one day I'm going to Spain to search out my ancestors. Wouldn't you like to know exactly where you sprung from?"

"I suppose so." But right now Rem's priority was his reunion with Sara. And his meeting with his son. The thought made his insides shiver with apprehension and anticipation.

* * *

"Psst!" Rem shook his brother's shoulder, and Carlos' eyes shot open.

"What?" Carlos sat up, immediately wide awake.

"I'm off now," Rem whispered. "Thought I'd get going before the sun comes up."

"Right, good idea. Watch out, man." Carlos came onto his knees and laid a hand on Rem's shoulder. "Don't get into any strife." He looked about. "You sure this is the spot?"

"Yeah. The only thing that'll fox me is if the undergrowth has covered all the track. I'll catch up with you again as soon as I can. If anyone wants to know where I am, don't forget to tell them what we planned."

"Right." Carlos nodded. "You buried your woman along the trail and you want to go visit her grave. I doubt any of these codgers'll worry too much. They mind their own business, and won't do anything even if they are interested."

"I'm banking on that." Rem stood and cuffed Carlos about the ear gently. "Behave yourself. I don't want to lose you now I've found you again."

"Never fear. I don't want to go back to Sydney and the old treadmill, so I'll do all I can to stay out of trouble." He pushed himself up.

"See that you do." Rem hugged his brother, picked up the bag containing his water bottle and a chunk of bread, cheese and beef saved over the past couple of days. With a wave he stealthily left the campsite.

Carlos was more or less right: being a free man, no one paid him much heed. One of the travelers' daughters had been eyeing him with interest since they left town, and she would be about the only one to say anything.

Keeping an outcrop of rock in his sights, he trod carefully. The last thing he needed was to tread on a snake.

A rustle to his right made him jump, but when a large kangaroo bounded off, he grinned.

It was almost light by the time he reached the outcrop. He now turned left and hoped his instincts were guiding him in the right direction. The trees had grown so much since he passed this way with Lulu it was useless to try to use them as markers.

"Thank God," he sighed as he reached a pile of rocks he had put there all those years ago. Wild beasts had trampled the area, thankfully treading the grasses and bracken so the marker still stood out, the branch he set in its midst askew, but still there.

Now, he estimated he had about five hundred paces to go before he reached the clearing. Would the hut still be there? Perhaps another lone miner inhabited it.

After an hour or so of trampling through the undergrowth, Rem began to lose heart. He'd marked trees, broken stems from bushes and left branches to point his direction, and it became clear he had backtracked. Cursing, he retraced his steps until he found the last marked tree, and then changed direction. Sweat poured down his face, dripped from his chin and soaked his shirt.

Suddenly he broke into a clearing, and there it was.

The dwelling was barely standing, a wall completely gone, the roof sagging. Obviously no human inhabited it. A shiver raced over his skin when he thought of the man at the bottom of the mineshaft nearby. Taking a swallow from his water bottle, he looked about and took his bearings. It had changed so much, and a desolate air hung about the place. He shuddered, remembering Lulu and her sweetness.

At least she was at peace now. Pulling himself up, he turned and paced away to the place where they buried the gold. A sense of guilt washed over him as he began to dig. This was her gold, not his. Still, no sense in leaving it here; she would have wanted him to make use of it.

Sweat poured from every pore by the time he uncovered his cache. There was too much for one man to carry. Now he knew the whereabouts of the cabin for sure and that no one lived here, he could always come back at a later date. Once he saw Sara and his son, and they decided on their future, he would return. He packed as much as he could carry on his person, in his pockets, and then filled the cloth sack he brought along.

* * *

"Well, how'd it go?" Carlos rose from his place by the fire and held out a hand to Rem.

"As you see I got what I went after. We're made for life, boyo." Rem shook his brother's hand, and they both sat. The night was warm and they were well away from the dying fires built to cook the evening meal. "I had a bit of trouble finding the spot, but got there eventually."

"What you going to do with that?" Carlos gestured to the sack Rem placed on the ground at their feet.

"Keep it as near at hand as I can. I'll roll it in my blanket. As long as no one guesses what it is there should be no trouble. Did anyone wonder where I'd gone?"

"The teamsters were curious when you didn't show up for the noonday meal. I told them you'd had a touch of diarrhea and would catch up with us as soon as you felt better." Carlos laughed as he punched Rem's arm.

"That's as good an excuse as any, I suppose."

"The little fair-haired chit was asking after you. She knew I was your brother and got up the courage to venture near enough to question me. I told her the story about your wife's grave, and she looked mighty pleased when she found out you don't have a live wife somewhere."

Rem groaned. "Lord, that's the last thing I need. I'll have to tell her I have a sweetheart."

"I'll give her the eye; I reckon she'll prefer me to you when she finds out what a fine specimen I am." Carlos smoothed his hair back and pulled himself up straight.

"Keep away from her, Carlos. Wait until you're a free man before you start eyeing the innocent young girls of the colony. Take my word for it, it's the best path," Rem advised. "Now, no one must guess what I went after; there's no telling what lengths a man will go to for gold."

Now he had it in his grasp, Rem wasn't about to give up his wealth for anyone. "Let's get some shut-eye. I'm whacked." Rem went to retrieve his bedroll and meager stash of belongings. The women were in their tents, and the teamsters who were smoking their pipes passed a few ribald comments on his supposed condition but other than that no one paid him any heed.

Chapter Twenty

Rem set his bundle of belongings on the ground and wiped his sweaty palms down his trousers as he paused to gaze at the house Tiger Carstairs built for Bella. It fitted in with its surroundings as if it had been there forever instead of six years. Solid, it would likely stand forever.

He had left the teamsters and Carlos at the barracks. Bathurst now had an inn, a church, but still no bank. More settlers were coming over but it was still not too different to when he'd left. The area had been plagued by drought. How had Tiger fared?

Eager now to meet up with his sister, he picked up his bundle and strode purposefully toward the orchard, pausing again when he reached the spot where he'd first kissed Sara. It seemed so long ago, and he was a different person from the carefree young man back then. Would Sara think he'd changed? How could a man endure what he had and not change irrevocably? But one thing hadn't changed, and that was his love for Sara, the woman of his heart.

He saw Bella before she glimpsed him. As always, her serene beauty astounded him. She stood on the porch, wiping her hands on her apron. "Tim!" he heard her call. Then she looked in his direction and he saw her press a hand over her heart, saw her lips move. "Remy." His name burst out in a near shout.

"Aye, 'tis your no-good brother," he cried, dropping his roll and rushing toward her as she jumped the steps in two leaps to throw herself into his arms.

Tears fell unchecked down her face as she wrapped her arms about him, whispering his name over and over. "Let me look at you." Finally she stepped back a pace to stare at him. Her eyes missed nothing, he knew. "Oh, Remy, it's so good to see you. I thought I'd never set eyes on you again, you rogue." She sniffed and wiped at her face with her apron hem. "What have they done to you?" His Bella was never one to mince words.

"Nothing I want to talk about right now. You're looking good, plump as a mother hen. Where's Tiger? And Tim? And how many little 'uns have you got that I haven't seen? Has the count reached ten yet?" Rem wiped at his own eyes, unashamed of the tears dampening his cheeks.

"Not quite. Come on inside." She began to drag him up the steps. "Tiger's due back any time. He'll be so pleased to see you—and Tim will be overjoyed. He's never forgotten you, Rem, and is always asking after you. The little blighter is likely off fishing. The minute his schooling is over he's off with his dogs to the river bank."

"It's so good to be back." Rem sniffed the familiar aromas of pine, beeswax, and good meat cooking.

"Gracie, come see who's here," Bella shouted as Rem tossed his hat on the hallstand.

Bella's old housekeeper came from the kitchen, she too wiping her hands on her apron. She beamed when she caught sight of Rem. "Well, look what the cat's brought in," she cackled as she came to hug him.

Too choked to speak, Rem breathed deeply and let the air of happiness that pervaded this home sink into his beleaguered soul.

* * *

Rem had never been so nervous in his life. Dressed in one of Tiger's linen shirts and a pair of his tan breeches, he looked about as presentable as he was likely to get. Bella had trimmed his hair, but it still curled around his nape. He dismounted Tiger's sorrel gelding and straightened his shoulders as he tied the reins to the post before the house. A lad of about fifteen appeared from one of the barns and loped over to him.

"Shall I unsaddle yer 'orse, sir?" he asked as he touched his forelock.

Rem hid a grin. Sir? He shook his head. "No, lad, I'm not sure if I'll be staying that long." Uncertain of what welcome awaited him here, he was sure Sara's father would likely send him packing. "Is anybody home?" He held his breath, supposing she chose to go off visiting today.

"The young mistress is out back, playing with the boy in the garden," the lad said, turning as if to run off. "I'll tell her she has a visitor, shall I?"

"No." Rem caught at his sleeve. "I'd like to surprise her. I'm an old friend."

"Right you are." The lad took off back to the barn.

Rem gulped in a few deep breaths. Suddenly, he felt deprived of air. So long he had waited for this moment, and now it had arrived he was almost scared to approach her.

With a last resolute stiffening of his spine, he walked slowly along a path winding through a flowerbed, beneath wattles and gum trees. Someone had obviously taken the time to work on the garden. It was in a better condition than when he'd left.

As he turned the corner, Rem caught the sound of a woman's laughter drifting across to him. He would know that laugh anywhere. Then a boy's shout followed by childish giggles made Rem stop in his tracks. A lump the size of a round of cheese lodged itself somewhere halfway up his throat.

He strode on. And there she was. Sitting beneath a small shade-house, she wore a pink dress that showed off her creamy throat. Her midnight dark hair was piled high on her head. Rem had never seen a more beautiful sight in his life.

He cleared his throat and her eyes shot to meet his. Until his dying day, he would never forget her instant smile, the pleasure that lit her features when she saw him.

"Remy!" As she shouted his name she was on her feet, flying toward him, and then hurling herself into his arms. This was heaven. If he died this instant, he would die happy. "Sweet heaven, where did you spring from?" she demanded, laughing and crying at the same time. "Bella said you would arrive soon, but we had no idea exactly when. Oh, Remy, it's so good to see you."

Rem caught her close, covering her mouth in a kiss that was perfection. He savored the sweet taste of her, while his hands roved intimately, relearning her beloved shape.

When at last their mouths separated, he rasped, "I came as soon as I could." Keeping her within his embrace, he ran his hands up and down her spine. "It's so good to hold you again, my love. I have to tell you I thought this day would never come."

"I know. I felt the same. So much has happened. First, I have someone you should meet." She turned to beckon to the child, who stared at Rem from eyes that were a replica of Sara's. His shoulder length mane was the identical color to Rem's own, its curls as unruly as his were in his youth. "William, come meet my friend." Sara extended a hand.

The boy was tall for a near three-year-old, and sturdy. Pride swelled in Rem's chest.

"I heard we had a son," Rem choked out as the child came tentatively forward.

"How?" She gave him a quizzical look.

"I went in search of you when I got back to town. The woman at Ravenbrook's house told me you'd had a son eleven months before the fair one I saw with Ravenbrook."

"You saw my other boy? How is he? Did he look well?" She fired the questions at him as her eyes clouded with anxiety. "He sent me away, and I had to leave without my baby."

Rem placed a hand on her waist. "He had a young woman there to look after him."

"But was he well? Oh, Remy, I miss my baby," she wailed.

"He looked fine to me. Clean and well-fed. Hello." His son clung on her skirts now and Rem went down on his haunches. The boy's eyes were serious but showed keen interest.

"You my papa?" he asked in a childish lisp, and Rem nearly keeled over.

"What will I say?" Rem looked up at Sara imploringly as he laid a hand on the boy's dark head. The hair felt like silk beneath his fingers.

"I guess the best thing to say is yes," Sara said softly, coming down to his level and resting on her knees. "Might as well start with the truth. Yes, William, this is your papa. He's been hearing about you since he was old enough to speak, Remy. So he knew his papa would be tall with hair that matched his own." She put a hand on the boy's back and gently nudged him. "Give your papa a hug."

Rem's eyes misted until he could barely see his son's face as he opened his arms and pulled William close. "Hello, son," he whispered, his lips pressed to the softness of his hair, breathing in the scent of childhood, sunshine, and grass. His heart felt as if it would explode as he relished the moment.

"I never thought to see you again," he said to Sara, looking up over William's head. "And to find I had a son makes me the happiest man alive."

"I never thought I'd see you again, either." She ran a hand over his cheek, and Rem swallowed, emotion choking him. "Having my son was some consolation, and I thought that was all I would have for the rest of my life."

She nodded to the young girl who came from the back of the house, saying, "William, you go off now with Maisie."

"Hello," Rem said to the young girl who watched him with rounded eyes.

"Sir." She bobbed a curtsy. Rem laughed at her reddened cheeks as she took William's hand and they went off together, William telling her that the big man was his papa.

"She came with you," he said.

"Yes, she's been a good friend. Wouldn't stay behind in that house, even though she hated leaving my baby as much as I did." Her voice choked on that. "She loves William, and takes good care of him."

"I'm glad you had one friend in that house. Where's your father?" Rem had wondered this all during their reunion, fully expecting the man to come blustering in at any moment.

"Father's a sick man." She sighed, shrugging slightly. "He spends most of the time in his room these days."

"I'm sorry about that. He was never my favorite person, but I wouldn't wish that on anyone."

"He was never very patient, but now he's confined to bed so much his temper often explodes."

"Does your mother care for him?"

"My mother died while I was in Sydney living with Clive." She took his hand and led him to the bench.

"I'm sorry about that too." Rem hadn't held any affection for either of Sara's parents, but harbored gratitude for bringing his love into the world.

She waved his sympathy aside. "My mother was never a healthy person. She took sick with a fever and faded away. It's sad, but I have to be honest and say I couldn't feel any deep grief at her passing. Do you remember Josie?"

"Ah, yes, the dragon lady who wouldn't let you out of her sight?" Rem chuckled.

Sara smiled. "The very one. She also died, soon after my mother. Unfortunately, I felt little sadness for her either. And my father's vile foreman, Luxton, met with a mysterious end, it seems." She shuddered. "He was apparently found one day on the far side of the property with his neck broken. I know it's wrong to say so, but I was so relieved. If he'd still been around I couldn't have stood it here. All the men hated him, and it's my opinion he was done in by one or more of the convicts."

"What makes you think that, love?"

"Do you remember Dick, the watchdog who accompanied me on all my rides?"

"Yes, I remember him well, I wished him to blazes many times." Rem smiled, but when he saw how sad she looked, he wiped it from his face, asking, "What happened to the young lad?"

"Luxton whipped him one day, so the new lad told me, and the poor boy was in such a bad way the doctor had to be called in from the barracks. He was heard to castigate my father for allowing such brutality to occur on his property. They took Dick to the military hospital, and he never returned here. It was hinted that the laborers decided to mete out their own justice."

"Seems likely." Rem shuddered as he relived his own flogging. "Tell me how and why you came back." Rem caressed the hand he held, wishing to get as far away from those memories as possible.

Such sadness crossed her face that for a moment Rem wondered if she once harbored some feeling for Ravenbrook. His stomach muscles tightened.

"Clive packed me off as soon as my baby was three months old. He brought in a wet-nurse, and swore I would never set eyes on my baby again." A sob tore from her throat and Rem pulled her into his arms, pressing her face against his chest. "I didn't want his child, Remy, but once I held the mite in my arms I fell in love with him. He was so fair compared to William, who is so dark like his father." She drew back and toyed with the ribbon at her waist. "He forced himself on me. I never went willingly to him, you must believe that." Her imploring look tore at his heart.

Rem sighed his relief. "God, Sara, I'll kill him for what he put you through."

"No, Remy!" She clutched at his hand. "I told you once before, I don't want you facing the magistrate for such a crime. All I want is my other son back."

"You'll have him," Rem promised. "Some way we'll get him out of Ravenbrook's house." There had to be a way. How, he had no idea, but he would move heaven and earth to get her heart's desire.

"You never will," she cried dejectedly. "He swore I would never see him again. He raped me, simply to get his child in me, then threw me and William out, vowing he would break you if ever you showed up in Sydney."

Rem cupped her jaw. "Every man has a soft spot, and Ravenbrook's is greed. I have gold, Sara, lots of it. Somehow we'll find a way to get your child back, I swear."

"Thank you." She brought his hand to her lips and Rem pulled her close again. For a few moments they held each other, and Rem breathed in her scent, his eyes closed. Tears threatened to fall as emotion overwhelmed him.

"Where did you get gold?" she asked at length.

Rem related the full story about Lulu and how they buried the gold. "There's more there, Sara, enough to keep us comfortable for the rest of our days. Enough to set up our son's future."

"Clive will never divorce me, Remy," she said on a small sad sigh. "He swore no other man would ever wed me. He doesn't want me for himself but wants no other man to have me."

Rem swore softly as he got up, pacing away. "There has to be a way to get him to release you from this farce of a marriage." He ran a hand through his hair.

"Even if he did release me he'll never let me have my baby. And I couldn't bear to think that he might remarry and another woman would have my child in her care." Sara came over and laid a hand on Rem's chest. He caressed it, hating the sadness in her eyes. He would get her child for her or die in the attempt. "Did Clive know you visited the house?"

"No, I waited until he drove away. The woman who answered the door didn't know who I was so he'd have no idea it was me even if she told him I'd been asking questions."

"What will you do now?" she asked uncertainly.

"Whatever you want me to do, my love. My life is in these hands." Rem kissed each palm. "Do you want to stay here in your father's house? Or do you wish to return to town with me and hope we can find a way to make your dreams come true."

"I want to be with you, Remy." She stroked his cheek, adding with a touch of shyness, "If you want me."

"Want you?" Rem shook her gently and kissed her again. "You are my life. Everything to me. I would go back alone to try and get your child for you, but it would be perfect if you came with me."

"Then we'll go together." Her smile was radiant. "I hate my father for what he forced me into. He never speaks to me anymore and barely tolerates me in his house. If he could get up from his sick-bed, I swear at times he would toss me out as Clive did."

Rem called Edmund Greenwood a vile name beneath his breath. "God, Sara, what a mess he's made of your life."

She pressed her fingertips over his lips. "Hush, love, we're together again. That's all that matters."

"Yes, you're right." Rem kissed her lightly, his body flaring to life. "Did I tell you I love you with all my heart?" he whispered against her lips.

She sighed. "You told me when I was young and foolish, and I didn't believe you." Her wistful smile held regret and a plaintive wretchedness that touched him to the core.

"Do you believe me now, my dear one?" He kissed the corners of her mouth.

"With all my heart." Her eyes glistened as she cupped his jaw in her hands and then pressed her lips to his. Rem folded her in his arms, his heart brimming with emotions too long kept in check, his eyes overflowing with tears he was unable to stem.

Nothing else mattered. Somehow they would surmount all obstacles as long as they had each other and their shared love.

* * *

Rem dismounted, tethering the horse to a low branch. Shielding his eyes, he looked off into the distance when his horse whinnied and raised its head. His heart did a quick turn as Sara neared.

"Hello, love," he said huskily as he helped her dismount and then tethered her horse beside his own.

"Have you been waiting long?" She seemed nervous, and he wondered if she was experiencing the same heart-stopping emotions he felt right now.

"I've just arrived. But I've been waiting all my life for this moment. Come, let's sit over here in the shade." He led her to a spot beneath the drooping branches of the river gum and spread out a blanket. They sank onto it together.

Rem pulled her immediately into his arms. "Sweet heavens, it seems like an eternity since we were like this," he muttered as his mouth descended. Their lips fused, all the pent-up passion of years exploding. Rem pushed her gently back and half covered her body with his. "I'm sorry, love, I'm in a fever for you. I want to be gentle, to make this last, but I'm finding it hard to control myself."

"It's all right. I feel the same," she assured him, her hands trembling as she ran them over his ears, then around his neck. "I want you desperately. Make love to me, my Remy."

With a fevered haste, they undressed each other. Their coming together was like a conflagration, a meeting of two wild spirits. As they lay replete and panting in each other's arms, Sara ran her fingers over his shoulders then down his back.

When she encountered the first scar, the horror was clear in her eyes. Jerking upright, her glorious hair cascaded down her back as she stared at the ugly welts on his skin. "My darling, what did they do to you?" she cried.

"Sorry, love, I'm not a pretty sight, am I?" He grunted as he turned onto his back and pulled her over him.

She pressed kisses on his chest as her tears dampened the curls there. "You're the best sight my eyes have ever seen. What happened? Why were you flogged?" she asked on a choking sob, holding him tightly.

"Nothing much." Rem shrugged. The blanket felt rough beneath his skin. "A man didn't have to do a lot wrong up there to earn a flogging. I think I upset the corporal. I can't remember." But he remembered every one of those lashes—would until his dying day. "Let's not talk about that." Cupping her breasts, he ran his thumbs over her nipples. "Just let me love you. Now I'm with you I want to forget the past. Live for now and plan for the future. A future with you and our son."

She bent to kiss him, and Rem pulled her hard against his body. Only with her could he forget the past, forget all the pain and anguish once suffered.

"I never thought we'd be together like this again," she whispered, her lips hovering above his. "I dreamed of you night after night, remembered every tiny part of our last time together."

"It was all that kept me alive." Rem rolled them over, covering her precious body, his eyes holding hers as he planted gentle kisses on her face and throat. "I would remember the feel and taste of you. Remember your beautiful eyes"—he kissed each eyelid—"hot with wanting as they are now. Would lie on my bed and forget the heat and the stench of sickness and filth surrounding me and dwell in a world where there was just you and me. As now. You are my life."

"As you are mine, Remy. Now, love me."

"Your wish is my command." Rem let his mouth trail down her body, his lips rapacious as they worshipped every part of her, every curve and soft mound. "Having babies has made you more beautiful," he whispered as he paid homage to her beauty with his lips, until she shuddered with her need.

When he finally entered her, they both moaned aloud at the sheer ecstasy of it. Sara's long legs wrapped about his waist, and her arms encircled his body, her fingers lovingly running over the scars on his back.

And he was healed. With her love, he could become a whole man again.

* * *

"Come over here, woman!" Sara cringed as she eyed her father's prone body. She stifled a shudder. The room

216

smelt of sickness and decay. If she ever liked her father in any miniscule way, that liking dissolved long ago, and all she felt now was intense dislike and a smidgeon of pity.

"Why did you want to see me, Father?" She moved to stand by his bed. "How are you?" She asked the question out of duty and not any real desire to know how he felt. If perhaps he'd spared her a moment's pity for the morass he forced her into, she might have spared a thought for the pain he must be enduring.

He waved both queries aside with a flick of the hand he still had a small amount of use in. "I hear the convict half-breed has been sniffing around," he growled.

Sara pressed her lips together. He couldn't hurt her any more by his cruel words.

"What did he want?" he demanded.

"Remy came to see me and his son," she said clearly, her head high. "And for your information he is no longer a convict without means."

"Is that so? I suppose you're going to tell me he's a man of importance, eh?"

"Remy was always important in my eyes, Father. You were the one who was blind and refused to see past the fact that he was a convict. Remy is an honorable man, and I'm returning to Sydney with him. He will help me regain custody of my other son from that scoundrel you forced me to marry!" Her hands clenched into fists as she glared at him.

"Is that so? And just how does he intend to accomplish that, eh?" His mouth twisted in what she presumed was a smile, and his face looked like an ugly gargoyle.

"We have no idea at this stage, but one thing I'm certain of is that Remy will do all in his power to make me happy. Something nobody has ever considered worth the effort before."

Sara turned to leave, but was stopped at the door when he called, "Princess."

So stunned was she by his use of the pet name that she went back to stand by the bed. "Yes, Father?"

217

For a moment his mouth contorted as he seemed to fight for use of it; then he said gruffly, "Go to the top drawer of the bureau."

Sara did as asked and opened the drawer. Papers lay there in disarray. She looked back to him.

"Take out the bound papers," he ordered.

There was only one bound packet of papers, so she picked these up and held them out. "These?"

"Yes, fetch them over here."

Sara put them on the bedcover by the hand that had some use in it. He picked the bundle up and tapped it on the bed while he seemed to contemplate her for endless moments.

"These are the deeds to the emporium in town," he finally said.

Sara nodded, unsure what to say.

"You realize that as my only heir you get everything on my death, don't you?" he said.

"To be honest, Father, I don't want anything from you," Sara said bluntly. "All I ever wanted was to be loved and admired. You denied me both. You treated my mother as if she were of no account and treated me only slightly better. As far as I'm concerned you can give your emporium to the first charitable group that comes along."

The shock on his face, despite its grotesqueness, was something that would have been laughable if it wasn't so pitiable. Then he began to laugh, a horrible sound. The laughter turned into a fit of coughing. Sara supported his head and held a glass containing water to his lips.

Once he caught his breath, he lay back on the pillow and closed his eyes. Sara turned to go, but he called her back.

Waving the bundle of papers, he thrust them at her. "Take these, you fool. Never turn down wealth. Do as you like with it—give it away if you so desire. I have no use for it now." Morosely he glared around the room. "But think on this, woman. You have a son—something that was denied me. The property will be worth a fortune one day, and when I'm gone you can sell this place too if you want. But mark my words, one day you'll thank me."

His eyes closed as he dragged in a few breaths, the air gurgling in his throat. Sara doubted she would ever thank her father for anything, but he was right. If not for herself, but for her sons, she would take what he offered. He had given her little else in life of worth.

Lifting the bundle from his lax fingers, she turned and left the room.

Chapter Twenty-One

January 1832

"You right, son?" Rem tipped his hat at the boy excitedly waving his arms and bouncing up and down on the wagon seat.

"Yea."

Rem grinned. That seemed to be his son's favorite word, one picked up from Bella's boys. William followed Tim's every word and action. Rem lifted a hand to wave to Tim, now riding alongside one of the drays. Taller than the average twelve-year-old, the lad sat tall in the saddle. Bella had entrusted him in their care. She wanted him to have a good education and considered the best way to achieve that was to send him back to town so he could attend Kings School. This hadn't pleased Tim greatly, especially having to leave his beloved animals behind. He talked Sara into letting him bring along one of his dogs, and the dog now ambled along at his horse's side.

Tim was interested in animal husbandry and embarrassed Sara at times with his forthright way of discussing their peculiarities.

"How you faring, love?" Rem turned in the saddle to glance behind them. The teamsters were cursing at their oxen, as usual. They'd been on the road since sun-up, and the mountains loomed ahead.

"I'm fine. Don't worry about me. I'm getting used to doing this journey. I wish it wasn't so hot though." Sara lifted a hand to her brow, and Rem frowned. There'd been a fire raging near the new settlement of Blayney for two days, and he fervently hoped it didn't veer their way.

"I still feel guilty about leaving Tiger and Bella with a fire in the vicinity," he said. "But if we hadn't come along with this group it might have been weeks before we found traveling companions back to town."

Although the bushrangers seemed to have forsaken the mountain road, it was always safer to travel with a larger group. And with his stash of gold, the last thing he needed was to have his gear searched. He intended to pick up the rest of the gold when they passed the spot. He had paid Tiger, despite his brother-in-law's admonishments, for the wagon, horses, and enough clothing to tide him over until they reached Sydney.

Rem was mightily pleased to see Carlos settled in at Tiger's property. As Rem guessed, Tiger easily organized it so Carlos could be signed over to him. Bella was overjoyed to have another of her kin living in her house. All they prayed for now was that Bob, the young fellow, would soon manage to get a passage out here.

* * *

They made good traveling time, but Sara was weary when they made camp for the night near Fish River.

"Take William off to your tent now, Maisie," she said when she saw her son's eyes drooping.

Maisie was as pleased as she to leave her father's house. Sara only saw her father once after he'd given her the deeds to the store, and he barely said more than two words to her at that meeting. She feared his mind was failing along with his body, for he looked at her as if she were a stranger, which after all, was all she was to him.

"You look tired, Sara. What say we go to our tent, too," Rem suggested once they had eaten, and Sara returned his suggestive smile. All day she'd been filled with anticipation for the coming night. A night she knew would hold far more pleasure than the dreadful ones on the road she endured with Clive Ravenbrook, and the nights of misery when Rem was so near but out of her reach.

There were three teamsters and their wool-laden drays and three covered wagons in the group. One of the six soldiers traveling with them drove Sara's wagon. The only

221

other civilians were an elderly couple who had been living with their daughter in Bathurst, but due to the husband's illness were returning to town where they owned a store.

Sara didn't know if they thought Rem and she were husband and wife or not, and wasn't really worried if they knew the truth. She'd passed being coy a long time ago and decided to grab at her chance at happiness. Clive would never release her, so if others saw it as living in sin there was little she could do. That was their problem.

"Is William asleep?" Rem lifted the tent flap and waited for her to crawl inside before dropping it back into place.

"Yes, he and Maisie are curled up together like a pair of puppies."

"And Tim and his dog are snuggled together beneath the stars." Rem laughed as Sara straightened their bedding.

But his smile disappeared as she began to unpin her hair. His eyes grew hot as he watched her. "Let me do that for you." Tossing his shirt to one side, he bent to the task. "It's stifling in here, but I couldn't bear the thought of sleeping out in the open where others could see us. I want you all to myself this night, Sara."

"I want that to." What if she appeared wanton; she didn't really care. "I've spent too many years without you, Remy. Spent too many days and weeks thinking I'd never see you again. Never feel your touch. Would you undo my buttons?" She lifted the hair that now reached almost to her waist, giving him access to the fastenings of her bodice.

"Willingly." His fingers trembled. Sara shared his excitement. Tremors raced through her at his touch. He pushed her bodice over her shoulders, kissing his way down her spine as he bared her flesh to his mouth.

"Now let me help you," she said, turning to kneel before him. Together they undid his breeches, and by the time he'd tossed them aside, along with his boots, they were both panting.

Rem blew out the lamp. "I fear I won't be able to control myself," he gasped when they were facing each other on the blanket.

"I don't want you controlled, Remy. I want you so filled with desire you can't wait to be inside me. How I long to be in your arms, to be kissed and caressed by you. In the long lonely years we've been apart, I dreamed of us being together like this. Promise me, no matter what, that you'll never leave me again."

"Never, my love. I promise you this, I'll never leave you willingly again in this lifetime, and I'll love you for eternity."

"That's all I ask," she whispered as he caressed her until she was delirious with desire for him. "Nobody could ever excite me as you do. No one could make me weak with longing with just a kiss or a touch as you do."

With his hands and mouth, he brought her to the peak of her desire, and only then did he enter her warm, welcoming body.

His moaned words of passion were like a litany of praise. Sweat wreathed their entwined bodies, and the fire of their desire bathed them in a sheen of sweet abandon.

* * *

"Sara, where are you?" Rem let himself into the house they'd bought on Philip Street, near Saint James' Church and the courthouse. Sara fell in love with it on sight, and they'd been in it a week.

"I'm in here," she called from the downstairs parlor. "Come in and let me know what you think of these drapes."

Rem joined her, putting his arms about her and nuzzling her neck. "I love them," he muttered against her sweet smelling skin.

"You haven't even looked at them, you rogue," she said on a laugh as she turned in his embrace and looped her arms about his neck.

"Anything you choose will be fine by me, love. I have news."

"Of Clive?" The smile died on her lips.

223

"Mm." He kissed her before adding, "He's in debt, drinking even more heavily than ever, and is now regularly smoking opium."

"Where did you find out all this? Did you hear news of my boy?" She left him to sit in one of the only two padded chairs they possessed.

Rem sat on the other chair after pulling it up until they touched knees. "At one of the taverns, of course."

The furniture was on order from the craftsman, but they would have to wait a few weeks for it to be delivered. Meanwhile, they made do with the bare necessities. Rem proclaimed he didn't care if they never had chairs, as long as they had a bed. That was their first acquisition—a huge four-poster with elaborate hangings.

Having made herself known at the emporium, Sara now had a solicitor dealing with the formalities of ownership. The man and his wife who managed it were trustworthy and able, and she was content to let them carry on as before. Rem cared not a whit about the business but was pleased for Sara, who found one benefit of owning a store; she had instant delivery of all the goods required to outfit a house and first pick of any new stock that arrived.

Rem, meanwhile, was negotiating to buy a warehouse near the wharf and carried out most of his dealings with the vendors in a tavern. He found it was normal for transactions to be dealt with over a glass or two of ale or rum. Gossip traveled fast through these places and rarely did anything happen in the colony that wasn't discussed by all and sundry.

"It's common knowledge that the man in question has been barred from his club. His debts are so great the house is mortgaged to the hilt. The bailiffs took away some of his paintings." Rem rubbed his palms together.

"I can't believe it! What of his property in England? And his interests here in Sydney? Surely he can't be bankrupt."

Rem shifted uneasily. "Everything he owned here has been liquidated. Sara, rumor has it he intends to sail for England within a fortnight."

She gasped, a hand to her mouth, eyes stricken. "What you're telling me is he intends to take my son to England. We must do something. Remy, we must get him away."

Rem gripped her hands. She was shaking. "Of course we will, love. I'm sure he can't really want a boy along with him—not if all the rumors about his true state are well-founded. And I can't see that they can be wrong. Three people told me the same story. He'll accept gold, I'm sure of it."

In her anguish, she didn't appear to be listening to him. "He'll take my son with him, just to spite me. I know he will," she cried. "We have to get him away from that brute!"

"Of course we do, and I'll move heaven and earth to get him for you. You must believe me."

"I believe you." She let him pull her into his arms. "But how will you do this?

Rem had no idea. If all else failed he would kidnap the child. There were enough people in Sydney who would go to any lengths, do almost anything, for gold.

* * *

Sara worried her lower lip as she walked along the uneven pathway. Soon she and Rem would have a garden flourishing here behind the house. Would Rem find out any more today? He talked of arranging a meeting with Ravenbrook, perhaps making some sort of bargain. Ravenbrook must be eager for funds; surely he would accept Rem's offer.

"Go with Maisie, William." Sara patted her son's head. "I'll be in shortly. It's time for your lunch." Sara watched as Maisie walked away with him clutching her hand and babbling on nineteen to the dozen.

How she loved him. She sighed. The ache that never went away filled her soul. Could her younger son talk yet? He was only a baby still, but William was such a bright boy and had talked clearly when her baby's age. Did he ever

225

ask for his mother, or did he think his nursemaid is his mama?

It was so hot. Mopping her neck with her handkerchief, she turned to go into the coolness of the house when a sudden movement to her right startled her. Before she had a chance to turn her head, a cloth covered her, muffling the scream that tore from her throat. Someone tightened a rope about her middle, trapping her flailing arms, thwarting all movement.

"Get 'er legs," her captor growled, then her feet were yanked up, and she was hauled over broad shoulders. She kicked as her legs were released, but then the second person wrapped something coarse around her ankles. The one carrying her began to move. Sara screamed, but the sound came out as a croak. The stink of sweat, filth and urine filled her nostrils, making her retch.

"Put 'er in, quick." At the muttered order she was thrown unceremoniously into what she presumed was a carriage as she heard its springs creak. Without a moment's pause, the vehicle moved off. Sara struggled against the restraining band about her middle.

"Now, now, ain't no use in doing' that, me girl. Keep still and quiet and no 'arm'll come to ya." She was whacked on the bottom. Sara cringed away from his heat and stink.

It had been sultry for days, the February sun beating down relentlessly from a cloudless sky and today a hot wind blew. Since their arrival in town small fires had burned on the outskirts, the smoke billowing over Sydney. Sara began to perspire; in no time, the sweat soaked her underthings. She couldn't breathe and panic overwhelmed her. She would suffocate! Who were these thugs, and what did they intend to do with her?

Fear wrapped itself around her insides, clutching at her until she felt faint. Why would anyone want to capture her? Then it came to her.

Clive! Of course, only one person would hate her enough to want to harm her.

The vehicle halted; it hadn't traveled far, so they were probably still in the midst of town. "Up yer get." She was hauled over the man's shoulder again. She heard a gruff laugh and instantly recognized its owner. Brace. Yes, Clive was responsible for her capture. But what on earth could he hope to gain by this?

Roughly, she was dumped onto her feet and then the cloth was dragged from her head. But the rope still bound her arms. Her two abductors were rough types; both men unshaven, their clothes dirty and disheveled. What had Clive sunk to, to enlist the help of such cutthroats?

Oh, well, she was soon to find out. One of the men bent to release her ankles from their binding and shoved her in the back, pushing her in the direction of the sitting room.

Sara pulled in a deep breath and straightened her shoulders. Her nerves were so taut her stomach ached as she was urged through the open door.

The room was bare of furniture, except for two wing-backed chairs flanking the fireplace, and a small side table. Her husband sat in one chair, a fluted glass held in his long fingers. His hair was now white as snow, his pale eyes expressionless. Sara marveled they hadn't bumped into Ravenbrook since being back in town, but presumed he rarely ventured out during the day. It was almost too much to bear, knowing her small son was so near, yet unapproachable. On the occasions when near the house, it took every shred of willpower to resist knocking on the door, just to see what her reception would be.

Perhaps she now had the chance to see her baby. But Ravenbrook was as trustworthy as a snake; there was little chance it would be so easy. She swallowed uneasily as she glanced about. The only happiness known in this house had been joy in her children.

"So, we meet again." Clive's mouth curved in a malicious little smirk. Her two captors had left and closed the door after them.

"What have you brought me here for?" Sara cried. "Have you sunk so low you would use brute force on your wife?"

227

"Wife? You are no wife of mine." He flapped a hand. "Take a seat."

"I prefer to stand," she snapped, glancing at the closed door. "Why have you done this? Remy will come after me—he'll kill you!"

"I'm banking on it." He sipped his drink, watching her over the glass. "You've grown more beautiful with the passing of time."

Sara ignored his compliment. "Ah, I see." She did. He had brought her here to hold her for ransom.

"I hear O'Shea has gold to throw about."

"I've heard you're in debt and have your creditors chasing you."

"True. So he has gold, and I need cash badly. Very badly." His long fingers toyed with the stem of the glass.

"You didn't have to do this, you know. You have a better bargaining tool. All you have to do is give me my son, and we would willingly give you all you asked in exchange."

His face darkened. "Do you take me for a fool? You will never see your son again."

"No!"

"Yes. We leave for England shortly. Clive will never know who his mother is. You're dead to him and always will be."

Sara let out a cry of despair. "Why? Why are you doing this to me? You don't want a boy hanging around. If you give me my son Remy will willingly give you all that you ask. He'll give you all his gold."

"I don't doubt he'll part with all his wealth in exchange for your sweet neck." He lifted a glass from the table and came to stand near her. She recoiled from the smell of cigars, sweat, and decay about him. His brows drew together. "You must be thirsty. This heat is abominable. I must say I'm looking forward to returning home. The cold of an English winter will be refreshing after this appalling heat. Your son will enjoy England. He will grow up as an English gentleman."

Sara bit back a retort. He was simply tormenting her. She would not rise to his bait.

Pulling out a kerchief from his pocket, he wiped his brow. "Here, drink this." He held the glass to her lips. She clamped them together. "Come, now, let's be civilized about this."

"Civilized? You?" she gasped out.

"Brace!" he yelled, and the door opened instantly. The hated driver entered. Sara noticed he held a cloth in one hand and a small bottle in the other. "The lady refuses to drink. Do as I suggested."

Before Sara had time to draw breath to scream, the cloth was jammed over her mouth. She heard Clive's sinister laugh, then nothing more.

* * *

Her mouth felt as if it was filled with sand, and her head throbbed as if someone had bashed her with a hammer.

"Wha...what happened?" Sara mumbled as her eyes shot open.

Dear Lord, where had he brought her? It was a small room, no larger than eight feet by eight feet, and not very high. She was tied securely to a post that supported the ceiling above her. Planks of wood were nailed across the single window, and leaves littered the rough boards beneath her, along with small branches and scraps of what looked like newspaper.

A scuffling behind her made her let out a squeal. Looking over a shoulder, Sara saw a rat scamper into a hole in the wall. The stench of animal droppings and filth made her retch.

"Clive!" His name came out on a hoarse shout as she struggled against her bonds.

It was so hot sweat dripped from her face, pooled between her breasts and legs. There was no answer to her call. The squawking of parrots filled the air.

229

The smell of smoke that had hovered about town was worse here. Sara shivered, despite the heat. Surely he hadn't left her to perish amid a fire. Even Ravenbrook couldn't be that callous. Or could he? She had no idea to what lengths he would go to get Remy's gold or to exact his revenge on Remy.

She tried to shout, but her throat became hoarse and who would hear her? He'd obviously brought her out of town. She strained her ears but could hear no sound of carriages or people. The town was always abuzz with both at any time of day or night.

Tugging at her bonds, she whimpered. They were so tight all her struggles did was chaff the skin of her wrists. "Help!" she yelled as loudly as she could manage.

"Now, now, my dear, there's no one here to help you. You might just as well save your energy." Clive's hated voice came from the other side of the door.

"Why have you done this?" she screamed.

"I should think that would be very obvious, you foolish female. I want the half-breed's gold. And I'll have it. Soon."

"But you could have had it all, if you'd just given me my son," she cried.

Silence, except for the birdlife and the occasional scamper across the boards.

"Clive!" The man must have lost his mind. Sara sobbed a litany of words as her head went forward on the rough post.

Chapter Twenty-Two

"Sara!" Rem tossed his hat onto the hallstand. He mounted the stairs two at a time and ran along the hallway, bumping into Maisie as she rushed from the nursery.

"Oh, Mister O'Shea," she cried, looking hot, flustered, and frightened.

"Hello William." He picked up his son when he ran after Maisie. "What's up, Maisie? Where's your mistress. Is she lying down?"

He went to turn the knob on their bedroom door, but stopped short as Maisie said, "No, she isn't in there." Agitation rang through her tone.

"Not in there? Then where is she?"

"We couldn't find her."

"Couldn't find her?' Rem gaped at her, feeling sick. Perspiration dotted his face. "What do you mean, couldn't find her? She can't be far away." Perhaps she fainted. A picture of her lying somewhere unconscious hit him, and he thrust William into Maisie's arms as he rushed down the stairs.

"Hilda has a note," Maisie called after him, a catch in her voice.

 A note! What the bloody hell was she ranting about? He skidded to a halt by the kitchen door when he almost bumped into the woman hired as housekeeper. Hilda held a scrap of paper.

"What is Maisie going on about?" Only then did Rem look at her face. Her lower lip trembled. As she waved the piece of paper he saw that her hand shook violently. His insides clenched as tight as a wound spring.

"Oh, sir, I went out to call the mistress in for her lunch and couldn't find her. Maisie brought young William in and said the mistress was going to follow." She sniffed. "I was just coming in, thinking she'd gone up to wash and tidy her hair when I found this. It was on the veranda post."

Rem snatched the paper from her fingers, his mind going numb with disbelief as he stared down at the few words written there.

"Ravenbrook," he snarled. "He wants gold. Good God! I should have guessed he would do something like this. The scum's taken her. I'll kill him."

Hilda looked ready to faint.

"Oh, sir, what'll you do?" Maisie wailed. She had followed him downstairs, William still in her arms. "He's as trustworthy as the lowest scum."

"How long ago did you last see her?" Rem demanded.

"It wasn't much more than half an hour, sir, five and forty minutes at the most," Maisie said. "You have to find her. That man's likely to do anything to her!"

Didn't he know it? Rem ruffled his son's hair, grabbed his hat and slammed out of the house.

They only had stabling behind the house for two horses, Sara's mare and his gelding. In less than a minute, Rem had his horse saddled and was heading for Ravenbrook's house at a canter, the hooves of his gelding throwing up clouds of dust.

It was stinking hot and sweat soaked his shirt, whether from the heat or the panic filling him he wasn't sure. Trembling with anger and fear, Rem tumbled from his horse when he reached Ravenbrook's house. He rapped on the door and shouted until the sour-faced housekeeper opened it a crack. It only then occurred to him that he hadn't contemplated what he would do if he couldn't find out Sara's whereabouts. What if Ravenbrook had already killed her?

The panic grew until he could taste his fear, could feel it coiling through him like a dark tide. "Where is he?" Rem pushed the door wide, uncaring that she stumbled back. "Where's Ravenbrook?"

As she straightened, pulling at the sides of her mobcap, she stared at him blankly, and then shrugged. "I dunno," she muttered.

He grabbed her by the shoulders and shook her. Rem saw red before his eyes, and shook her again until her teeth rattled. A man came from one of the rooms, goggle eyed, and she said sullenly, "Ask him."

The man turned as if to run. Rem pushed her aside and lunged for him, shouting, "Where's Ravenbrook?" Rem grappled him for a moment then, when he had an arm twisted and secured behind the man's back, demanded again, "Where has that bastard taken Sara?"

"I don't know," he squeaked. "They were carrying someone out to the carriage, that's all I know. Brace was driving. I dunno where they went, honest."

"I trust your word about as much as I trust your master's," Rem spat, shaking the man, and then forcing his arm further up his back until he squealed like a pig. "Tell me, or I'll break your bloody arm!"

"I'm not sure." His head went back and forth. "Honest, I don't know, mister."

"What makes me sure you're lying?" Rem forced the arm up even more, and the man screamed.

"All right, don't hurt me no more. I'll tell you."

"That's more like it." Rem loosened his hold a fraction.

"I heard him talking to Brace. The other two had scarpered."

"Other two?" Rem twisted the arm again.

"Two blokes who brought her here," he sniveled. "I ain't never seen them before."

Rem breathed in deeply to calm his anger and fears. God! What had she had to put up with? He would kill Ravenbrook for sure. "Well, tell me what they said."

"He mentioned a place where no one would find hidden treasure."

"And where is this place?" Rem snarled. He was capable of killing this fool at the moment.

"Ow! I ain't sure, but I think it's up the Parramatta Road, out of town."

"What is? Have you been there?"

"I think it's this hut we went to, but I dunno for sure."

"What do you mean, you aren't sure, you idiot!" Rem was fast running out of patience. But if he didn't find out from this cove where Ravenbrook had likely taken Sara then he would never find her.

"Well." He whimpered. "We went off in the carriage down the Parramatta Road and turned off in the direction of the river at the five mile post."

"And…" Rem shook him roughly.

"Brace told me to stay with the horses while he and the master went inside this hut."

"Right, we're going there."

"What do I have to go for?" he whined, crying out again when Rem shoved him, notching his arm up higher. "I don't know any more. I've told you all I know, mister."

"And I told you, I trust you little. You can lead me there. You, woman," Rem turned to shout at the watching housekeeper, who was either drunk or stupid. "Fetch me a rope. Go on, get on with it," he urged when she stood dumbly staring at him.

She disappeared into the kitchen, and for a moment Rem thought she wasn't coming back. Idiot! All she had to do was run and hide. But then, to prove her stupidity, she returned, handing him a length of stout cord.

Rem snatched it and tied the man's wrists behind his back. She smiled for the first time, and it wasn't a pleasant smile.

"Told you you'd get yer comeuppance, didn't I?" she sneered. Rem thanked the Lord she obviously had some score to settle with his captive.

"Yeah, and you'll get yours," he yelled as Rem pushed him through the doorway and down the steps. Her sniggers followed them.

What a household!

"Where's the boy?" Rem pushed the stumbling man to the back of the house.

"With his nurse. The master told the silly chit to stay out of sight, and she's still hiding," he said as they entered the stable where two horses watched them.

Rem shoved the man forward until he found a length of string. After securing the idiot to a post, he quickly saddled the cob.

"I can't ride." His captive moved from foot to foot, looking more scared than before.

"Well, now's the time to learn." Rem shook him roughly. "Come on." It took a moment to push the man awkwardly into the saddle.

Once mounted on his own horse, Rem led the other one along the street. Setting a fast pace he ignored the squeals and grunts coming from his companion as the horses cantered up Brickfield Hill. Once past the Turnpike and onto the Parramatta Road, Rem eased the horses back a trifle.

Smoke billowed in from the west and the air about them was hot enough to burn his skin. Rem tied his kerchief over the bottom half of his face.

The man began to cough harshly. "We'll be killed," he sniveled.

Rem grunted. "You'll be a dead man anyway if you're stringing me along with a lie; I'll slit your throat and drop you in the bushes. No one will be any the wiser."

"I ain't lying," he shouted hoarsely. "It's like I told you. You turn at the five-mile post. I'm not sure anyway that this is where they took her."

Rem was sure it was. Why would Ravenbrook come out into the bush looking at huts if not to seek a place to hide Sara away? Anyway, Rem didn't know what else to do. He prayed they were on the right trail.

They must be nearing the five-mile post. No sooner had the thought formed than Rem saw the sign, almost indistinguishable from the overhanging shrubbery. They turned onto a narrow track, and Rem thought for a moment they had taken a wrong turn, but then saw the carriage tracks scored in the dust. Through the gloom and smoke

Rem could make out a hut ahead. A vehicle stood nearby, the two horses harnessed to it anxiously stamping their feet.

"Is that Ravenbrook's carriage?"

His captive's head went up and down like a puppet. "Yeah, that's Brace up there."

The carriage driver flapped the reins and made to turn the horses.

"You mad?" Rem's companion shouted as Rem dragged both their mounts around to block the path. His legs worked like hammers in an effort to make the horse move to the side of the track.

Brace shouted. Then Ravenbrook poked his head out of the window and held a pistol aimed at Rem's head. His captive took the opportunity to break free, his horse kicking up clouds of dust as he made off at a gallop. Rem wasn't sure if he was intent on making his escape from him or his master.

Ravenbrook climbed down from the carriage, and Rem dismounted. "Where's Sara," he demanded, shaking a fist. "If you've harmed her in any way I'll kill you. I'll probably kill you anyway!"

"It seems to me you are in no position to threaten me." Ravenbrook laughed, looking down at the weapon he wielded. "No, I hold all the cards here."

Of course, he was right. "What do you want?"

"I thought I made that clear. I want everything you have. All your gold, of course."

One of the carriage horses screamed; the other pranced and fought the reins. Rem looked over a shoulder. The clouds of smoke and dust had thickened. The heat was now intense and oppressive. The squealing horse wheeled, reared, and once its hooves landed, bolted. Brace, cursing volubly, fought desperately for control as they thundered past and galloped full pelt down the track. Rem thanked the Lord he still held his reins when his own mount began to buck and snort.

Muttering a few calming words he faced Ravenbrook, who watched open mouthed as his only means of getting out of there disappeared into the growing gloom. Rem couldn't believe it when he said, "So, back to business," as if discussing the latest trading news.

"You are mad!" Rem laughed. "You're stuck out here in the back of beyond, with no one to offer assistance, and you think you can bargain with me."

Ravenbrook's smile wasn't nice. "Oh, yes. I hold a winning hand. I have your precious woman. I have a weapon." He glanced down at the pistol. Then, strolling over and keeping it aimed at Rem, he tugged the reins from him. "I also have a mount. Wouldn't you say I hold all the trumps?"

"Right." Rem held his hands out in front of him. "So, we bargain. What do you want in exchange for Sara's safe return to me? I'll meet all your demands."

"That's more like it." Ravenbrook wiped at his sweat-laden face with his free hand, glancing about uneasily. It was getting steadily hotter. "Word has it you have come into wealth."

"Word does travel fast here in the colony, doesn't it?" Rem wiped the back of his wrist across his brow.

"Always has. Now, if you want to see your precious Sara alive, you'd better go along with my demands." Ravenbrook waved the pistol.

The maniac was right. If Rem wanted to see Sara again, he had to go along with whatever he asked. "Fair enough. What do you want me to do?"

"Sign your wealth over to me."

"Done. Shall we shake on it?" Rem stretched out a hand, which Ravenbrook ignored. Ravenbrook laughed evilly.

The smoke clouds were growing thicker and blacker. Ravenbrook pulled a neckerchief over his face. It was so hot Rem's skin prickled, his throat felt so parched he could barely swallow, and his eyes stung. The heat was suffocating. A howling wind had sprung up, whooshing through the branches of the gum trees, setting up a frightening din. Sara had to be in the hut. And Rem had to get her out—and soon!

Dust and smoke tickled Rem's eyes and he rubbed them with a fist. The air was so dry each breath became laborious. Suddenly, a herd of kangaroos and wallabies broke from the scrub and thundered across the clearing where they stood. Rem used the diversion to rush at Ravenbrook.

"Not so fast." Ravenbrook pressed the muzzle of the pistol on Rem's chest.

"Sara's in there, you bastard," Rem roared. "You have my promise. You can have everything I possess—just let me set her free."

Thumping the arm holding the weapon he ran toward the hut, calling, "Sara!" Rem reached the porch as Ravenbrook yelled something. Rem wasn't sure if it was a blasphemy or order. He knew Ravenbrook wouldn't risk killing him and losing everything. He was mad but not that stupid.

"Sara, it's Remy." He pounded on the door, scrabbling at the board held fast across it. "Damn." Frantically he looked about and then jumped off the porch. He needed a tool of some sort. When he found a sizeable rock, he began to knock the board out of the way. It didn't take long to shift it. Then he thumped the door back on its hinges, ignoring Ravenbrook, now close behind him.

Sara was slumped in the middle of the dwelling, her arms secure about the upright post. "Sara!" His throat constricted as he went to her side, touching her face. Her skin was as hot as a stovetop. "Can you hear me?" Fear and the heat lodged the spittle in his throat. Her eyelids flickered, a mere wisp of movement, but it was enough to make him say a heartfelt prayer. "Sweet Jesus, speak to me," he pleaded, working to untie her bonds.

"Remy?" His name came from her sweet lips on a breath of sound.

Rem tossed the rope aside and dragged her limp body into his arms before she could topple sideways. "Yes, my love, it's me." He sat on the floor, cradling her in his arms, rocking backward and forward, his hands going up and down her arms and upper body.

"I thought you'd never come," she whispered hoarsely, burying her face against his shirt.

"How could you think such a thing?" Rem drew back so he could look into her eyes. Pushing her hair back tenderly he said, "I would follow you to the ends of the earth, don't you know that." It was getting as dark as a cellar in the hut, and if possible, hotter. A loud crackling and then a crash like thunder rent the air. "We have to get out of here," he said against her ear. "The fire is closing in on us."

Ravenbrook stood by the door, the pistol still aimed at Rem. "You bastard," Rem roared, pushing himself up. Without thought, he rushed at the man who had done this to his love. "You would have left her here to perish. You'll die for this."

Ravenbrook fired the weapon as Rem threw himself at his legs. The bullet whizzed by his ear, going upwards into the roof as he grabbed Ravenbrook about the ankles. They rolled over in the debris littering the porch and then fell onto the dusty ground. For a moment, Rem was winded. He looked up and realized the pistol had flown out of Ravenbrook's hand. He had to get it. On hands and knees, he reached for it, landing a punch on Ravenbrook's head when he tried to pull him back. They were both breathing heavily. As Rem reached for the pistol a cloud of dirt hit him squarely in the eyes, momentarily blinding him.

Rubbing at his eyes, he went onto his knees. Ravenbrook kicked him in the chest, sending him reeling backward. With a roar, Rem reared up, throwing himself at Ravenbrook. They grappled, rolling over and over. Rem felt as if he was in a dream, surrounded by heat, noise and dust. Then suddenly Ravenbrook was gone. Rem shook his head and rubbed his eyes again. Through slitted lids, he saw that Ravenbrook had mounted Rem's horse. The animal reared and spun, baulking at the rough treatment of Ravenbrook's hands on the reins.

The animal refused to move forward, and Ravenbrook slapped it across the neck, yelling, calling the horse vile names as it backed and sidestepped, eyes rolling, head tossing.

"You'll not get out of this," Rem shouted, but it was possible Ravenbrook didn't hear him over the howling through the trees and the roar of what Rem guessed was the encroaching flames. The din was horrendous as trees died and crashed about them.

He could barely discern the horse now, and heard Ravenbrook's cursing before the horse let out a loud scream and then danced in a circle, fighting the man forcing it to move into the darkness.

Shreds of what looked like black leaves blew into his face, and Rem realized it was particles of ash. Good God, the wind was blowing the fire their way. The horse finally got its way, unseating his rider, and careening toward Rem. Fearful the horse would bolt, leaving them stranded in the midst of the fire, Rem whistled shrilly. It skidded to a stop, and although still jumpy and glancing nervously about, stood his ground, one front hoof pounding in the dust. Rem said a silent prayer and staggered to the gelding's side.

Ravenbrook struggled to his feet, one hand raised as if to curse them. The heat suddenly intensified; then with a roar a tree to Ravenbrook's back went up in a ball of fire. Ravenbrook looked behind him, and began to run forward. He stumbled and fell. The tree plummeted down, and Rem winced as flames engulfed his enemy.

Chapter Twenty-Three

Rem secured the reins to a post then hurried back to Sara. He picked up his precious load and staggered to the door. The air was thick and stung his lungs. Putting her down he bent to tear a strip off her petticoat. Securing it over her mouth and nose, he then pulled his kerchief over his lower face. With difficulty he hoisted her into the saddle, where she slumped forward, mumbling incoherently. Vaulting up, he pulled her against his chest. Suddenly about ten kangaroos stampeded out of the blackness and bounded past, running blind in their terror. Rem managed to grab the reins before his horse took off after the creatures. It pranced about, squealing in terror.

"Right boy, take us to the river," Rem shouted and gave the gelding his head.

How they lived through that ride Rem would never know. The horse careened through the blackness, while Rem held onto his mane, clutching his precious woman as clouds of ash, leaves and dust bombarded them.

Rem didn't see the river until suddenly they splashed through the shallows, and the horse was up to his withers in water. Rem slithered down its side as they came to an abrupt halt, catching at Sara before she could sink beneath the surface. She spluttered and coughed and it was the best sound he'd ever heard.

"Sara." He moved nearer the bank until the water reached their chests. "We're safe now." He pulled her close and dragged their masks down so he could place kisses over her soot-blackened face. His laugh echoed across the water as she opened her eyes, smiling weakly.

"Rem? Why am I all wet?" she mumbled before slumping against him.

Rem pushed her hair back with a shaking hand. The trees on the far bank began to crackle then burn, some falling with a crash into the water. The horse stood a few feet away warily eying the fire on the far bank. Rem whistled, and when it came, Rem caught the reins. They would need a mount when this holocaust had passed, and he didn't want to risk losing his horse now.

"Good boy." He patted the sweating neck.

The fire roared on over on the far bank. He couldn't tell how near it came to their side of the river—it was too dark for him to see more than a few feet in front of him. It was like being inside a huge, filthy, billowing black cloud. It was a blessing the river was flowing well and hadn't dried up during the past hot spell of weather.

Now and then animals blundered wild-eyed from the inferno, swimming down-river when they found humans had invaded their retreat. A snake swam perilously close, and Rem held his breath as it drifted by, more intent on saving itself than attacking them.

"Remy?"

He blinked. He hadn't realized his eyes had drifted shut. Sara was looking at him.

"You're awake." He brushed wet tendrils of hair off her dirty face, grinning as she wrinkled her nose. "Do I look as big a mess as you?" he asked, tenderly cupping her face. She now stood on her own without his aid. Rem wriggled aching shoulders and stretched his arms wide.

"Have I been asleep?" she asked. He nodded, kissing her lightly on the lips. "You do look rather awful, and I guess I look just as bad." She reached to touch a strand of her bedraggled hair, grimacing when her hand came away covered in ash. "How long have we been in the water?"

"A while. I've lost track of time."

She glanced about. "Where's Clive? Did he leave us to perish?"

"He's dead." Rem glanced to the bank, where to his relief the sounds of the fire seemed to have lessened. Not so much of the deadly ash billowed their way and the trees

242

lining the far bank were just smoldering now. The worst seemed to have passed on this side of the river.

"What happened?" She put a hand on the horse's wither to steady herself. "I vaguely remember you carrying me from that smelly hut, but the rest is a blur."

"This old fellow bucked Ravenbrook off." Rem rubbed the horse's blackened face. "A falling tree landed on him."

She shuddered. "Oh, Remy! I know he was hateful, and I wished him dead many times; but that was an awful way to die."

"It surely was. But the man was a monster. I doubt he had time to suffer; it happened so quickly, which is a more merciful end than the one you would have endured if I hadn't found you when I did. And he took a shot at me. If I'd died then so would you have, with no one to help you."

Another shudder rippled through her, and Rem wrapped her in his arms. "Are you cold?" he asked when she began to shiver wildly. Despite the heat from the fire, the water was cold. Rem glanced about as her teeth chattered.

"No," she said, but he knew she lied. She was suffering from shock. Lord, if they didn't get out of this water soon she would catch a fever for sure. "What time do you think it is, Remy?"

"I'm not sure. It's hard to tell. If we could see the sun, I'd have more idea. It'll probably be getting near twilight soon." He had to get her out of this water and head back to town before night came down, and the temperature dropped.

"I think we'll chance heading out now," he decided. "If the worst comes to the worst we can always head back to the river if we meet up with the fire again." He took a deep breath, looking about.

Fewer animals had passed by since she'd revived, and the wind had dropped to a dull bluster. "Come on, we'll give it a try." Holding her hand Rem tugged on the reins with the other. Their feet had sunk in the mud, and Sara's skirts weighed her down. This combined to make their progress to the bank slow and unwieldy.

"I think this old fellow wouldn't be so eager to get out of the river if the fire was still about," he said as they dragged themselves up the bank and sat down side by side on the charred ground to empty the water from their boots.

"I must look a mess," she grumbled as he took clumps of her skirts and twisted the worst of the water out.

He took off his shirt to wring that out. "My darling, you've never looked more beautiful."

She laughed, and Rem laughed too—joyously. They were alive!

"The smoke must have made you temporarily short-sighted," she said.

"Not me, love." Rem pulled her into his arms and murmured against her tangled hair, "I thought I'd lost you."

"Oh, Rem, and I thought I would never see you or my children again. Ravenbrook must have been insane." She choked back a sob.

"He surely was. If he'd only come and asked for all my gold at any time, it would have been his. I'd give anything to keep you safe."

Their lips met for long moments in a celebration of everlasting love.

"We'd better get going," Rem said when they drew apart to look into each other's eyes. It was still intensely hot, each breath burning the lungs. "Here, let me pull this up." Rem gently eased the cloth about her mouth and nose. He had no idea how long it would take to reach town—or even if they would get there before nightfall. "I wish we had a container to fill with water."

One thing was certain; they couldn't spend the night here. Sara had to get out of her wet clothes. He cupped his hands, assisting her into the saddle; then hoisted himself up behind her, taking her precious weight in his arms.

For the first mile or so Rem began to wonder if they should have stayed where it was comparatively safe. There wasn't as much smoke now, although small patches of undergrowth still burned. He was careful to guide his horse around the worst places.

After a while, it started to clear so they could see more than a few feet in front of them. Dead birds littered the ground where they had fallen out of the skies. Many creatures lay burned before they could escape the path of the fire. Now and then Rem dismounted to put a badly burned survivor out of its misery—a sickening task.

His idea to keep the river on his left proved difficult. It twisted and turned, and they had to cross small inlets and creeks. Without the sun to guide them, he had no way of knowing if he was heading in the right direction. Once he could see further ahead, he put the river behind them, heading south, praying his instincts were right and they would hit the Parramatta Road eventually. The air was pungent with the stench of dead animals, smoke, and smoldering undergrowth and trees.

When it grew darker, Rem feared they might be going around in circles. He gave his horse his head, trusting in the animal's instincts rather than his own. Sara fell asleep, and although he relished holding her in his arms, they ached fit to drop off with the effort of keeping her from falling out of the saddle. Every part of him throbbed with fatigue and soreness; every muscle cried out with pain. His head ached and his eyes were so bleary he had trouble keeping them open.

Suddenly the gelding's ears pricked and Rem peered into the dimness. A shout came from ahead and then a horse whinnied loudly. His mount answered the call and picked up his pace. Shapes loomed ahead, and then took on the forms of men, women, children and horses. The people waved, and Rem waved back, saying a silent prayer.

"You made the river?" one of the men called as he neared. "Praise be to God, so did we."

Rem slid from the saddle, easing Sara down, and gently settling her on the ground.

"Remy?" She opened her eyes, clinging to him.

"Yes, love, I'm here."

"Are we home?" she looked about.

"Not quite. But we're on the road; we'll be home in no time at all. I just have to go and meet these people."

Hand outstretched, Rem approached the man who had spoken to him.

"Have you any idea how far from town we are?" Rem asked.

"I'd say a few miles. This is my wife, and these are my children." He gestured to three boys and two girls, all grime streaked, their clothes filthy and torn. "We lost our house, barn, and most of our stock."

"I'm so sorry." What more could he say.

Rem went back to help Sara onto the horse, mounted, and then lifted one of the smaller boys up behind him.

The slow, weary procession headed past the Turnpike Gate late into the night.

* * *

The clock in the hallway chimed three when Rem carried Sara into their home. Hilda and Maisie came running from the kitchen, Tim behind them.

"Oh, ma'am, thank the Lord! Are you all right?" Maisie cried, anxiously following Rem as he carried Sara up the stairs.

"Yes, Maisie, I'm fine now. But I had a few desperate hours. What are you doing out of bed, Tim?" Sara asked as Tim trailed them into the bedroom.

"I couldn't sleep, Aunt Sara, until I knew you were safe. We've been so worried." The scamp looked as if he'd been through the mill, his blond mane tousled and his eyes red.

"I'm safe now, thanks to your uncle here." She smiled up at Rem and then frowned as he made to lay her on the bed. "No, I must get out of these filthy garments first, Remy," she scolded. "I need a bath."

"I'll fix it, ma'am." Maisie bustled out.

"I'll help with the water." Tim came and put his arms about Sara, saying, "Thank goodness you're safe. We were really frightened, you know."

Sara put a grimy hand on his cheek. "I have to say we had a few frightening moments too, Tim. But everything's all right now. Everything will be perfect from now on, just you wait and see."

Tim grinned; then hurried out.

"Let me help you out of those clothes," Rem said huskily once the door closed. He fetched her robe and tenderly undressed her, wrapping her in the robe. By the time he'd discarded his own filthy coverings the tub filled with hot water sat in their bedroom.

"Are you sure we shouldn't send for the doctor." Maisie fussed about and tested the scented water's temperature with a finger.

"I'm perfectly all right now, Maisie. There's nothing wrong with me that a nice long soak in the tub won't cure, believe me."

Rem gently ushered a doubtful Maisie from the room, saying, "Now off you go to bed, Maisie. I'll look after your mistress, don't fear. If I think she needs doctoring then we'll send for the doctor immediately. For now all she needs is some tender loving care." He closed the door after the maid and the housekeeper and turned to Sara. "And I intend to give her plenty of that," he vowed, helping Sara out of her robe and into the bath.

Rem washed Sara's hair; then with some of the promised tender care, he soaped every inch of her.

He joined her in the tub and scrubbed at his own skin. By the time he toweled her dry and slipped her nightgown over her head she was asleep.

Despite his fatigue, it was hours before Rem slept. All he could see in his mind's eye was Sara tied to that post in the hut. Rem knew he would have nightmares all his days thinking what would have happened if he hadn't found the hut where Ravenbrook took her; if he hadn't arrived before Ravenbrook left. Knowing the man's evil streak it was odds on he would willingly have left her there to perish once he got his hands on the gold. It was probable he would have killed Rem too once he was of no use to him.

Wicked such thoughts might be, but he couldn't harbor a shred of remorse at the bastard's horrendous end.

"Remy."

He blinked his eyes open. His love was watching him, her eyes dreamy and her cheeks flushed.

"My darling. How are you feeling?" He pulled her close and kissed her gently.

"I'm fine now." She caressed the scars on his back. "I was thinking. We will be able to get my baby back, won't we?"

Rem hated the tremor of fear in her voice. "Of course. The child is yours. There can be no magistrate in the land who will deny you the right to your son, love."

"I've decided I'll change his name to Jeremy. Do you mind?"

"Mind?" Rem placed a kiss on her forehead. "Why should I mind? And the child will grow up thinking I'm his father. We'll never speak of that bastard who sired him again in our home."

"Oh, Remy, I love you so. I want lots of your children."

"As many as you desire," he pledged. "Whatever you ask I'll give it to you. We'll have eight just like Bella and Tiger if you wish."

She pushed him in the chest and chuckled. "I think perhaps four or five would suit me."

"Then four or five it will be."

Rem wrapped her in his arms. A kookaburra warbled in the tree outside their window, welcoming the new day, and Rem laughed along with it.

The End

If you enjoyed this book, please leave the author a review.

Also published by BWL Publishing Inc.

Settlers Series
Bk1. Mystic Mountains. Bk2. Distant Mountains.
Bk3.Challenging Mountains. Bk4. Annie's Choices.

Wild Heather Series
The Laird
Travis

Beneath Southern Skies Series:
Lonely Pride
A Dream for Lani
Leah in Love (and Trouble).

Challenge the Heart Series:
When Fate Decides
A Heart in Conflict
Kate's Dilemma.

Stand Alone
Remnants of Dreams
Amid the Stars
When Destiny Calls
Maddie and The Norseman
A Call Through Time
Powerful Destiny.
Laurel's Gift
Amethyst
Crying is for Babies
Sweet Bitterness.
For the Love of Faith

2022 Bestselling Author
Tricia McGill

Award winning author Tricia McGill was born in London, England, and moved to Australia many years ago, settling near Melbourne. The youngest in a large, loving family she was never lonely or alone. Surrounded by avid readers, who encouraged her to read from an early age, is it any wonder she became a writer? The local library was a treasure trove and magical world of discovery through her childhood and growing years. Although her published works cross sub-genres, romance is always at their heart.

Tricia's love of animals has always shown up in her books. Tricia devotes as much time and money as she can spare to supporting worldwide conservation groups and is passionate about supporting those who do all they can to preserve our wildlife for future generations, especially elephants and orangutans who seem to be getting the raw end of the deal even in this enlightened age. She also volunteers for a local community group that helps disabled adults and children to connect to the internet with provided computer equipment. When people ask what she does in her spare time, she usually replies, "Spare time, what is that?" www.triciamcgill.com

http://triciamg.blogspot.com
https://www.facebook.com/authorTriciaMcGill

bookswelove.com